Protecting the Duke
The Rakes of St. Regent's Park #1
By
Karyn Gerrard

Table of Contents

Protecting the Duke (The Rakes of St. Regent's Park #1)

Copyright © 2021 by Karyn Gerrard

Vers.1.4

KG Publishing

PRINT: ISBN: 978-1-7772205-9-4

Cover art by The Write Designer

Author's Note

THE RAKES OF ST. REGENT'S Park is a new series, with a couple of previously standalone historicals revised to fit the series. There will be more books, how many? Who knows. ☺

In the late Victorian age, women couldn't join the Metropolitan Police in London except as a matron. It wasn't until 1915 that Edith Smith became the first female police constable with full power of arrest.

Like Eleanora Galway in my story, many women joined or created private investigative agencies. Lady detectives were also popular in fiction books during the Victorian era, starting in the 1860s.

Rory Kerrigan makes an appearance in this book. You can find his story in *The Copper and the Madam* (Blind Cupid Series #3), which also takes place in 1897.

The Matrimonial Causes Act of 1857 finally gave women the right to file for divorce, although it was limited. A woman had to prove more than one cause to obtain a divorce; a man needed only to claim adultery. A revision in the act in 1878 allowed a woman to separate from her husband on the grounds of cruelty. She could also claim custody of the children. The Married Women's Property Act of 1884, at last, recognized that women were not property belonging to the husband but independent persons.

THE RAKES OF ST. REGENT'S Park

Rakes of St. Regent's Park Series

IN A PRIVATE MEETING place, in an old bank office behind Colosseum Terrace on Albany Street, a group of gentlemen attended a gathering. It had nothing to do whatsoever with financing, investments, or stocks—unless you counted moral bankruptcy. The central rules of this club: no serious attachments to anyone, and the pursuit of one's own pleasures, especially of the carnal variety, were to be of the utmost importance.

But weariness and boredom were setting in. Along with something more worrying: loneliness. A disquiet of the soul. These bad-boy peers of Victorian London were damaged, hiding their inner torture beneath a thin veneer of devil-may-care dissoluteness.

It takes an exceptional group of women to capture the hearts of such men. To see past the outer shell. The ladies are determined to live and love in their own way, with no relinquishment of their independence and no compromises. How satisfying to find that deep down, these progressive men are in total agreement.

Summary

THE FACT THAT WOMEN couldn't join the London Metropolitan Police was an injustice to Eleanora Galway. She found her way around such an obstacle: by forming a detective agency. When a note arrives from a duke concerning a mysterious and gruesome delivery, Eleanora agrees to investigate.

Despite the pursuit of pleasures by The Rakes of St. Regent's Park, weariness and boredom were setting in. Along with stark loneliness. No one felt this more than Christian Bamford, Duke of Allenby. Once the Galway Agency arrives, Christian is fascinated by Eleanora and her razor-sharp deductive mind and bold confidence. She attracts him as no other woman has done before.

When Christian proposes assisting her with her inquiries, Eleanora initially balks. But the temptation of being in the darkly handsome duke's company is hard to resist. Swept into an adventure and a passion neither had counted on, blending unlikely lives, occupations, and societal standing seem insurmountable. But for the independent Eleanora and the progressive-minded Christian, nothing is impossible. Not even love.

Chapter 1

LONDON, ENGLAND
   September 1897

A company of gentlemen attended a gathering in a private meeting place in a former bank office behind Colosseum Terrace on Albany Street.

The conference had nothing to do with financing, investments, or stocks—unless you counted moral bankruptcy.

The men were unofficially known as The Rakes of St. Regent's Park.

In attendance were men of varying ages and ranks. The membership ebbed and flowed during the past fifteen years. Some men had gone to war, others married and moved on to a less profligate life. Part of the current group had formed a close bond in school, all the way to Cambridge University, until this very day.

Presiding over this particular assembly was Christian Bamford, Duke of Allenby.

Their informal organization consisted of two dukes, a baron, a Canadian businessman of the gentry class, a marquess, and a viscount.

Not just anyone was allowed within this privileged circle. First and foremost, the other members had to genuinely like the fellow, and these formidable men did not easily give their friendship, trust, or reveal their emotions.

Any peerage associates must be firmly established landholders from another age, centuries of tradition, and all the rot. Snobbish, perhaps, but one must adhere to British customs in these matters.

Exceptions were made and had to be approved by all the members. Such was the case with Brandon Knight, a wealthy businessman, and entrepreneur who recently returned from Canada.

The last prerequisite is the foremost pursuit of one's pleasures, especially of the carnal variety. There was time enough to settle down and see to the title's responsibilities. Meanwhile, they would enjoy all life had to offer rich, pampered men of considerable means.

With certain restraints, of course.

Christian believed excess to be a sign of weakness, and losing control could lead to complications and unwanted attention. They decided they would convene once a week to keep each other in line. During these unceremonious meetings, they shared their experiences and recommended brothels or other places of vice. There was nothing like male bluster to liven up a conversation.

Besides, what was the point of these conferences if you couldn't boast of your sexual or gaming conquests with your friends?

A servant, Phillips, moved about the round table, filling their glasses with claret or scotch. In the center was a tray of beefsteak sandwiches and slices of cheese.

Christian looked up from his newspaper at the men gathered.

Directly to his left and slumped in his seat was Warren Cowley, Viscount Huxley. Warren had recently inherited the title and was still adjusting to it all. Warren was the least handsome of the lot, not that it mattered to Christian, but it certainly mattered to society. Though outwardly unassuming, Warren possessed a voracious sexual appetite. Since Warren was judicious, Christian tolerated his particular immoderations.

Next to him was Damon Cranston, Marquess of Brookton and heir to The Duke of Chellenham. Christian narrowed his gaze as he stared at the blond Adonis reaching for a slice of cheese. Society often compared the sinful marquess to the fictional Dorian Gray from an Oscar Wilde book. Damon had laughed it off, but Christian wondered. His scandalous reputation was the talk of London.

Damon was his closest friend. Christian had erected a protective wall through the years, but Damon had him surpassed in that regard. Christian often pondered what went on behind that impenetrable shield. It was telling that he considered someone as emotionally closed off as him as his closest friend. But that was for an examination at a later time.

Next to Damon sat Merritt Redfern, Viscount Tolwood, and heir to the Earl of Shelton. Merritt was not a full member but an apprentice, or prospect if you will. With curly auburn hair and an abundance of freckles, he still had the fresh-faced innocence that appealed to certain older women, which was Merritt's current preference. One affair had him bedding a woman of sixty, and he had heartily recommended it.

Sitting next to Merritt was Asher Colborne, Baron Wenlock. Asher's barony was the oldest in England, dating back to the medieval age, and one of the richest. Asher's particular carnal predilection was seeking out tawdry tups in the seedy back alleys of the East End of London.

Not something Christian was the least bit interested in, but to each his own. Christian's family also could be traced back hundreds of years, as could Damon's. Such long bloodlines came with responsibility, something the men were most definitely avoiding.

Another member of the group was Brandon Knight, the aforementioned businessman. He had been in Canada for several years—not by his choice—and made his fortune there. Though Brandon hadn't revealed the particulars, Christian had a distinct impression that the circumstances were grievous enough to leave deep internal scars. Brandon's carnal tastes were much like Christian's. Sex with strangers, move on to the next liaison.

Gideon Broyles, Duke of Watford, was the only remaining original member of The Rakes. He had relinquished the leadership of The Rakes to Christian eight months ago, as he had grown blasé about running it. The duke was more of an elder statesman of their little assemblage.

Gideon was rather fond of flagellation brothels that featured light birching. Or so Christian had heard. Again, it was not something Christian desired, but he believed whatever gave someone pleasure was their own business.

Beyond that, he would never judge his friends. At least, he tried to hold to that belief.

Christian had grown bored of late and had spent this past week at his town house—alone. Reading books—of all blasted things. Before he knew it, he would acquire a slobbering hound dog to sit at his feet. To say he had nothing to report this week was an understatement. Glancing around the table, Christian wondered if the others felt as jaded as him.

"That will be all," Christian told the servant, who bowed and left the room. "So, gentlemen, shall we begin? Have we all been careful in our various dealings this past week?"

Another rule of the club: always use protection regarding sex. It wouldn't hurt to remind the membership of it.

"What does it matter if we do or not?" Merritt stated, shrugging.

"You'll never become a permanent part of the group with an attitude like that, Merritt," Christian admonished. "First off, there are diseases to avoid—and any possible children."

Damon grunted and refilled his glass. "Yes, children. Avoid at all costs. If it does happen, however, never deny the child. Never refer to them as a mistake. Or a by-blow. God, I loathe that term. People should not shunt children around. They become lost in the morass of society or tossed aside like rubbish. This child will be of your blood and deserves care and acknowledgment. At the most, love and acceptance."

This concise show of emotion was the Damon he had known all these years. He showed compassion, understanding, and wisdom when you least expected it, and it didn't happen that often.

"You sound as if you know of which you speak," Asher said.

"Me? God, no. I'm extremely cautious in my libidinous dealings. My father, the duke, not so much." Damon frowned, then sighed wearily. "There are at least three siblings of mine out there in the world, borne from three different women of various classes. I've tried to find them. Or perhaps my father lied about it. I would not put it past him, the miserable cur."

The room was silent.

Damon squirmed in his chair as if realizing he had revealed too much. "Carry on," Damon said gruffly, downing his drink and pouring another. "I do not wish to discuss my father in *any* way."

Then Christian would do what his friend asked. "Warren? Your latest conquests?"

"Too many to mention," he grumbled. "I'm beginning to believe I have a true sickness."

"When was the last time you had sex?" Damon asked, a grin tugging at the corner of his mouth. Already his mood had shifted, typical of Damon, as changeable as London weather.

"You mean today?" Warren replied drolly.

Laughter broke out around the table but soon ceased when Warren did not join in.

"What is it, Warren?" Christian asked.

"I believe I will be extricating myself from this group for at least a short period. I might head to Huxley Estate, as I need to rest and reflect."

"Well, that has blasted well put a damper on the meeting," Damon pouted.

"Leave him be, Brookton," Gideon's deep voice rumbled. "He can do as he pleases."

"Is something the matter, Warren?" Christian asked.

"*Everything* is the matter, but I am not inclined to discuss it here. Move on." Warren sounded weary, and Christian decided not to pursue the subject.

"I also have an announcement," Brandon Knight interjected. "I cannot put off my plans any longer, and I will be heading to Herne Bay in December."

"Where in the deviled hell is Herne Bay? Never heard of it," Christian asked.

"Southeast England, on the coast, Kent, specifically. I have a score to settle," Brandon answered, his eyes glowing with a determination Christian had never seen from him before.

"Revenge," Damon yawned. "How tedious."

Brandon's eyes turned chilly. "You know nothing of which you speak. I have scores to settle, and I aim to see it done before the year ends. I've spent enough time in London."

"Will you be returning after you have meted out your justice?" Asher asked.

"I'm not certain, and I will inform you of my plans." Brandon's eyes narrowed. "Don't mock me, any of you. You don't know the entire story."

"Save it for some snowy night by the fire," Damon said, his tone dripping with sarcasm.

Brandon stood eager for a fight, but Asher grabbed his arm.

"This is not the time for fisticuffs," Asher stated firmly. "Ignore Damon. He's not happy unless he is stirring the pot. Don't give him the satisfaction."

Brandon grunted and sat but shot Damon a murderous look.

Christian could feel it; change was about to take hold of the men. They had lived life to the full with gambling, drinking, and women, the totality of their existence. He never thought Warren would be the first to cede defeat, if only temporarily. The man must be exhausted.

And now Brandon would be leaving?

"No one has anything to share?" Damon asked, looking around the table. "Shall I expound on my various adventures since the rest of you seem to have lost all interest in the existence of this club? I attended a particular orgy at—"

A knock sounded at the door. Phillips entered, carrying a long, narrow box. "My pardon for interrupting, Your Grace. There has been a delivery."

"Set it here, Phillips, and leave us," Christian said.

The man placed the box on the table before Christian, then bowed and departed.

"Someone sending us flowers?" Merritt stated. "A thank you for a recent dalliance? Whom is it addressed to?"

Christian flicked open his small pocket knife and deftly slit the string and a corner of the brown paper wrapping. "To the Rakes of St. Regent's Park."

Damon rubbed his chin. "I always liked that name; it has a certain symmetry. But how did someone know to send it here?"

"Our meeting place is hardly a secret. We have hosted card games here and even allowed an acquaintance or two to use the place for a clandestine meeting. And do not forget that all the past members know the location. Merritt, will you do the honors?" Christian asked.

Merritt stood, tore off the paper, tossed it aside, then lifted the top. His face went as white as a sheet. He gagged once, twice, then staggered, turning away with his hand to his mouth.

The rest of them scrambled to their feet and had a peek. Inside the satin-lined box was a leg. A human leg sawed cleanly just below the knee.

"Fuck me," Damon whispered.

The men exchanged shocked looks. Christian could not believe this. Why would someone send such a macabre—thing?

Merritt ceased gagging, took a handkerchief from his pocket, and wiped his mouth.

Gideon bent at the waist to inspect it closer. "There is a small tattoo on the ankle. Judging by the length and curve of the leg, this belonged to a woman."

"Shall we call the police?" Merritt asked, his voice shaking. "There is a constable that patrols regularly along Albany Street. I can go and fetch him."

Police. No.

Christian did not want the Metropolitan Police trudging through their lives, overturning rocks that should be best left alone.

At least—not yet.

At some point, they would not be able to avoid it. But until then—no. The incident would be splashed all over the papers; their location would become a tourist attraction as many other places connected to grisly doings or deaths. Jesus, there were informal Jack the Ripper tours in Whitechapel, attracting large crowds—no. Just *no*. Christian was getting ahead of himself as usual, but still.

"I believe it best we keep it quiet for the moment. This delivery is nothing but a twisted prank," Christian replied.

"A prank? A woman's severed leg? Where is the rest of her? We may be talking about homicide! Cold-blooded murder!" Merritt bellowed as Warren laid a hand on his shoulder to calm him.

"Or the body part came from a hospital or graveyard. Sent for the express purpose of rattling us," Asher replied.

This delivery shook Christian to his core, but he would not reveal it.

"Job well done," Brandon murmured. "Consider me rattled."

Christian pointed at the box. "We should hire an investigation agency to examine this—before calling on the police. Better to keep this situation in *our* control. For now."

"Why keep the police out of it?" Merritt cried, still clearly upset.

"Do you wish the coppers delving into our lives? Do you want all this to make the papers? And you know it will. Those blasted reporters hang about police precincts for any sniff of scandal or gruesome doings." Christian grimaced. "Be damned if I want my life—or any of our lives—splayed open for London's perusement and amusement."

"Is perusement even a word?" Gideon asked.

"No, it is not. What does it matter? Christian's correct about the police," Asher said. "But which agency should we consider?"

Christian glanced at the newspaper on the table, and a large advertisement caught his eye.

~◇THE GALWAY AGENCY◇~

THE FINEST DETECTIVES are available for all your covert watching and secret inquiries, either for divorce or other matters of import, criminal or civil.

◇ *Confidential and discreet* ◇

◘ *149 Cleveland Street Appointments required* ◘

"I BELIEVE, GENTLEMEN," Christian stated, "I have just the place."

Chapter 2

A YOUNG MAN KEPT A close watch on the front entrance of the Bull and Lamb Tavern. Unnoticed by any passerby, he pulled his peaked cap low over his eyes with his fingerless-gloved hand as he expeditiously scanned the street. His vigilance was needed, for he was on a case—and in disguise.

The working-class bloke wasn't a man but Eleanora Galway of The Galway Investigative Agency.

Two men sauntered toward her, heading in the direction of the pub. Adjusting the front of her loose-fitting trousers while simultaneously hiking up her shoulders, Eleanora spit on the sidewalk. They kept walking and entered the tavern without giving her a backward glance.

Good.

She wanted to blend into the background. To Eleanora, a male disguise was uncomplicated due to her taller-than-average height, broad shoulders, fake bushy mustache, and adeptness at mimicking a masculine manner.

Masquerading as a laborer meant the strapping down of some parts and the padding and hiding of others. It also allowed Eleanora to smoke in public without censure. Not that she cared what others thought, but dressing and acting as a man granted her a sense of freedom, even though she owned and operated an investigative bureau.

Reaching in her pocket, Eleanora removed a small paper pack of cigarettes she'd purchased at Rothman's small tobacco kiosk on Fleet Street. She then struck a match against the brick wall and lit one. Drawing deep, she exhaled with pleasure.

"Ellie, do I smell smoke?"

Althea, her younger sister, stood guard at the head of the alley. She was well hidden in the shadows but near enough that they could speak in low tones without being noticed.

"Yes, Althea. It's part of the costume, and I don't do it that often. No admonishment if you please."

Her sister sighed. "Is the subject still inside?"

Mrs. Anna Kitchener, their client, mandated attestation that her husband, Jacob, was having an affair. They required proof positive of adultery and any other grounds needed for a divorce.

Many of their cases involved women and marriage. The business had soared with the changes in various marriage acts and laws and a loosening of women's rights (though not nearly loose enough for Eleanora).

According to their client, Mr. Kitchener refused to consider divorce. Commensurate to his wife's blunt statement, the marriage had fallen apart months ago. They no longer shared a bed, not that the couple had shared it more than three times. Too much information, perhaps, but it gave Eleanora a clear picture of their subject's mindset.

"Yes. I can see Kitchener. He's standing at the bar, nursing a pint. Speaking to no one," Eleanora murmured, the cigarette dangling from her lower lip.

Before beginning the surveillance, they had done a cursory background check on the man. They did so with nearly all their clients, for knowledge is power.

Mr. Kitchener worked as a solicitor at a prominent law firm in Westminster, a famous enterprise with an elegant address and clientele. The few former clients she approached had spoken highly of him and claimed his reputation was commendable.

Kitchener was a thin, prudish-looking man who wore spectacles. Eleanora had deduced at the start of her surveillance that he hardly looked the part of an adulterer. But since forming her investigative agency five years past, she had often been surprised on more than one occasion.

Outward appearances meant nothing.

Regardless, her gut instinct was seldom wrong. And her gut told her there was more going on here than a possible adulterous husband.

The subject downed his beer and headed for the exit. Taking one last draw on the cigarette, Eleanora dropped it to the cobbles and ground it out with her boot.

"Althea, we're up," she mumbled.

Her sister emerged from the darkened alley, dressed in appropriate clothing a young woman would wear for a leisurely walk with her beau. Althea's costume included a wool skirt, straw bonnet, and a tattered shawl. Tucked away in her reticule was a Bull Dog revolver. Althea was a dead shot, even better than her. Eleanora preferred a knife and had one hidden in her boot and tucked up in the sleeve of her coat.

Eleanora looped her arm, and her sister slipped hers through it. They blended into the humanity of London, like a working-class couple out for an evening stroll. It was a masquerade they often used and had much success with since her sister was much shorter.

Standing well over ten inches above five feet, Eleanora was taller than most men and solidly built. Perhaps she was too voluptuously shaped, for she had to bind her breasts, wear loose clothing, and use extra wadding to conceal her curves. It was a hindrance more than anything.

Mr. Kitchener stepped onto the footway, glanced at them, then hurried up the street. The sisters sauntered along behind, keeping a discreet distance. Passing by two more pubs, their subject showed little interest. Eleanora surmised he had a specific destination and needed the pint as liquid courage.

The way he twisted his hands showed his aggravation and anxiety. Was he heading to his mistress? Though if he had a mistress, why not agree to the divorce and—

"Sweet Mother," Eleanora muttered as Mr. Kitchener climbed the steps toward the entrance of a multi-leveled brick house.

"What is it? A brothel?" Althea asked.

"Of a sort. It's a molly house."

This turn of events was not a twist Eleanora had considered. Mr. Kitchener dallied with men? Her gut was right again about people not being as they appear.

"Molly—as in homosexual? I read that it is a mental illness, though I find that explanation dubious," Althea whispered. "We should proceed with caution."

Eleanora gave her sister a skeptical look. "Do not believe all the books you've read. That book's opinion is incorrect and offensive."

"I completely agree. But it was written by a German psychiatrist," Althea stated. "It was among Da's books."

Grief sliced through Eleanora at the mention of their late father. Hollis Galway, straight from Ireland, had been a chief inspector with the Metropolitan Police, D Division, Marylebone.

Lord, how she missed him.

"As I said, it doesn't mean the book is accurate. Even Da said that."

They stopped a few yards from the building.

"I stand corrected. What next?" Althea asked, her voice low.

"I'm not keen on giving this information to Mrs. Kitchener. Maybe he is seeing a law client," Eleanora replied in an equally low tone.

Her sister snorted derisively.

"Far-fetched, I know," Eleanora replied. "But our client is out for revenge, and she will see her husband ruined and humiliated publicly."

"It *is* against the law, Ellie, regardless of our opinion."

Eleanora straightened her peaked cap. "Well, the laws aren't always right, either. Stay here. Let me get the lay of the land."

Althea pulled on Eleanora's coat sleeve to halt her. "Remember what Da used to say, 'You cannot involve yourself in the private lives of your clients.' Kitchener's sexual preference is not our concern. Nor is what his wife will do with the information."

She knew her father's sage advice on this particular topic. But Eleanora could not—and would not—remain emotionally distant from her work or the people who hired her agency.

"I'll take it under advisement," Eleanora whispered as she gently shook off her sister's hand. Climbing the stairs, the sound of a piano wafted from the building, and as she moved closer, the distinct warble of a masculine voice singing in the falsetto style.

Eleanora knocked, then immediately slouched as she had observed many young men do.

The door opened. A tall, thin man stood before her—dressed as a woman—complete with a wig, makeup, and a fancy gown one might wear to a ball. The man's whiskers were visible through the heavy powder.

"Hello, my lad. All are welcome here. Come in! I'm Kitty Muldoon, your hostess."

Kitty stepped aside, and Eleanora crossed the threshold into the alcove.

"Ooo, you're a bit of rough; some of the toff gents will like that," Kitty stated, thoroughly inspecting Eleanora. "Unless this is a costume, like mine."

"Give over," Eleanora grumbled in a deep voice. "I'm not here for none o' that, and I need to talk to the awkward-lookin' bloke with spectacles that came in not five minutes past. I'm not here to cause no trouble."

The sounds of laughter and merriment carried into the hallway. Eleanora heard ribald lyrics from the backroom: "riding on top—of an omnibus." Eleanora bit back an amused smile.

Kitty's false eyelashes fluttered flirtatiously, all while tapping Eleanora's arm with a fan.

"Do you promise not to be a nuisance, my sweet ruffian?"

How bizarre could this situation possibly be? A woman dressed as a man, talking with a man dressed as a woman.

"I swear it," she answered, giving Kitty a sly smile. "A few minutes of the bloke's time, and I'll get gone, no mistake."

"Are you certain you won't stay?" Kitty whispered. "You're a charmer."

"Thanks, but not tonight, love."

Kitty winked and moved off, no doubt to fetch Kitchener.

Curious, Eleanora followed part way, enough to catch of glimpse of the backroom. The expensive decor resembled any upper-class parlor, with velvet curtains, plush chairs, and a crystal chandelier.

Men dressed as women sat in the laps of other men. A few were kissing, and many were drinking and smoking and having a grand old time. To each their own was always Eleanora's thought on such matters of sexual preferences.

Have fun, lads.

Mr. Kitchener emerged, looking decidedly suspicious.

"What do you want?" he snapped, annoyed at having his entertainment interrupted.

"I am here to warn you." Eleanora stayed in disguise, using the same deep voice she had used with Kitty. Considering her voice was deep for a woman, lowering it another octave or two wasn't a hardship.

"Your wife hired me to follow you," Eleanora continued. "And will want to know of your proclivities. She will use it to her advantage. Give her the divorce she seeks, and I will not reveal what I have discovered."

Fair enough arrangement in Eleanora's mind. Mr. Kitchener's secret life would remain safely in the shadows, Mrs. Kitchener obtains her divorce, and The Galway Agency collects its substantial fee.

It was a win-win-win situation for all concerned.

The irritated Mr. Kitchener narrowed his eyes with suspicious anger. Eleanora recognized the look. Jacob Kitchener contemplated an escape and was willing to fight to achieve it.

Without hesitating, he let loose a roundhouse blow Eleanora missed by ducking to the side. She then kicked the man's legs out from under him, and he fell to the carpet like a sack of potatoes. Eleanora straddled him, her knife slipping from her sleeve.

Holding it to his neck, she whispered menacingly, "None of that, now. Or I'll slit your gizzard, sure as shite."

She had heard a sailor down by the East End docks make the same threat to another man, and she had used it ever since. It was effective intimidation, and Mr. Kitchener's eyes widened with fear.

"Now, will you talk without causing a fuss?" she asked.

Kitchener nodded, his head bobbing nervously.

"Here, what's all this, then?" Kitty cried. "Take a room in the back if you're up to playing around. No roughhouse here and not in the front hall!"

Kitty had not seen the knife, and with a sleight of hand, Eleanora slid it into its holder under her coat sleeve. And judging from Kitty's reaction and the "what's all this" tone, Kitty could be a copper. How interesting.

"A slight disagreement, love. I promise that we'll behave. Right, sir?" She glared at the man under her, giving him a slight squeeze with her thighs.

"Absolutely." He nodded for good measure.

Eleanora jumped up and held out her hand to Kitchener. He took it, and she hauled the slightly-built man to his feet with no effort.

"All friends again."

She straightened Kitchener's collar to prove the point.

Kitty gave them a dubious glare but left them alone.

With an exhale, she released the man's clammy hand. The dampness had seeped through her thin gloves. "You will inform your wife tonight that you will grant the divorce. Have my payment ready by three o'clock tomorrow afternoon when I stop by to collect it," Eleanora demanded.

"How much of a payment?" he squeaked.

"Just the rest of the fee owed to my investigative agency—nothing else. If all goes well, there will be no need to reveal anything I've discovered to your missus."

Mr. Kitchener straightened his spectacles, giving her a dubious look. "Why are you doing this? You could have blackmailed me."

"The Galway Agency does not traffic in such doings, Mr. Kitchener. Nor do we ruin lives if we can help it."

Eleanora reached into her coat pocket and slipped the man her business card.

"The Galway Agency. Legal (civil or criminal) or confidential advice or investigations, privacy assured," he said, reading the card.

"Should you need our services, do not hesitate to contact us. We have a pact, then?"

Mr. Kitchener met her gaze. "Yes. I will have the payment ready for you."

Eleanora turned to leave, then halted. "Do not seek out such flamboyant places as this, Mr. Kitchener or your secret will be secret no more. There is a guild on Bryanston Street in Marylebone. The Sportsman Club. It's private, circumspect, and should serve your needs. Tell them The Galway Agency sent you." Touching her forelock, Eleanora slipped out the door, not waiting for a response.

Althea was still standing in the same spot, next to the stairs. "You took long enough."

Eleanora smiled. "All straightened out. We will collect the fee tomorrow afternoon and close this case. Shall we catch a hansom and head home?"

The home was at 149 Cleveland Street, near London's West End. The location was upscale for the daughters of the late Inspector Hollis Galway of the Metropolitan Police, but their late mother came from a bit of money and afforded them this address.

They ran their business from this multi-storied brick flat. Next door, the George and Dragon Pub made a convenient place for any clandestine meetings. And to buy a nice steak and kidney pie if there was no time for a proper meal.

Arriving home, they found their cousin, Sybil Nolan, in the parlor, hands-on-hips.

"Where have you been?" she questioned, exasperated.

"On the Kitchener case, why?" Althea responded.

Sybil was part of their agency but worked more behind the scenes, keeping the books. Sybil's father, James Nolan, was their late mother's younger brother. Sybil's parents were living in Yorkshire, running a profitable sheep farm.

"Because we got a note delivered not fifteen minutes hence. Here. Look at the signature," Sybil cried with excitement.

Eleanora took the note, and Althea leaned in to read it.

Immediate assistance needed regarding a ghoulish delivery. Come at once. Will pay handsomely for your discretion and secrecy. Police must not be involved. The rear entrance is marked 2A.

Christian Bamford, Duke of Allenby

Colosseum Terrace on Albany Street

"How did you respond?" Althea asked Sybil.

"I bloody well said yes. I also said we'd be along sharpish, though not in those words. Didn't you see the carriage outside? The duke told the driver to wait."

"I thought I saw a crest on the door. Hard to tell in the dark," Althea mused. "Truthfully, I assumed people were engaging in a late-night rendezvous."

Sybil tapped the message. "It's a duke! Think of the fee we can charge. And we can brag that we serve the aristocracy."

"We had a knight as a client once," Eleanora stated, still studying the note. "Sir Reginald Ramsay."

"A knight is *not* a duke," Sybil responded.

True enough.

"Ghoulish delivery? Of what, a dead body?" Althea questioned with a touch of sarcasm in her tone.

Eleanora could only hope.

How she craved to sink her teeth into a meaty case much like the ones Scotland Yard detectives investigated or those detectives within the CID, the Criminal Investigative Division. Their father had trained them well. However, the rules stated that women could not join the Metropolitan Police, at least not in their desired capacity. Being a low-paying police matron did not appeal at all. Undaunted, she decided to take matters into her own hands and start her investigative agency.

Their father and uncle, also a copper, proudly supported her and Althea in their endeavor. Eleanora had yearned to prove that they could solve a complex crime as well as any man. Better even. She wanted them to understand that their faith had not been misplaced.

But their father had passed away before she and Althea could show him what they could do.

Perhaps Eleanora wanted to prove it to herself more than anything.

"Ellie? You have a strange gleam in your eyes," Althea said. "What *are* you thinking?"

"Let's go—all three of us. Why even send a carriage? We could walk there within minutes," Eleanora urged, growing excited at the prospect of a possible dangerous case.

"Shouldn't we discuss this further?" Althea said. "Honestly, Ellie. For someone with a well-ordered mind, you act impulsively at times. It's getting late."

Althea snatched the note from Eleanora and waved it in the air. "How do we know this note is legitimate? What if we are being called out to an isolated place and assaulted in the worst way possible? Even if this note is from a duke, despite the fancy carriage. I've heard of Allenby and his circle of friends and read about him in the paper. Rakes and ne're-do-wells, all of them. This appointment could be a ruse."

Eleanora crossed her arms. She did not like anyone reminding her that despite her overall self-discipline, she could be impetuous.

"And *you* are being overly cautious, Sister. We cannot wait until morning. This letter is regarding a 'gruesome delivery.' We have to address it now—this very minute. We have our weapons, and we can all handle ourselves. I suggest we depart."

"Wait, you can't go like that," Sybil admonished.

"I don't have time to unwrap and change clothes," Eleanora replied. "The mustache alone will take about fifteen minutes to remove." She touched the bushy mustache that concealed her full lips. She would need to find a better-quality adhesive for each time she removed the false facial hair; it had left red welts. "Make haste."

Althea and Sybil sprang into action gathering notebooks and pencils.

A duke. How exhilarating.

Allenby.

She had never heard of him, not that she kept up on peers and their doings as Althea did. The gossip in the papers had never interested her.

She could only pray it would be a compelling case.

Chapter 3

THE THREE WOMEN STOOD before Colosseum Terrace on Albany Street, and why a duke had called them here past ten o'clock at night was a puzzle indeed.

The lit street lamps offered some illumination, but a heavy fog and the complete silence gave the location an eerie atmosphere. In the distance, a dog bays at the moon.

Perhaps Althea was right, and Eleanora was too hasty to insist they come here.

"In the rear, the note said," Sybil specified.

The driver cleared his throat, and the horses whinnied in response. "Go on ahead, miss. Just behind the main building."

Eleanora looked up at the driver and gave him a brisk nod. "Thank you."

Eleanora was surprised by the labyrinth of alleys and lanes nestled behind the building. A whole other world existed, and one not seen from the street.

Developed in the early 1800s, St. Regent's Park was the idea of Prince Regent George IV. Stylish white stucco town houses surrounded the area like the ones facing the street. The park opened to the general public in 1835.

"There, 2-A," Althea pointed. The facade had the same design as Colosseum Terrace. Eleanora knocked, and a man wearing a livery opened the door.

"The Galway Agency to see the Duke of Allenby," Eleanora declared.

The butler, or whatever he was, looked down his nose. "Do you have a card?"

Eleanora whipped one out of her pocket and held it up for the snobbish servant to see. "Don't leave us standing on the cobbles; take us to His Grace immediately," she demanded.

The butler had a slight curl to his lip, strange for a servant to show any emotion, especially disdain, but he nonetheless stepped aside.

"This way, sir."

Granted, they looked like a motley crew with her and Althea still in disguise. The butler gave them a dirty look though he rapidly arranged his features to show indifference. The disrespect caused Eleanora's blood to boil, but she fought the response.

Focus on the matter at hand. Should Eleanora continue to act like a man or reveal her identity to the duke upon meeting?

The servant led them up two flights of stairs into a large area. This space was unquestionably the playroom for pampered peers. On either side of the large fireplace were leather settees. Around the room were a few round marble card tables, with two billiard tables against the back wall. Fancy gold wallpaper, velvet draperies, and crystal light fixtures finished the look.

On the opposite side of the room was a bar with multiple crystal decanters and matching glasses. Above it was a massive painting of a scantily-clad woman sprawled suggestively on a velvet fainting couch.

Seven men stood by the table; which one was the duke?

Eleanora studied them closely. What an eclectic collection of various ages, heights, hair colors, and builds. And levels of attractiveness.

Her gaze landed on the tall blond. This handsome specimen had to be the duke; how could it not? The blond Greek God was six feet tall or an inch above it. He was perfect beyond measure. But Eleanora dismissed the notion of him being the duke immediately. Though arrogant in his stance, he didn't hold the imperious self-assurance she imagined a duke would possess.

Next to him was an equally tall man with black hair. He was attractive in a brooding way and possessed the male beauty of the fair-haired one. His clear blue eyes had a frosty look of disdain. The cleft in his chin was a nice touch. Impeccably dressed, he wore a fancy signet ring on his little finger, evidence of a high-ranking peer.

The others were looking to Cleft Chin for direction. He must be their leader. His expression was not arrogant as such but self-assured, comfortable in his skin, a man who wanted for nothing. The way he stood with shoulders back, the haughty air—yes, this had to be the duke.

Although, there was another older man with a touch of silver at his temples, showing the same attributes as a high-ranking peer. But he stood back from the others with an expression of complete indifference.

The other five men were either tall or medium height, running handsome to pleasant-looking enough.

Cleft Chin held out his hand. "Mr. Galway? I am Christian Bamford, Duke of Allenby. This is Damon—"

"Women? What kind of agency is this?" Blond Greek God bellowed as he pointed at Althea and Sybil.

Before Eleanora could respond to the duke's offered handshake, Althea stepped forward and gave the Blond God a murderous look.

"I will have you know that most investigation agencies employ women," Althea admonished. "Do you think we are not up to the task? Women are as capable as men in investigating, more so even.

We are patient, methodical, and intelligent. Attributes most men sadly lack—especially those of the upper classes."

Oh, Althea, couldn't you hold your quick temper for this meeting?

Eleanora thoroughly agreed, but they needed a wise plan from a business standpoint.

Blond God's nostrils flared as his eyes narrowed at the insult. He either wanted to throttle Althea or kiss her senselessly. How utterly fascinating.

The duke pointed to the other men. "The misogynist is Damon Cranston, Marquess of Brookton. The freckled fellow next to him is Merritt Redfern, Viscount Tolwood. Next to him is Warren Cowley, Viscount Huxley, Asher Colborne, Baron Wenlock, Mr. Brandon Knight, and standing at the rear, Gideon Broyles, Duke of Watford."

Sweet Mother, they are of the peerage, except one.

And she had guessed correctly; the older man *was* a high-ranking peer.

"Pleased to meet you, Your Grace." She turned toward the others. "Your Grace. My lords. Mr. Knight. My assistant and sister, Althea Galway, and my cousin, Sybil Norton."

Eleanora removed her hat, pulling away the few pins holding her hair. Her wavy brown locks fell just past her shoulders. She kept her hair shorter than most women, but the length was helpful for her laborer disguise, as certain men sported longer hair.

Giving a slight bow, she said, "And I am Eleanora Galway, chief owner and operator of The Galway Agency. Forgive our clothing, Your Grace; we were on a case when we received your note. I'd rip off this fake mustache, but it would remove my upper lip with it." She smiled at her joke.

The men have yet to respond.

They stood, mouths gaping, staring at her as if she had sprouted another head.

Well, this was an inauspicious start.

CHRISTIAN COULD NOT believe his ears.

Eleanora?

This was a woman?

Credit where it was due. It was an astonishing and convincing disguise. There was not one feminine attribute visible. Hell, she could practically stare him in the eye. Miss Galway could easily wrestle any of them to the floor and pin them there.

Why did that idea send a blast of desire through him?

The shade of her hair was an attractive chestnut brown with a few threads of gold as if someone had weaved each strand in perfect iridescence.

She stepped closer, and the unmistakable odor of cigarette smoke invaded his senses. Hard to tell if she was pretty. The huge mustache took up the lower part of her face, and she must have smudged grime in places with no hair.

"Your Grace? Your note stated you had a ghoulish delivery. Unless you no longer wish to employ us."

Eleanora Galway's voice was deep, husky, even sensual if he wanted to go that far—no wonder he had thought her a man.

"Allenby? You *cannot* seriously be considering hiring this—agency?" Damon stated, his voice incredulous.

"Well, *I* am certainly intrigued," Asher smiled with amusement.

"I agree with Brookton; this is not the done thing," Merritt whined.

"Quiet. All of you." Christian had to think. What to do? How could women handle a delicate matter such as this?

That was not accurate and completely unfair.

Hell, he behaved as if he were as much a misogynist as Damon. Which he wasn't—time to prove it and act on his true beliefs.

"Allow me to show you what was delivered. Then decide if you wish to take the case. It's there on the table." Christian pointed to the rectangular box. "Your complete discretion is warranted."

Miss Galway—Eleanora—stepped forward, as did her sister and cousin. Why he thought of this young lady by her first name was puzzling.

They peered inside, exchanged astonished looks, then studied the contents.

"Did it come with a card, Your Grace?" Eleanora asked.

Not a flutter or stutter from this woman; he admired that. Nor from the sister and cousin. Christian decided then and there to hire them if they wanted to take on the case. Damn the others' prejudicial and inappropriate opinions.

"No, only a brown paper wrapping," he replied.

Miss Norton looked about and, once she located it, bent to pick it up. "To the Rakes of St. Regent's Park," she read.

Eleanora met his gaze. "Is that the name of your club, Your Grace?"

Was that amusement or disdain flashing in her light brown eyes? Or a combination of both?

"We haven't an official name, though others refer to us as such," he responded. "Will you be taking on the case? We want to know who sent this—and why."

The three women gathered in a small circle and conferred, murmuring in a conspiratorial manner.

Warren gave him a look: "You cannot be serious about this."

But he was—deadly serious.

Christian waved Gideon over while glancing at the other men. "What do you think? I'm inclined to hire them."

Gideon turned so no one could see his reaction. "It's your club, old sock, do as you please. It might be diverting, and I agree that this option is far more desirable than bringing in the police. However,

I know of one discreet police detective, and he could make some inquiries for us."

"Hold that thought. We could hire another agency if the ladies are not up to the task. But I think they will be. I believe this body part is a morbid trick, nothing more."

Eleanora strode to the table again, and Christian and Gideon moved closer.

The lady removed her glove and touched the leg with the tip of her finger. "Cold, as if it had been on ice before it was delivered. Pale hair and skin are evident on the leg, which could mean the victim has blonde hair."

Miss Norton took notes, her pencil stub moving across the page as Eleanora spoke in a professional, detached tone.

"A butterfly tattoo on the ankle," the sister interjected.

Eleanora leaned in closer. "Blue in color, black trim on the wings. Tiny and poorly done. Amateur work, and not done by an artist. The toenails are ridged, showing pitiable health, and not trimmed neatly. Could be an unfortunate."

A street prostitute.

So far, Christian was impressed by her deductive skills. She certainly had all their attention now, for Damon, Warren, Brandon, Asher, and Merritt had moved nearer, hanging on her every word. She even had Gideon's attention.

"A clean amputation using the circular-cut sawing method. Not frenzied. Reasons for medical amputation: gangrene. A deformity. Untreatable ulcers, arterial diseases, diabetes mellitus, and the complications therein. Or an accident resulting in a crushed leg, though not the case here."

"Can we lift fingerprints?" Althea Galway asked.

"Not certain it is feasible on skin. Make a note," Eleanora stood up straight and met his gaze. "Did anyone touch this limb, Your Grace? Besides me, obviously."

"Are you taking the case?"

"We are, Your Grace."

"Good. Then cease with the 'Your Grace' and no 'my lords' either. It grows tedious. Call us by our title names. And no one touched the thing, though one of us touched the top of the box and the brown paper beside the footman," Christian replied. "Will a fifty-pound retainer be adequate for a start?"

She smiled, showing brilliant white teeth under the fake mustache. "More than adequate."

Thankfully, Christian happened to have a roll of pound notes with him. He held it out to her. "There are nearly twenty pounds there, and I will have the rest delivered to—?" Be damned if he could remember the address.

"149 Cleveland Street. We will take this leg with us."

"Please make use of my carriage once again. Merely instruct Michaels to take you home. It would be safer than trying to hail a hansom or walking at this time of night," Christian said.

"Thank you, that is much appreciated."

"If I may ask," Christian said as he stepped closer. "What are you going to do with the leg?"

"We have a surgeon we use in various cases, and we will ask him to perform a thorough examination. He's Canadian, late of the North-West Mounted Police."

"Police?" Merritt cried. "We said no police!"

"I assure you, Tolwood, the man is not affiliated with any police here in London," Eleanora stated firmly.

She remembered the names of their titles after hearing them only once. Christian liked that she spoke with bold confidence. An amused smile formed at the corner of his mouth.

"Who delivered this package?" Miss Norton asked.

"Our servant, Phillips. He is the footman mentioned," Damon answered, stepping closer to Miss Norton. "Actually, he is part of my massive staff—of servants." He winked, but Miss Norton chose to ignore his feeble double entendre. "Well, he works for us here a few hours a week for extra recompense."

Miss Norton poised her pencil. "His full name?" she asked coolly.

"Blast it if I know—Huxley?" Damon replied.

Warren moved toward the wall and pressed the button. "How would I know a servant's given name?" he mumbled.

As they waited for Phillips's entrance, Eleanora covered the box with her sister's shawl and tucked it under her arm. Althea Galway folded the brown paper and tucked it into her reticule. An awkward silence settled over the room. Miss Norton was still scribbling notes.

"We will conduct interviews with each of you shortly and send word when we require a meeting. It will take place at Cleveland Street as we have our office there. Please give Miss Norton the addresses of where you currently reside," Eleanora stated.

The cousin marched up to each man and jotted the addresses when Phillips entered the room.

"You rang, Your Grace? My lords?"

"Miss Eleanora Galway has a couple of questions regarding this box. Answer her truthfully," Christian said.

"Your full name and address?" she asked.

Phillips gave her a surprised look but arranged his features into servant indifference. Christian's lip curled. He had never cared for this man. Though he was adequate in his duties, perhaps it was time to find someone more suitable to work here—one he could at least tolerate.

"Aloysius Phillips. I am employed at the Marquess of Brookton's town house in Mayfair as third footman and have been doing extra duties here for the past eight months."

Footmen were often referred to by their first name; he could see why Aloysius used his last.

"And this parcel?" Eleanora asked.

"Delivery took place about eight o'clock by a dirty-faced youth. They are often used to deliver parcels and letters. That rabble all look alike under the filth of the streets."

He was not the only one who didn't care for Phillips's manner. Neither did Eleanora, for it was plain by her expression.

"So there is a third person who touched the parcel. Did you bring it upstairs immediately?" Eleanora asked.

"No, miss. I was busy seeing to the food and drinks, and I brought it here about thirty-five minutes past eight."

"That will be all for now. We will be questioning you later and in more depth."

Phillips gave her a brisk nod.

Turning to him, Eleanora said, "I believe we have all we need now. I will be in touch soon, Allenby. Good evening."

Bowing slightly, she departed, with her sister and cousin following close behind.

"What in hell just happened?" Asher asked.

"Phillips, you may go. In the future, when there is a delivery, it is to be brought up immediately, understand?" Christian barked.

"Yes, Your Grace."

With the footman's exit, the others turned toward him, talking simultaneously.

Christian raised his hand. "Let us sit and continue to eat. Besides, I need a drink."

He grabbed the whiskey decanter and splashed a generous amount into his tumbler. Once the men were seated, he passed it around.

"What possessed you, Christian?" Warren asked. "An all-female agency? I admit it is unique, but what if this is not some gruesome joke but something far more nefarious and treacherous?"

"I agree," Damon murmured, slumped in his chair, sipping his whiskey. "A bad business."

Gideon slipped on his gloves and tucked his walking stick under his arm. "I've had enough of this meeting; I am off to visit my other clubs. Brandon? Are you coming with me?"

"Yes, I believe I will," Brandon Knight replied. "I need a diversion."

"Then we wish you a good evening," Gideon said.

The two men departed.

Christian took a generous gulp, the burn tearing down his throat.

"Listen, all of you, Christian declared. "It's time to adjust your various prejudices toward women. They are capable of more than men give them credit for, and we should allow them a chance to prove their talents."

"That was a cracking good disguise," Asher exclaimed. "Had no idea it was a woman under all that. Blasted tall, too. Looks as if she could hold her own."

"Maybe Galway isn't a woman. We didn't see actual proof," Damon stated laconically. "Perhaps they have perpetrated a complete scam, and they just walked out of here with all our names and addresses and twenty pounds as well."

Merritt laughed. Then he sobered. "What if Damon is correct? They've got the leg, too."

Christian picked up the newspaper and passed it to him. "Then it is an expensive scam indeed. Look at the ad; it isn't cheap. And the business card. Easy enough to check. Twenty pounds? Mere pocket change to us. I will be checking into them first thing tomorrow morning."

"This drama has put me off this gathering, and I cannot even remember what we were discussing," Damon scowled.

"Spare us your bragging of yet another orgy," Warren snapped irritably. "Your adventures grow tedious in the telling. I rather wonder if you are embellishing in most cases."

Damon snarled at Warren, and Christian rolled his eyes. You would swear they were all ten years old and wearing short trousers. The sniping, usually teasing in nature, was getting out of hand.

"No sexual tales tonight. We are in a crisis in more ways than one. Warren wishes to retire to his country estate due to exhaustion, and God knows what. What shall we do?" Christian looked around the table at the other men.

They didn't reply.

"Warren, I believe you should not venture to your country estate until this situation with the morbid delivery resolves," Christian said. "Will you stay in London?"

"I am not certain," he replied, rubbing his forehead. "But I refuse to attend any upcoming social events. What is on our calendar this coming week?"

Christian reached for the journal and flipped through the pages. He would have to attend at least one event as it would placate his mother.

"Tomorrow night is the soirée musicale at Asher's town house."

"I can postpone the bloody thing," Asher interjected.

"Not at all. Merritt and Damon will attend." Christian replied.

"Yes, by all means, pencil me in," Damon replied drolly.

"Friday night is a ball at the Earl of Pembroke's. I will attend that one." Christian picked up the pen, dipped it in the ink bottle, and scrawled his name next to the event. If he remembered correctly, the earl's balls gathered quite a large crowd, so he could quickly become lost in the multitude and slip out early. "Anyone else wish to discuss anything?"

"It appears you will be our representative for outside society this week, Christian. All I want is to go to my town house and sleep for a week," Warren declared. "Contact me when you have news. Otherwise, all of you—leave me be."

Though tempted to interrogate Warren, he would respect his requested privacy.

As for this damned ball, Christian was heartily sorry now that he had volunteered to attend. There would be no one there to interest him, at any rate. No matter. A brief appearance, then he would slither out and do as Warren said—sleep for a week.

Tomorrow?

Check into The Galway Agency and the fascinating women attached to it. But the most intriguing of the trio to him?

Miss Eleanora by far.

Chapter 4

"OPEN AT ONCE!" SYBIL pounded furiously on Dr. Corbett Buchanan's door. An animal-like grunt from within was the response.

"Easy, Cousin," Eleanora murmured. "Let's not make a scene."

They had just returned from the Kitchener residence. A contrite Mr. Kitchener, with his satisfied wife in attendance, paid them their fee and stated they would seek a divorce. One case is down, now to focus on the one before them.

Sybil turned to face her. "Why you continue to use this drunkard, this lumberjack from the wilds of Canada is beyond my understanding. He lives in a brothel, Ellie. Couldn't we find a more respectable—"

A gruff clearing of the throat interrupted Sybil.

Leaning against the doorway was "her Canadian," as Eleanora called him, the man she used when medical matters needed addressing in any particular case.

He looked the worse for wear, eyes bloodshot, rumpled clothes, and—Eleanora inhaled, the distinct odor of sexual activity, along with tobacco, alcohol, and sweat. Not a pleasant combination by any stretch of the imagination.

Corbett lit the cigarette stub dangling from his lower lip. "Well now, darlin', can't say I ever felled a tree, so lumberjack doesn't exactly fit. But I've certainly been to the wilds of Canada, and no mistake."

Sybil flushed in response.

Eleanora had noticed her cousin's flustering in Corbett's presence more than once.

"We require you, Doctor," Eleanora stated. "A carriage is waiting downstairs to take us to my uncle's precinct. His dead room awaits."

Not all police stations in London had a medical examination room. But her uncle, Reece Galway, was of a like mind to his late, older brother: forensics would play a prominent part in policing in the years ahead, and Eleanora believed the same. Her uncle was an inspector at J Division, Bethnal Green.

"I'm hardly in a fit state to examine a corpse," Corbett said. Absently, he wiped his nose with his sleeve as he drew deeply on his cigarette stub.

Sybil curled her lips in disgust.

"I've hot coffee, and you can swill it on the way," Eleanora said. "Strong, as you like it. Uncle sent one of his police conveyances for us to collect you. The journey to the East End should be long enough for you to sober up sufficiently, and I will double your usual fee."

"Well, why didn't you say so?" He dropped the cigarette stub and closed the door behind them.

After they stepped outside, Corbett grabbed the sides of the horse trough, bent at the waist, and plunged his head into the water.

He stood upright, and the air whooshed from his lungs; then ran his hands through his longish wet hair, slicking it back from his face as water droplets sprayed every which way as if a dog were shaking his fur after a brisk swim.

"Now he smells of a horse on top of it all," Sybil complained.

"Nothing wrong with smelling of a horse as I often slept with one out on the prairies," Corbett replied.

"I don't doubt it," Sybil retorted. "Probably the only creature that would deem to share your bed."

She marched toward the carriage, leaving Eleanora and Corbett standing by the trough.

"I believe she likes me," Corbett said, a sardonic tone to his voice. *Yes, she does.*

But Eleanora didn't voice her opinion. "Shall we depart, Doctor?"

Corbett opened the door, allowing Eleanora to enter first. She sat beside a fuming Sybil, and Corbett climbed in and sat opposite.

Unscrewing the glass container, she poured a generous amount of coffee into an enamel mug and passed it to the doctor as the carriage pulled away. His hand trembled as he took the proffered cup.

"Not sure how hot it is, but it will serve the purpose. Drink," Eleanora coaxed gently.

He gulped it all down, hardly taking a breath, then held the mug toward her. "More."

She refilled it and watched as he drank. Although he retched briefly, the Doctor held out the mug again.

Corbett sat back, drinking this mug more slowly. "You ladies on a case, I assume?" he asked, placing the cup next to him on the seat and lighting a cigarette.

"Yes, we will reveal more once we reach the station," Eleanora replied.

"Out socializing last night? I imagine that a dapper young man accompanied Miss Sybil. Dinner? Perhaps then to a concert?" He waved the match and tossed it out the open window.

Corbett must be feeling better, for he was teasing Sybil. Her cousin met his gaze, fury plain on her face.

"Once a man learns of my family background, most slink away. Nor do they ask me to any respectable venue. Not that I would have gone anyway," Sybil replied, her voice laced with cold disdain.

"Family background, what are you on about?" Corbett asked, looking genuinely puzzled.

"I'm the daughter of a sheep farmer. Deemed to be part of the lower classes."

"What in hell has that got to do with anything? Are you ashamed?" Corbett snapped.

Sybil bristled. "Absolutely not. I don't hide it. I'm merely stating that I come across prejudice regarding my station."

Corbett snorted. "Prejudgment is everywhere you turn. This country's class system and social hierarchy are poisonous, and it's *not* what I believe."

Sybil stared out the window.

Corbett alternated between gulping down the black coffee and smoking as he looked out the opposite window.

Eleanora found studying humans absorbing. Here was a classic example of two people attracted to one another but perceptibly denying it.

What did they know about Buchanan beyond that he came from Canada's East Coast and served in The North-West Mounted Police as a surgeon on the Canadian Prairie? He had hinted that he was involved in the second Riel Rebellion a decade earlier but would not elaborate on any details. How he wound up in London living above a brothel would be an enthralling tale.

The fact remained; as her cousin had stated, he was a drunkard. However, when sober, or at least halfway there, Eleanora had discovered an accomplished physician. He possessed a plethora of forensic knowledge and skill. Corbett Buchanan's fees were reasonable, and he was available at all times of the day or night—a definite bonus.

Buchanan's eyes never left Sybil, who stared out the window at the passing city streets. There was a yearning there on both their parts, and Eleanora was astute enough to recognize it.

The carriage pulled up to 458 Bethnal Green Road. The familiar sight of the light brick and sandstone building gave Eleanora a thrill.

The fancy gold streetlamp on the sidewalk had the word "Police" painted on the glass.

If only women were permitted to enlist with the police force. Yes, there were about fifteen police matrons, but Eleanora would only join if given all the rights to investigate and arrest as men had. But women weren't allowed, so she would have to take these small moments when she could.

Walking up to the front desk, Eleanora nodded in greeting. "Good morning, Sergeant Wilmot. We are here to see Inspector Galway. He's expecting us."

The bushy-bearded sergeant turned to a young uniformed officer. "Tell the inspector Miss Galway and company is here. Cut along now."

The young man hurried toward the rear. Moments later, her uncle emerged from the back office.

Eleanora's breath caught in her throat.

It did every instance she saw her uncle, for he was so similar in looks and bearing to his older brother—her late father—her heart hitched. It made her grieve all over again. After three years, you would think the feeling had lessened, time supposedly healing all wounds and all that rubbish, but not in her heart.

Her mother had died not long after Althea was born, so all they had growing up was their father and Uncle Reece, who had lived with them for a time. To lose Da to a damned cancerous bowel was a devastating blow. He hadn't even known he was sick, except for feeling more tired. Once discovered, he was gone in less than three months.

Sighing, she swallowed back the sorrow and smiled at her uncle in greeting. At forty-three, her uncle looked years younger, surprising considering the complex division he policed in. Taller than even their father, at close to six and a half feet, it was not difficult to see where Eleanora got her height.

"Ellie, Sybil, good to see you. And Dr. Buchanan. Right this way."

Her uncle led them to a transformed office. Though cramped, he had spared no expense in the renovation. The tiled room had a cement floor. Her uncle oversaw the conversion of the storage area into cold storage—thanks to regular ice deliveries. Uncle Reece opened the door, slid out the box, and set it on the examination table.

"What's this?" Corbett asked, pointing to the oblong package.

"A body part, more specifically, a leg. I think it's a woman's leg," Eleanora replied. "It was delivered to a group of gentlemen at their club who hired us to determine about the macabre consignment. Uncle, the fingerprinting has been done?"

Fingerprinting was being used sporadically by a few intrepid officers like her uncle, but the Metropolitan Police had yet to accept it overall.

He pointed to the wooden chest on the table opposite, "Got the kit from Hawksley's on Oxford Street. Unfortunately, I got nothing feasible off the box except partial prints. We can fingerprint the viscount and the footman and compare only where the gentleman grabbed it to open it."

"Perhaps we should. Sybil, make a note. None of us touched it, and I wore gloves, and we wrapped the box in Althea's shawl for the trip home."

Corbett cocked an eyebrow in disbelief. "You ladies took home a severed leg and stuck it where—in your icebox for the night?"

"Until we could bring it to Uncle Reece's cold storage. Is there any information to be gleaned from the leg?" Eleanora asked, focusing the Doctor's attention on the matter at hand.

With his cigarette dangling precariously from his lower lip, he gently removed the leg from the box and laid it on the exam table.

"Clean cut, possibly professional." He slowly rolled the leg over and grunted. "This is a lady's leg due to the length of the tibia and fibula." Corbett leaned in closely. "She was dead when the perpetrator removed the limb. See the dark patch of skin on the back of the leg? Blood settles in the extremities, *livor mortis*. She was lying on her back when she died, and the skin has not deteriorated much."

"It was cold to the touch when we answered the call, and I surmised whoever sent this kept it on ice until delivery. Could it be a body part from a hospital and used as a ghastly prank? Or is there something more nefarious at work?"

"Hard to tell without the rest of the body...Ah. There's a tattoo on the ankle."

"We took note of that," Sybil replied.

Uncle Reece leaned in for a closer look. "Buchanan, I have managed to allot some miscellaneous funds for a salary. You could work here part of the week and be on call the rest."

"Excuse me, Inspector, a reporter from *The Times* to see you," A young officer declared from the doorway.

"Take him to my office and tell him I will be along directly. Make sure he stays there," Uncle Reece replied.

"Yes, sir."

"Inspector, you seem a decent sort. But I've had enough of working for organized justice," Corbett stated. "I labor on my terms as an outworker. No one to order me about. Occasionally do some doctoring, and it suits me fine. No man will command me ever again." Corbett replied in a determined but not disrespectful tone.

"As you wish, Doctor," her uncle responded.

"More time for drinking and whoring," Sybil muttered crossly.

Eleanora pushed her cousin's shoulder to silence her.

"Well, darlin', it comes in handy. This small butterfly is on the ankles of some of the ladies working at The Chrysalis. They are the elite of the club. For special guests, big money. They are clean and fancy; you get my drift."

Sybil wrote furiously. The blush crawling up her cheeks was apparent.

"The leg, however, shows a different fate. The unkempt nails, the ridges which I believe show lack of certain nutrients," Eleanora interjected.

"Maybe. You will find the same if you remove most underprivileged people's threadbare socks—if they own socks at all. If you're considering going to The Chrysalis and asking questions, I advise against it. The club is exclusive, and they won't let you in. You could ask your gentlemen clients about it; they could obtain you an entrance." Corbett met Eleanora's gaze. "Are they of the peerage?"

She nodded.

He whistled low in response. "Could be a practical joke, knowing what amuses these nobs. Then again, be careful."

Uncle Reece strode into the room as Buchanan gave the warning. Her uncle gently clasped Eleanora's upper arms; he was one of the few men she had to glance up to meet his eyes.

"I second that. When you discover this is not a prank and you need my assistance or wish to involve the police, do not hesitate to contact me." He laid a gentle kiss on her forehead. "I have a couple of men at other divisions I trust implicitly, and they can discreetly assist with any queries. Rory Kerrigan at L Division, Lambeth, and Edmund Reid at H Division, Whitechapel. Let me know."

"We will, Uncle," she replied softly. "Doctor, are you coming with us?"

"I want to examine this limb more thoroughly and get a blood sample. Afterward, I know of a place near here to get a decent steak pie. I'll find my way from there."

Eleanora motioned toward Corbett, and Sybil stepped forward, holding a couple of pound notes.

"Your fee," Sybil stated.

Corbett trailed his long fingers along Sybil's upturned palm, and, to Eleanora's astonishment, her cousin did not pull her hand away. Their gazes met, and Eleanora could swear that electrical sparks crackled between them. As swiftly as the attraction flared to life, Sybil turned, the spell broken, but not before Corbett snatched the notes from her hand.

He grasped Sybil's shoulder and leaned in, "I know you can take care of yourself, but be careful, darlin'."

She hesitated, then nodded, making her departure without looking back.

Once out in the main room, Eleanora took a closer look. Workers dressed in overalls were installing something of import regarding all the banging and activity.

"What is all the commotion, Uncle?"

"Telephone lines, if you can imagine. It will ring here at the station. Up Glasgow way, they're experimenting with police boxes. In small kiosks, the uniforms can use while walking the streets. Our precinct was selected for a tryout by the higher-ups."

Eleanora smiled. "I don't believe telephones are a fad, Uncle."

"No, you have the right of it. Telephones *are* here to stay, blasted nuisances. Coming for dinner Sunday? Bring your sister and cousin, of course."

Uncle Reece had married two years past to a widow that Eleanora had taken an immediate liking to. Wilhelmina was in her mid-thirties and the widow of a copper under Reece's command. One thing led to another, and they fell in love.

The police officers at J Division raised an eyebrow at first. Eventually, they came around and were genuinely happy for their inspector. They were also glad the young woman was not left destitute as so many police widows are.

"Of course. Seven o'clock?" She smiled in reply.

"Absolutely." Her uncle instructed one of the uniforms to hail them a hansom.

Eleanora pulled Sybil aside. "I believe it's time to dust off 'Constance Baxendale, niece of Sir Reginald Ramsay.' We need information on these Rakes of St. Regent's Park and The Chrysalis, and the best method to gather gossip is at a toff ball or gathering."

"Sir Reginald will allow you to continue to use the disguise?" Sybil murmured.

"Yes, it's part of his fee. I still have eighteen months to go. I took the liberty of sending word early this morning, and he responded immediately. There is a ball at the Earl of Pembroke's town house this Friday night, and I will be going in his stead. Not that he attends many social events."

"What about a fancy gown? You only have the two."

"I haven't worn the brown and gold one; it will suffice."

Sybil furrowed her brow. "Well, it's more copper and gold, but what if one of those Rakes of St. Regent's Park shows up?"

Eleanora shook her head. "I highly doubt it; I assume it is not their sort of thing. I won't be staying long anyway. Young men usually arrive late at these gatherings, and I will be long gone."

While part of her held upper-crust society in scorn, another was delighted to be stepping into another persona.

Honestly, she should have been an actress on the stage.

Moving about among the elite? Drinking champagne and eating frosted cakes until she burst? Harmless flirting with all sorts of men and gossiping with the women?

Empty pursuits by empty people, she couldn't imagine living such a hollow, superficial life twenty-four hours a day. But for a few hours, Eleanora could look beyond all that and revel in the gathering of facts.

That is where her actual enjoyment lay.

She couldn't wait.

Chapter 5

IT WAS HALF PAST FOUR, and already Christian was late for his weekly afternoon tea with his mother. Hurrying past Huntington, his butler, he cringed, seeing the man standing outside the door to the parlor, which meant his mother was already inside waiting to pour.

"There you are, Christian. The tea is growing cold. Take a seat," his mother gently admonished.

"Apologies, Mother. I had errands to run."

Thanks to a contact at Scotland Yard, he ascertained that the agency had a good reputation. Most clients were women because many men scoffed at using young ladies for such a task. One, in their closed minds, that was too arduous and indelicate for any woman.

Christian never held such misogynistic beliefs. Due in part to the lady sitting opposite. The Duchess of Allenby lived life on her terms, speaking her mind regardless of what society thought, and she had brought Christian up to do the same.

The duchess was married at eighteen, a mother at nineteen, and a widow at twenty-seven. She had traveled, had taken the occasional lover, and found time to be an affectionate mother when the mood struck her.

She smiled as she passed him a cup and saucer. "Have a scone; I know how much you love them."

"I will."

"I have a couple of serious subjects to broach with you, my dear. Perhaps you wish Huntington to bring the decanter so you can add a splash of whiskey to the Darjeeling."

Christian groaned teasingly. "Oh, God. As grave as all that?"

"You turned thirty last month; you are not getting any younger. Surely you will not wait until you are fifty-six to set up your nursery as your father did," she murmured, biting into a treacle biscuit.

His father: a man he had barely known.

Like most aristocratic marriages, his parents allied; it was *not* a love match. Once his mother became pregnant, she retired to the country estate while his father stayed in London.

When his father deemed to make an obligatory visit, Christian had been trotted out for a shake of the hands and a pat on the head, only to be summarily dismissed if he tried to speak. By the time Christian turned nine, the duke was gone—a sudden stroke.

The happy country life with his mother came to an end shortly thereafter. He was sent off to school the following year while his mother traveled. Lonely—and in his young brain—abandoned, he sought company with like-minded lads. Hence his little exclusive group, Christian, Damon, Warren, Merritt, and Asher, had met at school. They had been more of a family to him than anyone. Men of the peerage often referred to each other by their title names. But since he had known most of the rakes since childhood, they used first names when alone.

Sipping his tea, he glanced at his mother. Being who he was in society, he would have been sent to school regardless. That was not fair about the abandonment thought.

Society entirely expected Christian to attend school. Necessary, even.

But he hadn't liked it.

Christian couldn't fault his mother for wanting to enjoy life. She had been young and beautiful. At forty-nine, she was still striking.

Through the years, they shared good times and happy memories. But to him, it was never enough.

Damn it all for still being a needy schoolboy.

There was no denying it; he craved affection, the touch of another.

He always had, no doubt, always would.

"Ah, the nursery. No, Mother. I will not wait until I am decrepit, but give me another year or two before I'm shackled."

Sighing, she sipped her tea. "I do not want you to marry as I did. I want you to find a woman who will love you completely and give you all the attention you deserve. Thinking back, I could have done more. As a widow, I had more autonomy than even a married duchess. It was selfish of me to swan off so often. I do apologize."

His mother spoke with deep emotion, and her eyes glistened with unshed tears. His mother was sincere, and it touched him.

"I would have been away at school at any rate. We had holidays and summers together," he replied softly, "They are wonderful memories I shall cherish. If you feel alone, you may move back here. That is if you wish to."

What was he doing? Giving up *his* freedom?

Or perhaps he craved company in this cavernous residence beyond his servants. That uncomfortable—and not unfamiliar—feeling of loneliness crept in, and he immediately dismissed it.

"Alone? My dear. I am *not* alone. That is the next subject I wish to tackle. But first, promise me you will try and find a woman worthy of your love. You have plenty to give, and do not let it founder. You must attend more social events to meet such a young lady."

"I'm attending the Earl of Pembroke's soirée," Christian replied.

He *should* start looking for an appropriate candidate for duchess instead of waiting another year or two. After all, it was his duty, and when in his late father's company (on a rare occasion), the duke pounded such responsibilities into his head. He always remembered his obligation to the title, family, queen, and country. As she was doing now, his mother had also expounded on his ducal commission.

"I will make a serious inspection of the young ladies in attendance," Christian added.

She beamed at him, and he basked in the warmth of it. "Excellent. It is a start. Now, I know emotions can be tedious. Outside of my love for you, I never experienced a deep love. Nor any romantic feeling."

Christian raised an eyebrow as he reached for a cheese and cucumber sandwich.

"I may not have had as many lovers as you think," his mother continued. "You know the gossips exaggerate. But I'm involved with a man now, and drat it all, it's turning serious."

"How serious?"

"He has asked me to marry him."

Christian blinked rapidly, the shock causing him to lose his ability to speak momentarily.

Good God.

"Marriage? What about this freedom you revel in? You will give it all up once you agree to matrimony. Who is it? A young, sensitive painter? A bespectacled, somber barrister? An aged and rich marquess?" he teased good-naturedly.

But inside, that feeling of loneliness insidiously made an appearance once again. How pathetic at Christian's age to want to be the only recipient of his mother's affection.

Good God, indeed.

His mother waved her hand dismissively. "I would never give up my freedom. Nor would I give up my position in society. After all, I married a duke; my son is a duke."

Christian chuckled. "You have been seeing a duke? Whom, precisely?"

There weren't that many dukes. Christian's mind rapidly conjured up the names of various dukes as if he were flipping through the pages of *Debrett's Peerage*.

"Gerard Linton. The Duke of Coldbridge. He mentioned that you had spoken once during one of your rare appearances at Parliament."

That was something else that must change; time to take his responsibilities in the House of Lords more seriously.

Coldbridge.

Right, he remembered him now.

The man was tall, distinguished-looking, with an abundance of silver hair. He was in his mid-fifties, handsome in his way. Also, chilly and standoffish. The title name fit.

"My first impression of Coldbridge was not entirely good," he said straightforwardly.

His mother smiled as she sipped her tea. "How amusing, he says the same about you."

Christian bristled at the statement. "And what did His Grace say?"

"You showed no interest in the matters before the house, and your attendance was sporadic at best. Gerard takes his duty seriously."

"How could you consider giving any sort of affection to such a cold fish?" None of his business, but he didn't want his mother to enter into another loveless arrangement. She deserved so much more.

The duchess's back straightened, and her mouth pulled into a taut line. "I assure you he is *not* a cold fish. Once you break down that outer barrier...."

Her look turned reflective; her features softened.

So, she *was* in love with him.

"Will you marry?" Christian asked.

"I'm considering it. Even if I do not, I am through with the restless traveling. If I decide to accept, I will be the Duchess of Coldbridge. Gerard has his heir and a spare; he has been a widower for eleven years. He claims he never intended to marry again, nor had I. Falling in love is exciting and frightening all at once. I need a little time to adjust. Oh, Christian, I believe I *do* love him, most desperately."

Christian set his cup and saucer on the table beside him, sat forward, and gently grasped his mother's hands. They were trembling, which caused his heart to swell with emotion.

"Then marry him at once, and be happy."

She smiled tremulously. "I do so want the same for you, Christian."

Kissing her hands, he released them and sat back in his chair. Happiness with another was something that lay beyond his reach.

Or so he believed.

He never experienced any tender feeling of romance toward another. Duty demanded that he make an alliance to carry on the name. Ensure the title—what a cold outlook and future.

But it must be the path he traveled, and he had procrastinated long enough.

But he would make an effort at the ball and socialize with marriageable young ladies. There wasn't any likelihood he would meet someone at the ball that would be interesting enough to catch his interest.

None at all.

ELEANORA GLIDED INTO the ballroom of the Earl of Pembroke's massive town house, nodding to those who acknowledged her. Tonight, she was Constance Baxendale, widowed niece of Sir Reginald Ramsay. She had already passed the gauntlet of the earl and his countess, sending her uncle's regrets.

Eleanora had worn this persona before, and her excuse for her lengthy absences between social events? Her travels to far-flung areas of the world. Posing as a young widow allowed her not to be subject to closer scrutiny, granting certain societal freedom.

No electric light was in this room; however, one was in the front hall. Numerous candelabras circling the perimeter provided the ballroom's soft illumination. It looked like a party from another age.

The subdued lighting caused the gold wallpaper to shimmer with a life of its own. Large mirrors and portraits of dead ancestors took up most of the wall space, along with silk cream curtains covering the windows. The ceiling had fancy gold leaf trim and crystal chandeliers.

Eleanora silently reminded herself to jut out her chin, hold back her shoulders, and take care of walking. She was not used to satin slippers and polished marble floors.

"Miss Baxendale!"

Eleanora turned toward the direction of the high-pitched screech: Lady Lillian Castle, second daughter of the Earl of Windham. Chatty young woman, she would be perfect for extracting specific facts.

"Lady Lillian, how delightful to see you," Eleanora said, using her well-practiced posh-snobbish tone.

"What a glorious gown; it matches the beautiful shade of your hair. I recently stopped by Sir Reginald's, but he said you were journeying in Canada. What an adventure! All those wretched moose and fur trappers. How rugged it must have been!" The words tumbled out of the high-strung heiress without her taking a breath.

She and Sir Reginald had agreed to use the Canada story, though he'd never mentioned someone had stopped for a visit. Eleanora would have to bring that point up at their next meeting.

Regarding Canada, she pried snippets of general information from Corbett Buchanan on the geography and whatnot. Eleanora had stored away a multitude of facts on the commonwealth country.

"My dear, only part of Canada is wilderness. I visited the cities exclusively. Montreal, Toronto. Halifax, on the East Coast, and Saint John, also a port city, Canada's first city, don't you know." She tapped Miss Castle's arm lightly with her gold fan. Corbett was from Saint John, so she had a few facts on that city tucked away as well. "Delightful society. Canadians are so polite and welcoming."

"I had no inkling. I thought those pioneers lived in log cabins and hunted for their supper," Lady Lillian stated. "Great Britain's untamed colony."

It took all Eleanora's self-control not to roll her eyes. Unfortunately, ladies of the upper classes did not receive the same education as young men. It was not right. In Eleanora's few dealings with society elites, she had often been shocked at the lack of imagination and the disdain for facts and curiosity about anything outside their protected sphere.

"Saint John is called 'The Loyalist City.' All those who stayed loyal to the crown during the Revolutionary War had a place to go and live once it ended. I attended the Loyalist Ball in a room much bigger than this one. Wonderful food. And Canada is a country; it has been since 1867; it is *not* a colony."

"How astonishing," Lady Lillian replied, her eyes glazing over with boredom.

It was time to change the subject.

"What have I missed in my absence? A friend wrote to me of some scandalous doings, usually involving the Marquess of Brookton."

Eleanora picked who, at a glance, she surmised was the most scandalous of The Rakes club. The blond Adonis fit the bill.

Lady Lillian brightened immediately. "Oh my, so much to catch you up on. You mentioned the most notorious rake of them all. Brookton and his friends are wild, to be certain!"

Eleanora edged Lady Lillian toward the far wall next to a massive potted fern to ensure privacy.

"Do tell, my lady," Eleanora murmured. "How wild?"

"Well, Brookton haunts the East End, attending every debauched club and musical hall he can find. No wonder he's referred to as 'Dorian Gray,' you know, after that scandalous book by the equally scandalous author. Is the novelist still in prison? I cannot remember." Lady Lillian's cheeks flushed; her voice was excited.

Eleanora had read *The Picture of Dorian Gray* by Oscar Wilde and found the gothic tale fascinating. The author was in prison for gross indecency, but she did not want to interrupt her ladyship and steer her off-topic.

"Nevertheless, regarding Brookton, there is talk of an illicit affair with an infamous actress," Lady Lillian leaned in closer, glancing about to ensure no one could overhear. "And her twin brother! Both at the same time!" She smiled victoriously at revealing her salacious gossip.

Eleanora gasped, placing her gloved hand over her mouth in counterfeit shock. "How scandalous indeed. No decent young lady of society would give him any consideration," Eleanora huffed with mock indignation.

Lady Lillian arched her eyebrows. "My dear, this makes him even more of a catch. Alas, he rarely attends social events such as this. None of them do; more's the pity. Nothing livens up a dull gathering than a pack of handsome men."

This salient fact of an immoral peer being more appealing than one who lived an honorable life was something Eleanora could not wrap her head around.

God above, I could use a drink.

Anything to get her through this tedium. Or better yet, a cigarette.

Imagine the scandal if she lit up one in the middle of this affluent congregation.

"And what of the dark-haired one with the pretty blue eyes? I cannot recall his name," she whispered to her ladyship. "Is he disreputable as well?"

"Well, a few of them are dark-haired. Do you mean one of the dukes?"

"Yes, the younger of the two."

"Ah, you must mean Allenby. I haven't heard anything recently, but he is nearly as scurrilous as the marquess. He certainly is unapproachable. He was so cold in his countenance that one could catch a chill standing next to him. He stands about when he deems to attend an event, looking down his nose at us all. Although handsome and a duke, he will soon seek a suitable bride. The man can hardly avoid it. All the young ladies await his entrance into the marriage mart with bated breath."

Eleanora had deduced most of this information at their first meeting.

Allenby was composed, aloof, every inch a duke. And quite handsome. But cruel? No, Eleanora did not think that of Allenby.

"They must have left many enemies in their wake, considering their disreputable behavior," Eleanora ventured.

"I'm not certain about enemies, though there is resentment in certain circles..." her voice trailed off. "Well, I am all astonishment. The Duke of Allenby just walked through the door wearing his usual expression of remoteness."

Eleanora straightened.

Sweet Mother.

She did not expect this at all as he could expose her disguise. Inspecting her surroundings, Eleanora located the balcony doors.

Blast it, just as she was close to discovering relevant information. How to slink unnoticed toward the exit?

"Miss Baxendale, he is heading this way!" Lady Lillian cried excitedly.

Oh, damn.

Chapter 6

WHEN CHRISTIAN FIRST entered the ballroom, his mother's words about finding a suitable bride replayed in his mind. He had agreed with her assessment—duty and whatnot.

His gaze landed on small clusters of young ladies chatting. A few others sat alone in chairs along the far wall, looking uncomfortable, as if they would rather be elsewhere. He understood the sentiment. Protective mamas and chaperones kept a close watch on those young ladies dancing.

Christian loathed this aspect of society.

His interest started to wane despite having every intention of milling about with marriageable young ladies. No, he needed to do this. It was time to act as a duke and see to his duty, whatever in the deviled hell that meant.

Sighing, he clasped his hands behind his back as his gaze landed on a statuesque young lady partially obscured by an oversized potted fern. His eyes narrowed as every nerve ending in his body came alive, crackling with sensual energy and awareness.

An actual reaction, and he did not expect it at this gathering.

Christian moved nearer, his concentrated gaze never wavering. The young lady was athletic in build, well-proportioned indeed. But her beautiful shade of brown hair. Where had he seen it before?

When he pondered where he might have met or observed the veritable Amazon, she turned slightly, and it struck him like a blow across the face.

Eleanora Galway.

Here.

Christian's interest increased a thousand-fold as his heated stare took in her lush figure. How had she managed to hide those curves under her laborer's disguise?

She turned and faced him; her eyes widened but swiftly schooled her features into bland apathy. Her skin looked like fine porcelain, but he would bet his moderate fortune it would be soft to the touch. Her lips were plump and lush, and the urge to kiss her senseless washed over him.

Next to her, a young lady whispered furiously, and Eleanora bent slightly at the waist to listen to the much shorter woman.

Ah, of course.

Lady Lillian Castle.

Her screeching voice reminded him of an agitated parrot squawking non-stop for crackers. However, he could use her to gain an introduction.

Suddenly, this dull affair had piqued his interest.

And curiosity.

What part was Eleanora playing now? And why?

Christian moved through the assembly with a clear purpose in mind.

Eleanora stepped out from behind the fern, and he got a full view of her. The copper and gold gown hugged each curve.

And she had the most glorious breasts.

She must have bound them to keep such abundance hidden under the oversized coat she had worn the night they'd met.

His raw and visceral reaction tempted him to fall to his knees before her.

Worship her. Surrender completely.

Easy now. A little control would not go amiss.

Purposefully, Christian exhaled, willing his rapid heartbeat to slow and his unbridled erection to lessen. Thank God for his formal evening coat, as it hid the evidence.

Christian stood before them and bowed. "My lady. How good to see you again?"

Though be damned if he could remember *where* he had seen her.

Giggling, she held out her gloved hand, and he politely bent over it before releasing it.

"Your Grace! What a delight to see you here! Does this mean you are at last seeking a bride?"

Squawk-squawk indeed.

Lady Lillian Castle's squealing voice cut clean through his spine, and he inwardly cringed. It certainly assisted in killing his arousal.

Instead, he focused on Eleanora, who shook her head slightly as if to warn him.

"And who is this? Would you introduce us, Lady Lillian?"

"Certainly! This is my dear friend, Miss Constance Baxendale, niece of Sir Reginald Ramsay. Are you acquainted with him? Perhaps not, as he is only a knight. Miss Baxendale, this is the Duke of Allenby."

"Sir Reginald and I may have socialized once or twice," he murmured.

Eleanora held out her gold-gloved hand. "A distinct honor, Your Grace."

He took her gloved hand, and heat passed between them. The flame traveled through all parts of him; what a strange but not unwelcome sensation.

Did Eleanora feel it too? Her expression did not change.

The flame turned to a raging fire. Those sinful lips and Eleanora's throaty voice stirred his cock. Instantly aroused again—to the point of torment.

"The honor is all mine, I assure you. Christian Bamford, at your service." He laid a brief kiss on her knuckles before reluctantly releasing her hand.

The small orchestra struck up a waltz.

"Are you otherwise engaged for this dance?" he asked her.

"No, I am not," she replied frostily.

Yes, she is good.

Eleanora was every inch the glacial heiress, right down to the posh accent. Her husky voice had his heart thumping against his ribcage. He held out his arm, and Eleanora lightly placed her hand upon it, allowing him to lead her to the dance floor.

"What are you doing," she ground out softly through gritted teeth.

"I could ask you the same thing, Miss Galway."

"I'm *not* a good dancer. You will expose my charade," she whispered furiously.

Gathering her as close as propriety allowed, he whirled her about the dance floor, a slight gasp of surprise leaving her luscious lips.

"I am an exceptional dancer, all part of my blue blood upbringing and training." He gave her a teasing wink.

Christian abruptly swirled her along the perimeter of the room, and a smile curled about her lips, her eyes bright.

"Everyone is watching us," Eleanora whispered as she gazed at the crowd.

"Of course we are. After all, I'm a duke." He gave her another teasing wink. "Everything I do causes speculation as I haven't danced with a young lady at a social event such as this for quite some time. It would excite comment and will undoubtedly make the society pages."

"Drat it; the last thing we want is to draw attention," she admonished, fingers digging into his shoulder.

"Too late." Christian dared to pull her close enough that the hem of her gown landed between his legs with each turn about the marbled floor.

Eleanora was almost looking him in the eye; he liked that. Her waist was trim, her shoulders broad, and he liked that too. By God, she felt right in his arms.

A warrior goddess.

In his mind's eye, he pictured her clad in armor and wielding a sword, leading an attack on a horde of barbarians. The thought aroused him further.

"You look exquisite tonight," Christian ventured, his voice low and hoarse. "You're shimmering like a gold ingot. The gown is lovely and complements your coloring and, dare I say, your luxuriant figure?"

Yes, he was flirting and teasing and having more fun than he had in an age.

"Or perhaps you're similar to a butterscotch sponge cake with chocolate ganache. I wonder if your succulent lips taste as sweet?"

Eleanora laughed, and he was pleased that she was taking his light-hearted banter in the way he intended. Her full-throated chortle caught the attention of all around them, and Christian joined in as he pivoted her in the reverse direction. As far as he was concerned, he could dance with her all night.

Everywhere Eleanora touched him, her hand on his shoulder, her other hand resting lightly in his, ached with awareness.

Her laughter ended with a dazzling smile covering him with a flourishing warmth that summarily flared to a roaring flame once again.

How tempting to nuzzle her soft neck and inhale her glorious scent. Eleanora was not awash in lavender, as was the fashion these last years, but hers was more of a spicy mixture, and it appealed to him.

Christian wanted to know: did she apply it directly to her soft skin or garments?

The thought of her elegant fingers trailing across her naked skin made him moan softly. Thankfully, the loud music masked his indecorous reaction.

Gently, he squeezed her hand, his thumb caressing her knuckles. Eleanora's eyes widened. Her hand resting on his shoulder moved slightly in a circular motion, caressing him. Every part of him was aware and alive as never before.

Briefly, he pulled her closer until her breasts mashed against his chest. The contact seared, and his eyes narrowed with desire.

To Eleanora's credit, she did not pull away. Instead, she trailed the tips of her fingers along the valley of his spine. He growled in response.

The spell broke as the music came to a crescendo. The dance ended far too soon. Christian came to an abrupt stop, and their gazes locked. The room was quiet, or perhaps all faded away, leaving no one but him and Eleanora. Her chest was rising and falling from their exertion. Several beats passed before their hands slowly moved away from their shoulders and waists.

Eleanora curtsied with her head down and murmured, "Tomorrow afternoon at three o'clock. Come to 149 Cleveland Street. I have questions."

"So do I, Miss Galway. Many of them."

She whirled about and glided away from him before he even could escort her back to Miss Castle. Perhaps it was for the best, as they had attracted far too much notice. But he couldn't help himself; he had to hold her in his arms.

It had been absolutely *glorious*.

Seeking, then finding the balcony doors, he strode outside, taking great gulps of humid early autumn air. Ever since he had become aware of women in a sexual way, he had never had such a stark reaction as the one he had just experienced with Eleanora Galway.

Not ever.

Completely foreign.

This flirtation was not wise.

Christian had employed Eleanora to discover the truth about the body part delivered to his club. Is that why she was here? Had she located a suspect already? What had Miss Castle whispered in her ear? No doubt filled her in on his disreputable reputation, one he had been coasting on for months.

He will obtain answers tomorrow. In the meantime, keeping his attraction under wraps would be best. How he would be able to achieve it was another matter.

It shouldn't be problematic. Christian learned at an early age to hide behind his diffident ducal mask.

It was time to do so once again.

Chapter 7

ELEANORA'S INSIDES were fluttering like mad.

It was an inappropriate response when one was holding a question-and-answer summit with a client. But a little vigilance would not go amiss after her brief encounter with the Duke of Allenby at the ball the previous night and her heated reaction to being held in his arms.

What a magnificent dancer.

Being in his arms had given her a decided thrill, which she was not used to experiencing in *any* situation. When Allenby had brought her against his solidness, there was no mistaking his arousal, and it had stoked her passion to higher heights.

It was as if hundreds of butterflies had unfurled their wings within her stomach. And the flutters had continued the entire time she was in Allenby's arms. And after she had returned home.

When Eleanora first saw him at his club, she had hardly given him any mind. Well, she had noticed his looks. The man was wonderfully put together, with his fine blue eyes and handsome face. How could you not notice him?

But the ball had changed everything.

Her hands trailed across her middle, hoping to calm the wobbles in her stomach. All this over anticipating the arrival of a man?

Yes. This particular man.

The duke had sparked her interest and desire as no man had before. And for that reason, it merited further investigation.

Eleanora wore one of her best afternoon tea gowns and also managed to style her hair. Was it obvious what she was doing? That she wished to make a good impression on Allenby?

Eleanora had spent the morning in the kitchen—baking. It was one of her favorite hobbies. She could barely boil water for tea, let alone make a full meal, but she was a proficient baker. Baking was calming, allowing her to compartmentalize her thoughts concerning various questions or clues.

One question occupying her mind this morning?

The dark duke and all the deliciously wicked things she wanted to do to him—and with him.

The truth? Eleanora was not a virgin.

Along with her independent mind, she concluded early on that she would probably never marry, so why deny herself the pleasure of physical relations? To date, she had two—she would not call them affairs exactly, dalliances?

Yes, that fit.

She had enjoyed carnal relations and equally appreciated that there were no deeper emotions to complicate matters.

Yet, Allenby stirred up a maelstrom of confusing feelings. All from a dance and harmless flirting? How strange that she was experiencing a case of nerves as if she were a young lady of society waiting for her suitor.

Utter bollocks.

"There you are," Althea called out, pulling her from her thoughts. "What is all the to-do? Baking? Mother's tea service? Your best afternoon dress?"

"We've never had a duke on the premises before," Eleanora replied, trying to keep the emotion from her voice.

"Hmm. You have yet to inform me of what transpired at the ball." Althea plopped into one of the chairs and picked up the wildflower-patterned china, giving it a close inspection.

Sybil entered the room and joined them.

Eleanora snatched the plate from her sister's hand and placed it on the table. "Allenby showed up."

"At the ball?" Sybil's eyes widened. "What did you do?"

"I played my role, and he went along with the deception. We danced. A waltz. The duke left soon after, and I found some information from a third party."

Eleanora sat at the table and relayed the conversation with the chatty Lady Lillian.

"After the waltz, she clamped onto me. I downplayed the dance, and over a glass of punch, she revealed that although society sought out the rakes as possible matches, certain peers and others resented them. How much of the dislike translates to sending a severed leg to their club? It's hard to gauge?"

"I cannot picture some stuffy old marquess sending a body part as a prank," Sybil stated.

"Neither can I. Which leaves the possibility of a younger peer? One of their acquaintances from school or later," Eleanora replied. "Or former members of the club."

Althea shrugged. "Could be anyone, even current members of the club. How many people have they slighted through the years—or worse? We are all aware that these aristocrats believe that they're above the law. How often had Da and Uncle Reece stated their frustration about how these privileged few get away with the lot, no matter how serious? The manner in which they blatantly and smugly lie, how will we know if these stuffy aristos will even tell us the truth of any worrisome encounters? Remember the Cleveland Street Scandal?"

Althea had the right of it.

Eleanora nodded in agreement. "Exactly, and it is why we are gathering information on them. And yes, I remember the scandal. Point taken."

At the opposite end of their street, some distance away, a post office was identified as a front for a brothel, and the messenger boys were male prostitutes. It was quite a scandal in the papers most of 1889, with peers of all ranks, right up to royalty, accused as customers. But no convictions arose since those in power swept the scandal under the rug because of the privileged men involved.

Typical.

"Before we continue, I have a letter from Mother." Sybil held up the open envelope. "I feel terrible for doing this to you, but I must leave for Yorkshire immediately."

"Oh, no. It's not bad news?" Althea said.

"Father is unwell. Nothing too serious; the doctor there says it is mild pneumonia. I haven't been home in months; I want to assist my mother. I shouldn't be gone more than ten days to two weeks, and I don't like leaving while we are working a case." Sybil frowned, clearly torn.

Eleanora clasped Sybil's hand. "Dear Cousin. Don't concern yourself. Take care of Uncle James, and hug him for us. Of course, we understand. You must go at once."

The frown turned into a sunny smile. "You both are absolutely lovely. Thank you. I'll start packing right away. Unless you want me to remain for the meeting and take notes?"

"No, Althea can do it," Eleanora said as she released Sybil's hand.

Sybil stood. "Then I'll slip out before the duke arrives. I'll be upstairs if you need me."

Their cousin departed, and Eleanora exhaled.

"Well, guess we will have to carry on," Althea muttered.

"Sybil will be back before we know it. Besides, I cannot see this case concluding before she returns."

"True. It will be next to impossible to discover who did this—if it is indeed a hoax or something more sinister, "Althea said. "Unless this becomes a pattern."

Eleanora arched an eyebrow. "More body parts? How morbid. We will know soon enough. In the meantime, we continue to explore all paths. Brookton will be here tomorrow at three o'clock, and I want you to take the lead in the interview."

"Why me?" Althea shook her head. "I doubt I can remain impartial. His attitude—"

Eleanora held up her hand. "Something sparked between you, and we should use it to our advantage."

"Yes, Ellie, something sparked. It's called revulsion. He is everything I loathe in a man. Besides, he's far too pretty; no man should be that flawless. It isn't normal," Althea exclaimed, her voice rising in irritation.

"Well, you could classify Allenby as pretty, too."

"And since when do we conduct such probing interviews with those that have hired us?" Althea continued, ignoring Eleanora's statement. "We usually inquire about our clients before jumping feet first into a case. You are steaming ahead without thinking this through, and it's not like you."

"I am, but we have to approach this case differently than others. These men are of the peerage: two dukes, a marquess, a baron, and two viscounts, along with a rich businessman of the gentry class. We cannot approach other peers to make queries. They all protect each other. Besides, something Lady Lillian said at the ball has been nagging me: these rakes have caused resentment in certain circles. I want to see what they have to say about it."

"And if they are not truthful?"

"Then we hold firm to our rules. We do not take the case of anyone who is not upfront with us."

Althea considered it and nodded. "Why not interview them all at the same time?"

"The men will open up more if we interview them individually. At the least, with the two main rakes, Allenby and Brookton."

"What about the older duke, Watford?" Althea asked.

"Did you notice he stood back from the rest, hardly spoke or offered any opinion? I have the distinct feeling he acts removed from most doings."

Althea nodded. "Yes, I did notice. Mr. Knight was near Watford as well. The rest looked to Allenby."

"If we need to interview the others, we will. I will conduct the conference here in the parlor instead of the office; it will put the duke more at ease. Hence the tea service. You will take notes, and I will do the same for you tomorrow."

Althea rubbed her temple absently. "I'm still not certain that this is wise. However, we will do as you suggest. Where is Mrs. Bartle, by the way?"

Their esteemed housekeeper-cook was in her mid-forties and almost as tall as Eleanora. Mrs. Bartle would not hesitate to bash someone on the noggin with her broom if they stepped out of line. Mrs. Bartle was not a live-in employee; she came daily, except Sundays, to do general household cleaning. She prepared meals in bulk so they could heat them at their leisure. It meant they lived on meat pies and stews, which suited Eleanora.

"I sent her home early. She roasted a nice chicken with vegetables so we would have enough for the next several meals. I also made rolls this morning. Don't forget that tomorrow night is dinner with Uncle Reece and Aunt Wilhelmina." Eleanora paused. "I had best send word Sybil will not be accompanying us."

Althea's eyes lit up. "I cannot wait; Aunt is a wonderful cook. And I smelled the rolls baking earlier, and I cannot wait for those either." She grabbed the handle of the covered cake platter. "And what's in here?"

The bell clanged loudly in the hallway.

"He's here sooner than I expected," Eleanora said breathlessly. "Quick, make ready. Fetch the pen, ink, and paper. Promise that you will take copious notes."

"I will." Althea jumped to her feet and hurried into the hall toward the study.

Smoothing her light green cotton and silk gown, Eleanora exhaled as she headed toward the front door. When she opened it, the sight of Allenby caused her breath to hitch in her throat.

The duke wore a tight-fighting long black coat, gray trousers, black Homburg hat, and silver ascot, and he looked utterly appealing. He gave her a crooked grin while tapping his leather gloves in his palm. Tucked under his arm was a newspaper.

He tugged on the brim of his hat. "Good afternoon, Miss Galway. I hope I am not too early?"

Eleanora stepped aside. "Not at all. Please, come in."

Once he did, she took the proffered hat, gloves, and coat; and arranged them on the mirrored hall tree. Catching a glimpse in the mirror, she was appalled to observe that her cheeks were flushed. And those flutters increased as well, drat it. Already she was losing control of this meeting.

Concentrate. Gain control.

Taking another cleansing breath, she led Allenby to the parlor.

He nodded as he gave the room a thorough inspection.

"I like this room; it's cozy. You have a gramophone." Allenby laid the paper on the table and strolled over to it. "HMV, the latest model. I have a variation of the same, except my horn is metal, not wood. Have you many discs?"

Eleanora came to stand beside him. "Only a few, mostly classical arrangements, and I like to play it when I read."

He turned and gave her a dazzling smile, causing her heart to stutter.

"I do the same as I find it relaxing. One would think it would interfere with concentrating on the written word, but it does not. Have you made the switch to electricity?" Christian asked.

"No, far too pricey. Have you?"

Allenby ran his finger along the wood surface of the gramophone. "Only a few rooms at the town house. The main parlor and my study. One day I will convert the entire place to electricity. But there is no rush. It is not catching on as rapidly as the telephone."

Eleanora clapped her hands together. "Isn't it a wonderful modern age we live in? So many innovations, it is hard to keep up."

"That is quite true. Mark my words; I predict motorized automobiles will become more common on roads and streets as we move into the new century. The Locomotives on Highway Act became law last year. Four years ago, I gambled on this prediction and bought into a new enterprise, now known as The Daimler Motor Company."

"How forward-thinking of you," Eleanora said, impressed that a duke would be interested in such developments in the industry.

"We will soon see if my prediction bears out. We've recently bought an old cotton mill in Coventry for engine and chassis manufacture."

"I would love to see a motor car in production," she replied eagerly.

"Then we shall arrange it soon."

Eleanora gave him a warm smile. "An automobile may be out of my immediate reach, but I will obtain a telephone before electricity as the device will be useful for my business. Speaking of which, time to begin our meeting. Please do take a seat, Allenby."

Althea entered the room, carrying a tray with the writing implements.

"Good afternoon, Your Grace. Or Allenby, as you prefer."

"Good afternoon, Miss Galway." The duke pulled out a chair for Althea and then did the same for her.

Independent, she may be, but Eleanora had to admit she enjoyed it when a man used proper etiquette.

Once they were seated, he handed her the newspaper.

"Look about halfway down. The society page."

Eleanora read: "'London Society was all atwitter with speculation of the reappearance of the Duke of Allenby at a fête at the Earl of Pembroke's stately London home. The darkly-handsome duke danced with only one young lady. Witnesses report they were talking and laughing intimately. This column has learned the statuesque heiress is Constance Baxendale, widowed niece of Sir Reginald Ramsay recently returned from a journey to the Canadian wilderness—'"

Eleanora's voice trailed off.

Blast it all.

She *knew* better.

Eleanora certainly did not interact with men except for the occasional flirtatious remark before moving off to complete her mission. She had kept a low profile when attending these social events to gather information. She talked to a small select number of attendees.

But when Allenby had asked her to dance, all caution had disappeared.

"Oh, Ellie. The society column of all things," Althea snorted. "This is a first, even if it is under a false name."

"Widow?" Allenby looked amused, and it annoyed her further. "Why were you introduced as a miss?"

"I explained to Lady Lillian at a previous meeting that I wanted to be referred to by my maiden name. Well, I cannot use that persona again. Saying I'm a widow makes it easier to attend these events alone. What a blasted aggravation. And we can surmise the talkative

Lady Lillian was the witness mentioned." Her brows knotted in frustration.

"Read on," he urged, the corner of his mouth twitching with amusement.

Sighing, Eleanora glanced at the paper again. "There's more?"

Althea's eyes twinkled. "Oh, do go on, Ellie."

"Very well. 'Sir Reginald informed the author of this column that his niece does not reside with him. He would not reveal where she is staying, only to say she frequently travels out of the country.' My God, they went to Sir Reginald's? Oh, he will not like that at all. 'Fear not, dear reader, for we will ascertain the location of His Grace's paramour.'" She looked up from the paper. "Paramour? Are they insinuating that I am a concubine? What do these reporters do, follow you about?"

Allenby gave a slight shrug. "It happens now and then. In this context, they mean more of a sweetheart or admirer than a doxy. Though I suppose the reader could take either way."

Eleanora slammed the paper on the table. "Well, hang it all; they could have followed you here!"

"I *am* well aware when someone follows me, and I took precautions," Allenby replied matter-of-factly.

Eleanora arched a dubious eyebrow at him. "Perhaps I should hire *you* for my agency."

"Perhaps you should," Allenby responded. "Why no men on your payroll?"

"I don't require any. We are all capable. My late father was a chief inspector with D Division, and he trained us well. My uncle is an inspector with J Division in Bethnal Green. He is supportive and assists us when able. And I have my Canadian and one or two others when needs must."

"Yes, your police surgeon. Before we begin, here is the rest of your fee." Allenby reached into his pocket and placed a small roll of pound notes on the table. "Have you made any discoveries?"

"A few. But I want us to conduct the interview first." Eleanora held up the teapot. "Tea? Or would you prefer coffee?"

"I drink both but prefer tea in the afternoon. Milk, if you have it, and no sugar."

Exactly how she preferred hers, though she didn't care for coffee. She passed the cup and saucer to Allenby, then did the same for Althea, who smiled knowingly.

Ignoring her sister, Eleanora lifted the cover off the platter. "I made the cake; would you care for a slice?"

Allenby leaned in to inspect it. "You bake?"

"Frequently. I cannot cook worth a farthing, but I love to bake."

"Ellie is a skilled baker. It's a wonder we have not gained weight over the years," Althea interjected.

Eleanora basked in the praise, and a little bragging would not go amiss because of it.

"Scones are my specialty."

The duke chuckled, and the masculine sound rumbled from his chest and reverberated in hers. How shameless of her, but the ease with which they conversed made him even more attractive. If that were possible.

"I adore them. Scones-that is. Apple is my favorite. Hot from the oven and served with clotted cream and apple jelly. And what is this masterpiece?" he smiled, the corner of his eyes crinkling.

He did have the most attractive light blue eyes. Absolutely stunning.

"Butterscotch sponge cake with chocolate ganache, of course."

The exact cake the duke had mentioned at the ball last night, and Eleanora couldn't resist baking it.

Allenby threw back his head and laughed heartily. It was the first time Eleanora had heard him laugh so profoundly; heat traveled through her at the joyous sound. This smiling, talkative duke was far removed from the one Lady Lillian had described. And from the one she had met that first night at his club.

What a fascinating discovery.

"Wonderful. I will take a large slice if you please." Allenby's laugh turned into a bracing smile.

Not in on the private joke, Althea glanced between them, puzzled. Eleanora would explain it to her sister later in the evening.

After passing him the plate, Allenby plunged his fork across the corner.

"Look how easily the fork moves through the sponge. It is light and airy; the ganache is shiny with just the right amount of thickness," Allenby placed the forkful in his mouth and groaned. "Unequivocally delicious."

"Your Grace, you sound like a country fair judge at a cake-baking contest," Eleanora teased.

"I cannot conceive of a better occupation. And do me a favor, Eleanora; call me Christian when we're alone like this. Allenby, in public if you like. Miss Galway, please permit me to address you as Althea."

Her sister smiled. "Of course, Christian."

Who is this charming man?

What had happened to the dark, brooding duke?

Not that he was all that brooding. Again, Eleanora recalled how his description at the ball. 'Unapproachable, cold in his countenance, remote.'

He turned out to be none of those things, not deep down where it counted.

Christian.

She had liked the name from the first time she'd heard it. It wasn't exactly proper, but to hell with it. From this moment forward, she would think of him as Christian.

For the next several minutes, they all ate quietly.

Although, Eleanora exchanged the occasional heated look with the duke. At last, he pushed his plate aside.

"Another slice?" she asked.

"Perhaps later. Let us begin the inquisition. I assume you will question me about my private life, and I also assume it's to ascertain why some anonymous person delivered a body part to my club."

How astute of him.

Eleanora nodded. "You have the right of it. Althca will be taking notes. Why form a club? What is its exact purpose?"

Chapter 8

CHRISTIAN TAPPED HIS fingers on the table's surface, his gaze firm on Eleanora. Revealing his innermost private thoughts rankled, he barely did with the lads.

Ever.

But for whatever reason, he wished to know this captivating woman better.

One way to achieve such would be to divulge certain aspects of his life. Plus, it may assist in closing the door on this ghoulish practical joke.

So much for wearing his diffident ducal mask; that prospect went to the wayside when Eleanora opened the door and warmly greeted him. And as soon as they shared a private conversation, one that had him feeling more relaxed than he had in an age.

I might as well get on with the inquisition.

"Part of our club was formed at Eton, a ragged group of lonely boys, starving for social interaction. I'm not being factious; we were a sad lot. None of us have any siblings. We all gravitated toward each other for the support, I suppose." Christian hesitated, then grimaced.

"Although, now that I reflect on it, it wasn't only the lack of siblings. Almost all of us had neglectful and or wretched fathers. Or no fathers at all. Our group consisted of Wenlock, Brookton, Huxley, and Tolwood. After university, we joined up with Watford. He is a founding member of the Rakes of St. Regent's Park and the last of the original group. The club had been around for more than fifteen years. We merged our little group with his."

"How many were in your group while in school?"

There were seven of us."

"So, all seven are not part of your group now?"

"No."

"What happened to the other two?" Eleanora asked.

Althea kept her head down, her pen moving swiftly across the paper. How mortifying. It was distressing enough speaking of this in front of Eleanora, but her sister too.

It had been an age since he had considered either of his former friends. "Hayes Addington, the heir to a baron, died from an apparent drowning when we were sixteen. Ford Whitney, the son of a baronet? The last I heard from him was close to seven years past, as he lives in India."

Was Ford a former friend? Perhaps so. They hadn't spoken face-to-face since 'The Hayes Incident.'

Eleanora's eyebrows rose. "Apparent drowning?"

"We were drunk and holding a bonfire on a beach during the summer break. Since no corpse materialized, Hayes was declared legally dead some years ago, and the title will pass to a distant cousin," he whispered. "Sooner rather than later, I gather, for I hear Baron Addington is not well."

Speaking of this caused a generous dash of guilt to arise. Old ghosts were hard to shake once they reappeared.

"How did he drown," she asked softly. "The heir, that is."

"Memory is certainly faulty when one drinks to excess. I believe I passed out, as had the others. When we awoke, it was dark, and Hayes was gone, only his coat and shoes left by the shore. The authorities concluded that an inebriated Hayes stripped off to go for a swim and drowned. His body no doubt carried out to the ocean thanks to the tides in the Thames."

"Why would he swim in the filthy Thames? Where were you when this happened? The exact location?" Eleanora asked.

"We were on the Isle of Sheppey near Kent. Brookton's family had a summer retreat there. Not any longer. The Duke of Chellenham sold the property soon after the incident."

"So not in London."

"No, not London. Regardless, the inquest concluded Hayes was missing, presumed dead by accidental drowning. As far as Whitney is concerned, none of us have seen him since that night on the beach. Everything is still hazy concerning the event. But we all shared in the blame. It is why overindulgence in any of our vices is strictly prohibited. I barely drink anymore, although I may have the occasional whiskey at the club," Christian stated.

"Why have you not seen Ford Whitney since the night at the beach? That would be how many years?" Eleanora asked.

"Fourteen. I do not know why we haven't seen Ford. When Ford didn't attend school the next term, we made inquiries with his father. The baronet stated that Ford traveled to India to be with his uncle and continue his education there. It was all rather sudden."

"Have you heard from him since?"

Christian had always found it strange that Ford disappeared without a word to any of them. Until that night, they were close and confided in each other.

"There were letters the first couple of years, and the baronet sent them by messenger. Ford mentioned that he misses us and that his life is productive, content, and satisfying. Actually, we all envied his gratification with his new circumstances. We haven't heard from him in years."

"This baronet's full name?"

"Sir Howard Whitney. Why?"

"In case we need to question him regarding the current location of his son. Is a baronet part of the peerage?"

"No."

"Then why include the oldest son of one in your exclusive group?"

Christian scoffed. "You make us sound like priggish snobs, which I suppose we are. I've been a duke since the age of nine. I formed the group at school and felt sorry for Ford, and sponsored his membership. Besides, Ford would become a baronet when his father died. I had no objection to Brandon Knight joining our present assembly."

"A duke at age nine? Sweet Mother," Eleanora exclaimed.

"My father was decades older than my mother, leaving her a young widow."

"Why did you feel sorry for Ford Whitney?"

"He was short, overweight, soft-spoken, an easy target for cruel boys. At first, we joined in with the teasing. But it was heading in a dangerous direction: the line so often crossed at these elite schools. We all stood up for him in one particular incident, and he started following us around like a grateful puppy. It grew from there."

Christian paused. Speaking of this was stirring up old feelings of lonesomeness and resentment. "In times of need, the lads and I turned to each other. We could count on each other when there was nowhere else to go or no one to turn to."

"Until the night of the drowning," Eleanora interjected.

His heart squeezed with regret. "Yes. We let Hayes down. That night we did *not* look out for each other. Not at all."

Eleanora caught his gaze and held it. There was no pity in her eyes, and he appreciated that.

"I have heard of resentment directed toward your group," she said. "You see, many outside your protective circle would find you all pampered and privileged, those who have theirs and don't give a hang about anyone else. Arrogant and pompous. Above the law."

Eleanora paused, giving him a reflective look. "Your description of looking out for one another would have an entirely different meaning to those of the lower classes, as in you would protect each other from rebuke. From justice."

Christian arched an eyebrow. The description annoyed him, and his blood simmered. "Is that what you believe?"

"On the surface, it appears as such. Those in your class often skirt any responsibility. This reckless behavior has continued for hundreds of years and will continue well into the future. Wealth is power, and power begets power, and it creates isolation from any atonement."

Her summarization of his frivolous life vexed him. However, hadn't he been concluding that he no longer wished to own such a worthless existence?

"I can assure you—as far as I'm aware—none of us have perpetrated any misdeeds that would involve the law. We are not thieves, assaulters, or rapists; we practice caution in all dealings, never indulging to excess...." His voice died.

Sitting back in his chair, he rubbed the bridge of his nose. "We are spoiled rotten and thoughtless to the feelings of others. We're everything you have described. I've no idea what the lads got up to these past years. All we do is meet once a week and blatantly lie about our conquests, either exaggerating or downplaying. The truth is much more pathetic. We are sorry excuses for human beings. There is no one particular incident I can point to that would warrant a body part delivery."

The cake he had consumed roiled in his stomach, for speaking the truth was far more of a dilemma than he imagined. He looked up. Christian found both sisters staring at him, but not with pity or disgust, thankfully. What possessed him to spill his soul?

Eleanora laid a hand on top of the one he had flat against the table surface. Immediate and much-needed warmth traveled through him.

"We all have regrets, and I admire your honesty. I will need more of it." Patting his hand, she motioned to Althea to attend to her notes. "You recall a tattoo on the ankle of the severed leg."

Christian was grateful for the topic shift. "Yes, a butterfly."

"My Canadian, Dr. Corbett Buchanan, informed us that tattoo is on the ankles of certain prostitutes of The Chrysalis, a high-end brothel."

In each instance, she said, "My Canadian," a red-hot poker of jealousy speared his heart.

Jealous? What in the hell was going on here?

Christian pushed the foreign emotion from his mind and focused on the tattoo. Right. Why hadn't he made the connection?

"I take it you have frequented this establishment? As well as your friends?" Eleanora asked.

"Yes." They had attended the club many times. Though for him, not often and not of late.

"Dr. Buchanan claims the brothel is exclusive and private, that only *you* may gain me entry and a meeting with the owner. We need to establish if her workers have left or gone missing lately. I want us to go now."

Wait, what?

"Now?"

She couldn't be serious. But by the determined expression on her face, she most decidedly was.

"Ellie, is this wise?" Althea questioned.

"Of course it is." She slid her gaze to him. "I assume they are open at all hours, correct?"

Christian rubbed his chin. "Well, from one o'clock in the afternoon until two in the morning."

Eleanora stood, her resolute look more determined than before. "Is your carriage outside?" He nodded. "Brilliant, then let us depart immediately. Althea, I believe it best you stay here. Too many people may spook the owner and make her less likely to talk."

"If you insist. I'll assist Sybil with her packing."

Christian shook his head. "A brothel is not a proper place for—oh, hell. Let us depart, then."

He strode toward the door, Eleanora right on his heels. As they gathered up outerwear, he could not help but observe her face's genuine excitement and pleasure. Eleanora Galway had a purpose in life, an occupation she enjoyed.

How envious he was of her resolve. But he also admired it.

The sweetness of her butterscotch cake was still on his lips; he drank in the dazzling sight. He adored her frank and open way of speaking.

And it heightened his attraction toward her even more.

Chapter 9

DURING THEIR CONVERSATIONS, it was easy to forget that Christian was a duke. Eleanora had never ridden in such a plush and fancy carriage. She studied him as he stared out the window, holding the velvet curtain aside with his gloved hand. He possessed a handsome profile, a well-formed chin, and a sharp blade of a nose: long lashes and high cheekbones.

Christian was entirely wrong for her, not even for a short dalliance.

Why did that enter her mind?

Because she was attracted to him—and not only for his looks, which is not wise.

Calculating his age from their conversation, he was thirty years old, four years older than she. Eleanora had thought him older somehow. Because of his bearing? Or the deeply-etched frown lines bracketing his mouth?

What he had revealed to her about how his group formed—touched her. He looked lonely and lost sitting here.

Or perhaps it was her overactive imagination.

As Althea constantly reminded her, Eleanora involved herself too much in the lives of her clients. Through the years, Eleanora discovered that someone blessed with good fortune, good looks, and even a title could still not be content.

How she would love to hear the duke's masculine laughter once again. Instinctively, Eleanora knew he did not do it often, proving that no matter how privileged, a person could still be unhappy. A group of lonely lads had found refuge and friendship until one summer night on a moonlit shoreline. At least she had a few avenues to explore concerning this investigation.

With one last longing look at the duke, Eleanora sighed softly. Any assignation with a duke, however brief, would not be prudent. How typical the first instance she found a man attractive in many months, he was utterly unattainable.

Shame, that.

He released the curtain and turned to face her. "Is your cousin going on a trip?"

"Sybil will be traveling to Yorkshire. Her father, my Uncle James, is not feeling well. Nothing serious, but Sybil wants to be with him. She could be gone ten days to two weeks."

Christian crossed his legs. "She doesn't live with her parents?"

"They bought a sheep farm in Yorkshire three years ago. Sybil did go with them at first but found she despised country life. She travels between the two locations, sort of a sixty-forty split of her time, all told during the run of a year. When in London, she stays with us and assists Althea and me in our work."

The carriage pulled up in front of a brick and stone multi-storied building. The door opened, and Christian climbed out first, turned, and held out his hand to assist her.

"Where are we exactly?" she asked.

"Basinghall Street."

"Not far from your club, how convenient."

Christian frowned and didn't reply.

Her sarcastic comment was too on the mark, perhaps. She must curb her tongue.

Once they reached the front door, the duke gave three short knocks, and the grille slid open. A pair of bloodshot eyes stared back questioningly.

"Allenby and guest. Jasmine."

The door creaked open, and a gigantic man stepped aside.

"Your Grace, welcome."

Jasmine must be a password; how clandestine.

Corbett had the right of it; she would never have gained entry. Christian led her upstairs before she could thoroughly inspect the place. Emerging from a room at the top of the stairs, a petite woman dressed in a plush lavender gown greeted the duke with a sly smile.

"Your Grace. You have brought a visitor. Will you require another girl to join you both?" she purred.

It took several seconds for Eleanora to understand the meaning.

Oh. A threesome, or another term: a ménage.

What could one man possibly do with two women? She had a vague idea. Had the duke participated in one before? Obviously. Reading about vice in her father's books was not the same as witnessing the surroundings in which such doings transpired.

"Not today, Bathsheba," Christian replied, his voice distantly ducal. "We were hoping for a brief and private meeting."

She stepped aside." Do come in, Your Grace, and your guest, and take a seat." She pointed to the plush circle of chairs in the corner of the large room. As she closed the door, she asked, "May I offer you something to drink? Or possibly tea or coffee?"

She was polite, and her accent was aristocratic, but it could be counterfeit. Eleanora could do the same when needed.

"No, thank you. Unless?" Christian looked at her, and Eleanora shook her head.

Bathsheba sat opposite, her hands clasped in her lap.

"This is Miss Eleanora Galway of The Galway Investigative Agency."

Bathsheba's shoulders straightened; a taut line formed about her generous mouth.

"As a favor to me," Christian continued, "Could you address her inquires?"

"Of course."

But her body language said the complete opposite. Bathsheba wanted nothing to do with this. Not at all.

"I will require your complete discretion. This conversation is private," Christian said sternly.

He used the "I am a duke, and you shall heed me" tone.

The madam nodded, a flash of fear in her eyes. Yes, he was intimidating, but not to Eleanora. No man would ever be, regardless of titles or societal standings.

"A butterfly tattoo is on the ankle of several of your sex workers. Why?" Eleanora asked.

Corbett had already told her why, but she wanted to judge the madam's character—and level of truthfulness.

Bathsheba's lips pursed. "I have strict rules of engagement. My elite girls are attractive, clean, and only for my best customers. The tattoo reflects that they have been employed here for one year and are healthy. My elite employees undergo countless rigorous physical examinations. And they are expensive."

She smiled knowingly at the duke, and a stab of resentment tore through Eleanora. No, it wasn't resentment but jealousy—of any woman who had ever been with Christian.

How strange. This unknown emotion would bear further reflection. Eleanora swiftly filed it away and turned her attention to the madam.

"Have any of these elite girls been dismissed or departed of their own accord in the past year? Or more?" Eleanora asked.

The madam's mouth twitched. Her pupils dilated. She was about to lie; Eleanora would bet coin on it.

"My employees are satisfied with their lot, and I am satisfied with them."

A complete non-answer.

"Someone has departed, or I would not be asking. Either that or you have a one-legged prostitute in your employ," Eleanora snapped. "Come now, speak the truth."

Bathsheba glowered, confusion showing on her face at the one-legged comment. Eleanora wasn't about to explain.

"There have been two in the past year," the madam replied. "One gave her notice as she had found a rich patron, another I dismissed for breaking the rules of the house."

"What rules?" Christian interjected.

"She was not using sheaths with certain customers, charging an additional fee, and pocketing the money," the madam replied, nervously glancing at the duke.

"What? You made certain guarantees. Now I find you're not diligent in your dealings." Christian was annoyed. "You guaranteed that all the ladies used protection in *every* circumstance."

Who could blame him? Eleanora was annoyed as well but for a different reason altogether.

How dare Christian meddle in her investigation?

"Thank you, *Your Grace*," Eleanora admonished, "Allow me to continue."

He raised an eyebrow at her, for the duke did not like someone speaking to him in such a blunt and reproachful manner.

Then he did the strangest thing; a smile curved about his mouth, and his eyes twinkled.

With what, amusement? No, she had seen that heated look before in men's eyes—and she had seen it in Christian's eyes: last night at the ball when they danced.

It was—desire.

Something else to ponder later.

"Pray continue, Miss Galway," he murmured.

"Thank you." She pulled a small notebook and pencil from her cloak's pocket. "Please give me a description of the employee you dismissed."

Bathsheba huffed. "Medium height, slim, blonde, but I believe she dyed her hair. Attractive, even beautiful, I suppose. In her early twenties. There is nothing else to say."

"There is every chance the employee you dismissed is now deceased, and I will not reveal the particulars. A blood test showed high traces of mercury and iodine in the blood, and I'm certain you are aware of what the combination portends. The person was suffering from syphilis, and taking that combination is believed in medical circles to stem the worst symptoms, if only temporarily."

"What!" Christian yelled, rising to his feet.

The madam looked horrified and worried. "I assure you, Your Grace, that I—"

"Give me the names of the women no longer in your employ," Eleanora demanded.

"I will not. I have a reputation to uphold—"

"I assure you, *madam*, I will make it my mission to tell all and sundry of the decided lack of accountability you took for your brothel. No one of any worth will ever darken your door again," Christian snarled. "The Duke of Watford will hear of this, and you know what his public disapproval will mean for your business. Finished."

Christian interfered once again in her questioning of Bathsheba. It took all Eleanora had to hold her tongue.

"Please, Your Grace, I thoroughly examined the girl before I kicked her to the cobbles! There was no sign of any pox; I assure you!" the madam cried.

Bathsheba sounded scared. As far as Eleanora could tell, she was telling the truth. Syphilis takes weeks or months before symptoms appear. She would be out of business and entirely ruined by one word from the dukes.

"The names?" Eleanora asked coolly. "I require—"

The madam was shaking her head.

"Give her the names, Bathsheba," Christian growled.

She dipped her pen in the ink bottle with shaking hands and scribbled the names. Christian snatched the paper from her hand, blew on it to dry the ink, and stuffed it in his pocket. Grabbing Eleanora's elbow, he brought her to her feet.

"Your Grace, have pity. I swear she had no diseases when she left here," Bathsheba whimpered.

"Which name is the one dismissed?" he demanded.

"The second one. Emily McCarthy. That is her real name. She used the name Lucinda with customers. Please, Your Grace. Do not repeat any of this!"

"What name did the other girl go by?" he snapped.

"Eurydice."

"If these names are not legitimate, I will return."

"Please, Your Grace...."

Christian ignored her and steered Eleanora toward the door and down the stairs.

Eleanora huffed, stuffing her notebook and pencil into her cloak, but she didn't fight him. Inside a brothel was not the place to make a scene.

Eleanora grabbed his arm and twisted it around when they stepped outside, causing him to yelp. Catching him off guard, she gained the advantage and pushed him into the nearby alley.

Releasing his arm, she poked him in the chest, her anger and frustration boiling. "Do not *ever* do that again." Eleanora kept walking and poking until the duke's back hit the brick wall. "I am in charge here; I will make the threats or demands and ask the questions. Understand?"

A ragged moan left Christian's lips; his long eyelashes fluttered.

Wait, this arouses him?

Momentarily stunned, she stepped in reverse, unsure what to do or say. In her younger years, not so long past, Eleanora had acted impulsively on more than one occasion. She'd learned to curb such behavior through sheer determination, especially when she opened her investigative agency.

However, impetuosity sometimes burst through, even though her sister and cousin tried to contain her worst impulses.

Standing here with Christian, all restraints melted away.

Leaning in, she laid a kiss against his lovely lips. The brief contact caused sizzling heat to travel through her.

His eyes popped open. Eleanora had shocked him. She placed her hands flat against the brick wall on either side of his head and kissed him again, nibbling on his full lower lip.

Yes, Althea and Sybil would have stepped in to stop this reckless behavior.

A good thing they were not here.

A deep-throated growl left his throat. Christian grasped her upper arms and whirled her about until she was against the wall. A shockingly potent thrill moved through her.

He gave as good as he got, and how *that* aroused *her*.

His kiss was hungry and ferocious, and the blistering flames roiling inside combusted into a scorching fire. Eleanora tunneled her fingers through his thick, silky black hair, knocking his hat askew, which caused him to moan once again. They were breathing hard, grinding against one another.

The hardness of his erection pressed against her, causing her insides to melt. He clasped her leg and draped it across his hip, taking the kiss deeper as he ground against her.

A loud bang against the bricks tore them apart. "What's all this, then? Enough of that. Move along sharpish."

It was a uniformed copper, carrying a baton and a Bull's Eye lantern. He looked them over as he tucked his truncheon into his holder. Seeing that Christian dressed as a gentleman, he touched the brim of his hat in a show of respect.

"Sir. Take it off the streets. If you please."

Christian gathered her close as if to hide her identity. The protective gesture caused her heart to flutter—yet another strange reaction.

"Right away, constable."

Satisfied, the copper continued on his beat.

"Sweet Mother," Eleanora mumbled into his shoulder.

"Indeed." Christian stepped backward, and their gazes met. Their breathing was uneven, the air crackling with sensual energy.

"Take my arm. We will head toward the carriage."

"I'm not sorry," she said breathlessly.

"For what, manhandling me or kissing me?"

"Both."

He gently trailed the tip of his finger along her cheek. "I'm not sorry either—for both. We will talk more in the carriage. Come."

Strange, her legs were as if made of jelly. Best to take the duke's arm. Casually, they strolled out of the alley.

Once bundled inside the carriage, the small window slid open. Christian instructed the driver to take a circuitous, leisurely route to Cleveland Street. Then he handed her the note with the names.

Eleanora glanced at the paper and then tucked it into her notebook.

"As much as I would like to continue to explore what sparked in the alley, we must talk about what happened at the brothel." Christian removed his hat and gloves and all vestiges of his loss of control as he successfully slipped on the mask of the aloof duke.

"What do you wish to discuss first, Your Grace?"

His mouth quirked. "What happened to Allenby or Christian?"

"I believe it best we remain client and investigator."

Christian scoffed. "Oh, hang it all, that's not what I want, and neither do you. I want to be involved in this investigation every step of the way."

"Absolutely not," Eleanora said firmly. "I never allow clients to become involved in investigations. This case is not a game to me. It is not my job to amuse a bored aristo. Not for any amount of money. Besides, why would you want to?"

"Why not? I can assist—in gaining entry to places that would be off-limits to you. Like the brothel."

"We have done that. There's no need for any further collaboration." Honestly, what on earth was he doing? Or thinking?

"Do you not think I am capable of conducting this investigation? If not, I will refund your money, and you can engage someone else. No doubt a man," she huffed.

That kiss had affected her far more than she thought. Eleanora was utterly rattled.

Christian gave her a skeptical look. "When have I ever shown any lack of confidence in your abilities? You do recall it was I—over the objections of the others—that employed your agency?"

Well, he was correct there.

"I can also gain access to people who would not otherwise give you an audience," he continued. "Like the baronet or any peers that may crop up in your inquiries. Besides, with your cousin gone, you could use the assistance."

The dark duke again had a point.

"I cannot be responsible for your safety. It is too much to ask, and the risk is too great." Eleanora shook her head, but inside, she was wavering.

Truth be told, she yearned to be in his company. To embark on an adventure with a man who had caught her interest like no other?

Tempting. Very tempting indeed.

But common sense had to be considered. It must prevail.

Never had Eleanora allowed her clients to become involved in *any* investigation. After Christian had gained her entrance to the high-end brothel, she should have made him wait in the carriage and kept him out of it altogether.

"I am capable of looking after myself. I should be the one to decide on whether it is too risky." Christian didn't sound angry, merely firm in his statements.

"What about all your duke duties and such?" she asked.

His eyes crinkled with amusement. "Parliament is not in sitting at the moment, so I am not needed."

"I heard that you rarely attended."

His eyes widened, then narrowed. "You've asked questions about me?"

"A couple of general and cursory inquiries, I do so with all my clients. Is it true?"

"Shamefully, yes, but I had decided a few weeks past to amend all that. I have already made certain other changes in my life."

Eleanora observed his body language. Christian was not acting defensively, as in crossing his arms or glowering; his tone was sincere. He was open and honest, at least with her. It was vastly appealing.

"What changes?" she asked softly.

"The rakish lifestyle. I had more or less ceased the various activities some weeks ago. I have the distinct feeling that others in our group have done the same. Believe it or not, meaningless encounters do become tedious."

"What about running your vast empire?" she asked.

Christian snorted. "It's 1897; most peers no longer possess enormous wealth. Luckily, I have a competent steward and a reliable land manager. They see I do not sink into financial oblivion as many peers have the past three decades."

Eleanora gave him a teasing smile. "Clearly, considering the lushness of this carriage."

He chuckled. "My one indulgence. At the turn of this century, the Bamfords owned ten estates and three residences in London. Under my advisors' wise advice, I sold everything not entailed and now only have my country seat, Bamford Park in Essex, the town house in London, and the smaller residence for my mother. My steward placed the money from those sales into investments, giving me a comfortable income. There is still a smattering of tenants in Essex, but it is not enough to earn the estate a living. The world is changing."

"That it is," she agreed.

"Since I am unencumbered now, why not use me in your investigation?"

"My gut instinct is saying no, and I always listen to it."

Christian crossed his arms. "I have another motive. I want us to become better acquainted."

Eleanora shook her head in disbelief. "And you thought assisting me would be one way to go about it?"

"It is certainly more exciting than going to the theater or a ball. Besides, we already attended a ball." Christian gave her a brief smile. "I *like* you, Miss Galway. I want to know you better. On a lesser note, it will give me something to do. A purpose. I cannot remember the last time there was any purpose in my life." Christian shook his head. "And here I am revealing more than I should. Once again."

The loneliness radiated off him. And blast it all if it didn't affect Eleanora, as her heart squeezed with empathy.

"I will think about it. I do not promise anything, mind."

"Fair enough. I will not press the matter any further—today. Regarding the case, I feel this may not be a macabre prank after all."

Though she agreed, Eleanora said, "It's far too soon to rule out anything yet."

Christian leaned in, regarding her closely. "How on earth will you track Lucinda? She could have gone anywhere after being dismissed."

"Have you ever been with her? I ask because of the pox." And she was curious as well.

The corner of his mouth quirked. "Always straight to the point. No. I haven't been there in over a year; I do not recall a Lucinda. As I said, my brothel activity has fallen sharply over the last eighteen months. I had best mention this to the lads, however. It is a rule between us that we do not venture forth on our sexual adventures without taking proper precautions, but who knows if anyone had at The Chrysalis."

"I never understood why anyone would engage in such reckless behavior, but I suppose it is part of the privileged class. Thinking you're all above any reparation for any of your actions."

A furrow formed between his brows. "Can we please lay aside your obvious disdain for my class? You're not exactly wrong. Yes, peers, particularly men, are feckless, reckless, and conceited. But having it thrown in my face constantly is increasingly wearisome. Let us leave it at that."

"You're right; I will not do it again. It's not just peers acting in such a fashion. But yes, let us leave it lay," she said, her voice gentle.

Eleanora could not allow her prejudices to enter this investigation or any decision to allow Christian to assist.

"As to your original point," she continued, "We start tracking this Lucinda by finding the other name on the list, Fiona Mapleton. I will also ascertain where the ladies of The Chrysalis congregate and find any information there."

"By wearing a disguise?" he asked, his tone lighter.

She smiled. "Of course. This type of gathering is usually at a pub. A few pints of bitter, and they will spill all sorts."

Heat emanated from his attractive pale blue eyes. "The kiss."

"Is this the part where you say it must not happen again?" Eleanora queried.

Deep down, she was apprehensive about what he *would* say because she wanted it to happen again.

Frequently.

There was another reason to allow him to become involved in this case: more opportunity for those fierce, heated kisses. But those wild kisses were also a detriment. It was not prudent to become distracted by an incredibly handsome duke.

Sweet Mother. Eleanora didn't know *what* to do.

"Perhaps this isn't wise." The duke stared out the window again. "Mixing business with pleasure is always grounds for complications. Or so I have heard."

Eleanora waited for him to elaborate further, but he didn't.

"I cannot promise it will not happen again," she stated.

His head whipped about, and he met her gaze. "What do you mean, exactly?"

"I cannot promise that I won't kiss you again."

"I have never met a woman like you. Frank, fascinating and extraordinary in every way."

His voice was low, his tone sensual, and it caused a shiver of desire to dance along her spine. The words he had spoken also sent a thrill deep to her core.

Impulsive.

She was acting rashly in speaking her mind regarding their apparent magnetism. But she considered Christian's proposal to work with her on this case. Staring at his muscular form, noticeable despite his layers of clothing, he had her ready to throw aside all restraints.

"What do we do?" she ventured.

"See where it leads," Christian rasped in reply.

"What? The case?"

His eyes came alive with blue fire. "Indeed, I speak of the case."

His desirous look had her tempted to wrap herself around him. Hold him close and nuzzle the substantial column of his neck. Muss him thoroughly and how her hands itched to run through his silky hair again. *A little restraint is warranted.*

"What comes next—regarding the case?" Christian asked again.

The change in subject was jarring, for she still thrummed with excitement.

Yes. The case. Focus, Eleanora.

"Tomorrow, Althea will lead the interview with Brookton. Huxley has not responded to our inquiries. In fact, when Sybil stopped by yesterday, no one answered the door."

Christian blew out a breath. "Huxley is having—issues. I will stop by his home tomorrow. Surely he will gain me entry."

"Good. However, you cannot share any information with your chums. Understand? I believe in forming a thorough report, not giving out information in dribs and drabs. And not until I say."

"Understood, Miss Galway. However, as I said earlier, I should share the information on the syphilitic Lucinda and The Chrysalis. Will you permit me?"

"Yes, but nothing else of the conversation."

"Understood, Miss Galway."

"I require a list of all former Rakes of St. Regent's Park members. Can you get that for me?"

"Yes, I can. Watford would know. Leave it with me." The carriage came to a stop. Christian pushed aside the curtain. "Home again. When will you contact me?"

"When I decide that I need you. If I need you at all." Eleanora wasn't cruel in her tone, merely straightforward. She made the short step to the cobbles.

Turning, she gave a slight bow. "Good afternoon, Your Grace."

Lord, how officious she sounded—and nonchalant. When in fact, she burned with desire, her emotions in a whirlwind.

She hurried toward the entrance, stopped, and returned to the carriage. The door was still open. Lifting her skirts, she climbed the two steps, leaned into the carriage, grabbed Christian by his lapels, and gave him a hungry kiss.

Before he could respond, she exited, ran for her front door, entered, and closed it. Breathing hard, she leaned against the wall. A slow but satisfying smile crept across her mouth. The duke was entirely delicious.

And Eleanora couldn't wait to taste more.

Chapter 10

"WHERE TO, YOUR GRACE?" his driver asked through the open sliding window.

Christian clutched the leather strap on the door and pulled it close. "Backchurch Lane."

The carriage moved forward, for Michaels knew where to go. The clop-clop of the horses' hooves kept him company as he journeyed toward Whitechapel.

God above—that kiss.

Having her take the lead had thrilled him, arousing him to the point of discomfort. Eleanora must have known of his desire, for she had eagerly ground against his stiff shaft.

Christian moaned at the thought of it. No amount of caution could stop him from returning such a passionate kiss. The desire that flamed between them could have consumed the surrounding buildings.

And then, for her to impulsively kiss him again just now? His passion had flared to unknown heights.

He wanted to kiss her.

Now. And more, so much more.

Christian was utterly captivated.

It was best to keep his emotions to himself for the time being.

See where this will lead, indeed.

Eleanora was attracted to him, perhaps as much as he was to her; there was no denying it.

Meanwhile, he would keep offering his services in assisting the investigation. For all the reasons he had stated. But most importantly, to be near Eleanora.

Revel in her bold presence. And for a chance to hold those luscious curves in his arms again.

When had he ever had such a reaction to a woman?

Never. Ever.

Once they arrived at Backchurch Lane, his driver climbed down and opened the door for him.

"The usual time, Your Grace?"

"Yes, one hour. You can stay here or get a bite to eat at the tavern on the corner." He slipped a handful of shillings into Michaels' gloved hand.

"Thank you, Your Grace."

Christian sprinted up the steps and was immediately permitted to enter. The madam, wearing a shimmering emerald green satin gown, smiled warmly.

"It has been a while, Your Grace. Care to make your selection?"

Christian made a superficial glance toward the women gathered in the small parlor.

He didn't particularly care and pointed toward a curvy, brassy blonde. "Her."

Once in the room, the best the small brothel had to offer, the prostitute started to unhook her corset.

"No," he growled. "I want none of that."

He tore off his coat, hat, and gloves and sat in the plush chair. He patted his lap.

"I want you to sit here, put your arms around me, and hold me. That's all I want. No talking, no touching, except your arms around me. Do you understand?"

"Yes, Your Grace," she replied demurely.

"What happens here is not to be repeated. I know you all like to exchange war stories. But you will not mention me—ever. I have ways of finding out."

"Yes, Your Grace."

Christian patted his lap once again. The prostitute sat, curled up next to him, placing her plump arms about his waist as she laid her head against his chest. Thankfully she was not heavily perfumed. All he could detect was fresh soap—the warmth of her spread through him.

He needed this.

The tender touch of another.

Affection, though, feigned on both sides. Christian laid his head back against the chair and closed his eyes.

During the next hour, he basked in human contact, pretending Eleanora was holding him, nuzzled against his chest. That it was her heartbeat working in unison with his. That it was her breath expelling in short bursts.

For he was desperately lonely.

Hiding inside of him was a vast emptiness. All the women in London could not fill it, regardless of class. How that void had come to be, he wasn't sure. His father's death? His mother's absences? No, they added to it but were not the cause. For as long as he could remember, he was lonesome. No doubt born that way.

Christian relived over and over the fierce kiss in the alley and the quick one in the carriage. For a brief moment—one forever seared in his mind—he experienced a fiery heat that had ignited him straight to the toes of his boots.

Could Eleanora Galway be the one woman to fill his vacant heart?

Why would such an intrepid, confident, independent woman want a needy bastard like him? If he were smart, he would cut all ties and find another agency to investigate this case before he made a right idiot of himself.

He had an expected duty to marry well.

Instead of roaming the streets of London with a lady detective, he should be seeing to securing a future duchess. And he should do this before he made the grave mistake of falling for the delightful Eleanora.

ALTHEA WAS PACING ABOUT the parlor. Brookton, the misogynistic marquess and heir to a duke, was close to an hour late. There was no tea service nor an offer of cake or biscuits. Althea had stated that she wanted this done, and the man departed in a manner of minutes. Eleanora agreed with the terms. All Eleanora would be is an observer and take notes.

"My dear, you are making me nervous. Come and sit down," Eleanora said. "I reiterate, we should not place a time limit on this meeting."

"No. The sooner the marquess is out of here, the better."

"Why?"

Althea plopped into the chair, exhaling. "I cannot bear to look at him. Outwardly, the man is too perfectly gorgeous. Inside? I will lay coin there is an empty pit, with an unquestionable rot of what is probably left of his soul."

Eleanora arched an eyebrow. "Gorgeous? I cannot deny the truth of it. But there is more to this. I've never seen you so agitated. It is as if you're excited by him coming here but also dreading it."

Althea shook her head sadly. "Oh, Ellie. I don't know *what* to think. Is it possible to be simultaneously aroused and disgusted by a man? I've never experienced such a range of conflicting emotions before." She looked up at Eleanora. "Or perhaps you can relate?

I've never seen you excitedly shimmer as you did yesterday with the duke."

"Yes, I can certainly relate, though Allenby does not disgust me. What is wrong with us? Attracted to clients—and peers, for God's sake." Eleanora shook her head in disbelief.

"We cannot involve ourselves in the lives of these troubled men," Althea stated firmly. "The less we have to do with them, the better. Blast it all for finding pretty men appealing. It is a fatal flaw in my character, to be sure."

And mine as well.

The front bell clanged, and Althea froze. Mrs. Bartle was here today, and moments later, she escorted Brookton into the room.

"His lordship, the Marquess of Brookton," the housekeeper announced imperiously.

Brookton entered the room, and Mrs. Bartle's eyes widened, fanning herself for only the sisters to see. He certainly lit up a room with his glorious presence—and he knew it well.

"Thank you, Mrs. Bartle," Eleanora replied.

The housekeeper closed the door.

Althea pointed to the table. "Take a seat."

Her sister wouldn't say "my lord" in every sentence.

"No refreshments? Or offer to take my coat?" he sniffed.

"You won't be staying long enough," Althea replied coldly.

After she sat, Eleanora pulled the ink, pen, and paper closer and studied Brookton. His eyes were glassy. Not enough sleep? Too much drink? A little of both? His clothes and toilette were impeccable, and the man had a top-notch valet, but he also cared for his appearance. A touch narcissistic? How could he not be?

He sat, slouching in his seat, the complete picture of an indolent peer bored to tears and would rather be elsewhere.

Eleanora sniffed the air. The duke wore an expensive cologne, an enticing woodsy blend, but she could not ascertain any alcohol.

Brookton was a virile and healthy specimen, at least at first glance. He also did not exhibit traits of an excessive drinker. There was no indication of reddened and distended veins on the nose and cheeks, the paunch around the middle, or yellowed skin.

"Do you frequent an establishment known as The Chrysalis?" Althea asked.

Eleanora dipped her pen in the ink bottle and started writing.

"Yes."

"Were you acquainted intimately with a prostitute named Lucinda?"

"Yes."

Althea glared at Brookton. The marquess looked aggravated as well. "Care to elaborate?"

"No."

"We are here to establish if there is anything you can recall that might be a catalyst for the delivery of a body part." Althea's tone was abrupt.

Try as she might, Althea couldn't remain detached and professional.

Eleanora could not look away from the marquess or her sister as their encounter fascinated her. This behavior was not like Althea at all. Both she and Althea were swimming in dangerous, emotional waters.

Brookton pursed his lips. "Be damned if I will sit here and rehash my past for your amusement. I have had many encounters. Because of it, I have no idea if anyone was offended enough to play such a grisly prank. And at the end of the day, I do not care. I'm only here because Allenby insisted. I cannot be of any assistance to you." Brookton picked up his gloves as if to depart.

"Then what about your scandalous affair with the actress and her twin brother? Either at the same time or separately. Do you prefer both men and women?"

"So? What if I do?"

"It is nothing to me. In the book *Psychopathia Sexualis* by Richard von Krafft-Ebing in 1886, he claims that those who prefer both genders are bi-sexual. Would you say you belong in this category?"

Eleanora drew in a sharp breath.

My God, Althea.

So caught up in this exchange, Eleanora had yet to take any notes. How tempting to interject, but she remained silent, her gaze moving back and forth between them. The air in the room sizzled with energy.

Brookton's jaw dropped open, but he hastily recovered. "Good Christ," he muttered.

"I ask such a probing question because a three-way relationship could cause resentment, jealousy, and ultimately, reprisal."

"You are basing this invasion into my private life on society gossip? I was briefly involved with the actress. It lasted two weeks and ended four months ago. Her brother was *not* part of the affair. Regarding my preferences, there were sexual activities in my past in where men were participants. If that makes me bi-sexual, so be it. If you must know, I prefer women, but I also do not deny myself *any* pleasure." He slapped his gloves on the table, then placed them upon it.

"I have heard of these worthless books," he continued, plainly annoyed. "They believe any act of sex outside the purpose of marital procreation is depraved. This prudish society already harbors an unhealthy attitude about sex. These so-called scholars are exacerbating the problem."

Well, the marquess was right.

Their father had often stated those books were merely one person's opinion and not necessarily based on any particular fact. Perhaps she should bear such advice in mind when dealing with these peers. There could be something inside this man beside the superficial devil-may-care rake.

"Why stuffy virgins would read such claptrap is beyond me. I believe on-hand experience is always best." He gave Althea a wicked grin.

Then again, perhaps the surface was the essence of this man after all.

"I would not be surprised to hear that you have a portrait in the attic," Althea murmured crossly.

His smile evaporated. "I am beyond weary of the Dorian Gray references. It's not amusing. And it is insulting. I may be debauched, but I would never sink into the depths of that gothic fictional character. Why I'm explaining myself to you—either of you—I have no idea." He ran his hands through his golden hair. "Do you have anything else? Any more salacious tidbits of tattle to regale me with?"

Brookton's voice shook on the last sentence. Althea was getting under his skin. For once, he was not the perennially jaded aristocrat. Perhaps some elaborate brew of emotion lurked below the surface after all.

The marquess was a puzzle, and Eleanora could see why Althea was fascinated. It also was a warning that they shouldn't become too involved in the lives of these troubled men.

Yes, troubled.

Althea had the right of it.

The more Eleanora studied Brookton, the more she concluded that he was not suffering from excessive drink or opiates but rather a disquiet of the soul. The dark circles, barely noticeable on his flawless skin, spoke of a lack of sleep. It could be from his sexual vices—worn out from all the illicit activity—but Eleanora believed it was more.

Perhaps Althea had come to the same conclusion, for her expression softened.

"Let us return to The Chrysalis. That first night when we mentioned the butterfly tattoo on the ankle, you knew it could be a woman employed at The Chrysalis. Why didn't you mention it?" her sister asked.

Brookton sighed. "I have no idea why. It seemed far-fetched. As it turns out, it was not."

"There were two ladies with this tattoo that left the employ of the brothel in the past year. Lucinda and Eurydice. You had an acquaintance with both?" she asked.

"My, how thorough you are." His tone was sarcastic, and Althea bristled.

"We are paid to be so. The question, if you please?"

Brookton tapped his fingers on the desk. "Yes, on multiple occasions for at least a year before they departed. I found other amusements elsewhere. I haven't been to The Chrysalis in many months."

Eleanora turned her attention back to her notes.

"And what can you tell me of the Isle of Sheppey about fourteen years past?"

"Who told you of that?" Brookton snapped. "Allenby, I suppose. The miserable wretch. I have no memory of that night."

Pinpoints of red dotted his skin. His mouth curled into a sneer. Now he was angry.

Eleanora was caught up in the discussion once again. No wonder Althea and Sybil took all the notes; she was rubbish at it.

"I only wish to know if you have had any contact with Ford Whitney outside of the few letters his father passed on to you over the past several years."

Brookton blinked twice, his incredibly long lashes brushing against his high cheekbones. Or at least they appeared to do so in Eleanora's mind.

"You believe Whitney may be behind this? It makes no sense. Granted, he disappeared suddenly after that night, but his letters were genial enough."

"You have answered his letters personally?" Althea asked.

"No. The letter was to all of us. I believe Allenby answered on our behalf. Whitney has a new life far from here. All is well with him. It's been years since we heard from him. I say good luck to him."

"Now, as to Hayes Addington, a body was never found, correct? Is there a possibility he hadn't drowned and is now out for revenge?"

Brookton's jaw dropped. Then he burst into laughter. "What an overactive imagination you have, Miss Galway." The laughter ceased, then he gave her a dubious look. "Fourteen years. Why would Addington stay away and allow his inherited title to pass to someone else? Give up the money left to him? His identity, his place in society?"

Althea shrugged. "Perhaps he washed ashore, unable to recall his identity, lost in the amnesia haze. He only recently regained his memory and blamed you all for his change in circumstance. Addington wants you all to suffer, to have your lives upended as his life was."

Althea's questioning of Brookton was far more effective and probing than Eleanora's interview with Christian. Eleanora smiled at Althea with admiration. She had to hand it to her sister.

What a bloody outstanding assessment.

Far-fetched? Maybe yes—or maybe no. Eleanora had thought of the same thing but hadn't mentioned it to anyone.

Bravo, Althea.

"I believe, Miss Galway, you have read one too many potboilers," he scoffed.

Althea let the sarcastic comment pass. "So, to sum up, no one has made any threat toward you—no matter how harmless?"

"Not that I can recall. I will consider it and inform you if I recollect anything of import."

"Any aspect of your debauchery we should be concerned with concerning the parcel?"

Brookton raised an eyebrow. "You seem too curious about my private sex life, Miss Galway. What do you believe—that I have a deviant bent along the lines of engaging in sex with those that have limbs missing?"

Althea's eyebrows shot up. "That is a thing?"

Brookton stood, pulling on his leather gloves. "To some, nothing is off the table as far as sex is concerned. Good afternoon, Miss Galway. Miss Galway."

"Wait..."

She stood, and Althea's long skirt entangled with the toe of her boot and the rung of the chair. Althea reached out to grab the table to stem her fall, but she couldn't grasp it.

Instead of hitting the floor, strong arms held her upright and enfolded her in a masculine embrace. It happened so swiftly; Eleanora had no time to respond.

"Are you well?" the marquess murmured to Althea, genuine concern in his tone.

"Do not think this is some parlor trick to have you rescue me from a faux fall. I don't play games," she whispered into the folds of his silky cravat.

Brookton nuzzled Althea's neck. "I would not care if it was a game."

Time stopped or appeared to stop.

A soft sigh—or was it a moan? —escaped Althea's lips.

"Sister, *are* you well?" Eleanora asked. Trapped in the man's spell, Althea remained silent. What were the odds? Both of them attracted to a duke and an heir to a duke?

Entirely inappropriate. And unwise.

They both turned to stare at her as if they had forgotten she was in the room.

"Yes. I stumbled, that is all," Althea replied, her voice shaky.

Brookton gently grasped Althea's upper arms and took a step back.

The spell—or whatever it was—shattered and dissipated into the ether.

Brookton's immaculate features settled into his usual detached look.

"Good afternoon, ladies." After he bowed, he turned so briskly that his long coat whipped about his legs.

He was gone.

Althea touched her flushed cheeks.

"My dear—" Eleanora began.

Althea waved her arm rapidly. "Give me a moment." Her sister grabbed the chair and sat, her breathing ragged. "We *must* refuse to go any further with this case."

"I disagree. This case is the most exciting one we've ever had. The money we make from this can keep us going for a year. When we close this case successfully—and we will—think of the rich clients."

Althea arched her eyebrow. "Is that all you care about, the money? Or are you smitten with the Duke of Allenby?"

Eleanora exhaled. "You and I tell each other everything. So, I will be honest. It's a little of both. Allenby intrigues me. And from what I've witnessed here, Brookton intrigues *you*. Falling into his arms, Sister?"

"I *did* trip; I do not play such wily games. Intrigue? My God. He's everything I loathe in a man: his wealthy class, arrogance, and blasé lifestyle; he's immoral to his core. By his own admission!"

Althea scowled, then sighed. "You're correct. We need this money and the possible future clients. But know this: I can never be alone with Brookton, for there lays the danger. To my sanity and most especially my heart." Althea clasped Eleanora's hand and gently squeezed it. "You should follow the same rule, Ellie. We cannot become involved personally. Not with these men."

Eleanora said nothing. Deep inside, she knew Althea was correct—on all counts.

But *her* heart was telling her the exact opposite.

Chapter 11

CHRISTIAN HAD BEEN banging on Warren's front door for five minutes. Frustrated, he started to kick the lower panel with his boot.

The door, at last, opened. The butler stood aside and allowed him to pass. A disheveled Warren stood in the hallway, bare feet, trousers, and dressing gown hanging open, revealing his bare chest. The man hadn't shaved in days.

"What in the deviled hell? Why aren't you answering your door?" Christian demanded. "The Galway Agency says that you refused to answer."

"What part of 'I want to be left alone' did you not understand?" Warren growled.

Christian moved to step around Warren to head to the study, but Warren blocked his way. "You are *not* staying. Say your piece, then go."

"I'm calling a meeting. Come with me to the club," Christian urged.

"No. I'm leaving London tonight. I've been packing and making arrangements. I've no time for one of your blasted meetings." Warren waved off his butler, effectively dismissing him.

Christian had never seen Warren like this. Agitated. Not in control. "Where are you going?"

Warren shook his head. "Fine, I will tell you, then you can inform the rest. I am off to the Bevan Sanatorium in Hertfordshire. I will be there for weeks, perhaps months. I am broken and need mending. Call it a breakdown, call it an unhealthy sex addiction, call it whatever you wish. More than anything, I need to be away from this damned city."

Shock covered Christian. Why hadn't he noticed his friend's change sooner? However, Warren—like the rest—was adept at hiding deeper emotions and tribulations.

"What can I do to assist?"

Warren blew out a breath of relief. "Thank you. Outside of our club, put it around that I'm traveling on the continent. Not certain how long I shall be gone."

"I will. Anything you want. What has happened to us? We used to tell each other things. Support each other," Christian murmured.

Warren shook his head. "No, we haven't. Not for a long time. We gravitated toward each other as children. What a privileged and carefree life we have all led. It's no wonder we became friends. The thread that held us together no longer exists. You know nothing about me."

Christian had no idea how to respond. Was it true? Had he lived in his friendship fantasy, oblivious to others' feelings?

The truth of it was that everything changed that summer night when they were sixteen. The group splintered, and nothing had been the same since. He had been too stubborn to see it. And arrogant.

Christian backed up a step. "Then I will leave you to your preparations." He turned to depart but halted. "If you need us—any of us—do not hesitate to contact us. Regardless of what you think, we care for you. *I* care."

Christian stepped outside and closed the door behind him. Sighing, he headed toward his carriage. Michaels stood by dutifully and opened the door.

"Albany Street."

"At once, Your Grace."

Once the carriage pulled away, Christian slumped in his seat.

Damn it all.

He had been correct the night of the delivery that there was a change in the air. Only he had no clue how much. Before he knew it, the carriage came to a stop. The door opened, and he strode toward the rear of the building. Once he entered the club, someone grabbed a fistful of his cravat and slammed him against the wall.

Damon.

His eyes were chips of cold blue ice. Standing inches from his face, Damon snarled, "What did you reveal to those women? How *dare* you bring up Sheppey? It has nothing to do with that damned package. *Nothing.*"

"Those women? They are competent investigators." Christian pushed Damon away from him. "Keep your hands off of me."

Damon gave an exaggerated bow. "My apologies, Your Grace."

"Oh, stuff it. What does it matter? Addington is dead. Whitney has been gone from the country for more than a decade. Eleanora asked if there were other group members, so I mentioned the incident only in general terms." Christian straightened his cravat as he spoke.

Merritt had bounded over from the bar during the altercation. "Where is Warren? Didn't he accompany you? And no more roughhouse the pair of you, or you will put me off my tea."

"I'll explain once we're comfortable," Christian answered. "Asher? Take a seat. Where are Brandon and Gideon?"

"I have no idea. I suggest we start without them," Asher replied.

Damon marched to the bar, opened the scotch decanter, and poured a generous portion.

Seeing Damon with his guard down was not something Christian was used to. The anger that had flared between them dissipated in a flash.

What had occurred during his interview with Althea and Eleanora Galway?

Holding up the decanter in question, Christian nodded, and Damon poured another and passed it to him.

Once seated with their drinks, Merritt cleared his throat. He was fidgeting in his chair, looking decidedly uncomfortable.

"You have something on your mind, Merritt?" Christian muttered as he sipped his scotch.

"I will be venturing forth into the marriage mart. After all, I am heir to an earl; time to accept my responsibility and whatnot. I intend to find a suitable bride. One that I will adore and will adore me in return. I know I'm not a full-fledged member, but it means I must distance myself from this club. Terribly sorry, old chaps."

Well. That's that, then.

Their group, club, whatever, neared its end. Christian couldn't help but feel a bit sad over the prospect.

Damon snorted. "What a pathetic lot we are. All the best, Merritt. Go forth and procreate. Ensure the line and do your duty." He knocked back his drink, reached for the decanter, and poured another.

"Thank you, Damon. It is something you should both consider as well."

Damon snorted once again but said nothing.

"About Warren?" Asher inquired.

"Ah. Warren is departing for Standon, Hertfordshire. A sanatorium," Christian replied. "Warren called it a breakdown and asked that we keep this information between us. If we comment on his absence, we must say that he is traveling about the continent and leave it at that."

"Jesus," Damon cursed, taking another drink.

Asher's eyebrows knotted. "Perhaps I should go and see him."

"No, my friend, he wishes to be left alone," Christian replied. "I have another piece of news. A blood test on the leg showed traces of mercury and iodine. That is a treatment for symptomatic syphilis. It's believed the leg belonged to a prostitute from The Chrysalis."

"Jesus," Damon groaned, finishing his scotch and pouring another.

Merritt whistled. "Oh, I say. That's a place we used to frequent."

"It is that. Have any of you ever been with prostitutes Lucinda or Eurydice?" Christian asked.

"Not that I can recall," Asher answered.

Damon raised his glass. "I've been with both, once at the same time. However, that was over a year ago, and I've never engaged in sex without sheaths. *Ever*. I would have shown symptoms by now, wouldn't I? Fuck it all, the pox. What next?"

What next, indeed?

Christian had no clue what lay ahead. Not with him, his friends, the case, and most significantly, the lovely Eleanora Galway.

Chapter 12

ELEANORA AND ALTHEA sat in the dining room three days later, partaking in a light brunch of leftovers from their supper with Uncle Reece and Aunt Wilhelmina. Wilhelmina had insisted on sending home a small basket of food, stating her loving concern that they were not consuming enough wholesome nourishment. They certainly had enough laid out in front of them today.

"Perhaps we should acquire a pet, a cat or dog. It would certainly assist us in eating this food. Remember we had a cat when we were children?" Althea said.

Eleanora chucked. "Mr. Mouser. The orange tabby did not catch any mice and eventually ran away. He also scratched us constantly. The wretched animal didn't even want us to pet him."

Althea poured them fresh cups of tea. She then proceeded to cut her chicken and pork into bite-sized pieces. "Yes, Mr. Mouser. Typical male, lashing out for no good reason and utterly useless."

Eleanora chuckled, then sobered. "Truly, you would like to have a pet?"

"Perhaps not a cat this time, but a cute little Scottish Terrier. I saw a picture of a white one that looked adorable and friendly. It would be nice to have a pet to curl up by our chairs when you read, or I do my needlepoint."

"When was the last time we indulged in such activities?"

Althea nodded. "Yes, you're correct. Too busy to care for a pet."

"Perhaps not. Let us think on it." Eleanora watched her sister closely. Althea had seemingly recovered from her emotional encounter with Brookton and was back to her old self. Contained and in control.

More or less.

A pet. Was Althea lonely? Was she tired of their detective agency? Of the long hours? Hard to tell from her blank expression.

"Now that you have slept on it, are you certain you wish to continue with this case?" Eleanora asked softly.

"Yes. I'm certain. But I will abide by my caution and not be alone with the marquess. The case will conclude soon enough, and I need never see him again. What attraction I'm feeling will pass, I've no doubt."

Althea was made of sterner stuff because Eleanora could not make such a firm proclamation about not becoming involved personally. How astounding that she considered allowing Christian to assist her, at least with part of the investigation. Best to avoid the subject altogether.

"As for our interviews with Redfern, Colborne, Knight, Broyles, and Cowley, you agree that we should postpone it indefinitely?"

Althea nodded. "The assorted dukes, viscounts, and the businessman? I believe there's nothing more the men can offer. But keep them on our suspect list by all means. Where do we go from here?" her sister asked as she buttered a roll.

"Allenby will ask Broyles, I mean, Watford, for a list of all former members. That will be the next step of our investigation if the current friends, members, and school chums are not suspects. As for the immediate future, we will wait for the doctor's analysis. I'm waiting on another report. He should be here any moment."

Althea frowned. "You're not still using that street urchin?"

"Althea—"

"No, let me finish. The boy is part of a criminal enterprise, the Blind Beggar Gang. He is a pickpocket and a thug. He is also part of the Strutton Ground Boys, extorting protection money from the tradespeople on Petticoat Lane. Why are we associating with a criminal, albeit an underage one?"

"For that exact reason. Archie knows the streets better than any seasoned copper. He hasn't steered me wrong in the two years I've used him."

Althea grunted. "As of yet. His loyalty is to his unlawful cohorts. Once our investigations wander into his borders, he will choose his criminal side, mark my words." Althea bit into the thickly buttered roll.

Their housekeeper entered, clearing her throat. "Excuse me, Miss Eleanora. That ragamuffin is at the back door again," Mrs. Bartle sniffed indignantly.

"Show him up, Mrs. Bartle."

She huffed. "With the state of those boots? I think not. I've just cleaned the hallway."

"Then have him remove them."

The housekeeper let out a sigh of resignation. "At once, Miss Eleanora."

Once Mrs. Bartle departed, Eleanora said, "I will heed your warning, Althea. You make a valid point. Uncle Reece mentioned they would soon break up those gangs on Petticoat Lane. I want to guide Archie toward another path before that occurs."

She no sooner spoke the name when the boy stood in the entrance with Mrs. Bartle behind him, wrinkling her nose.

Archie stood barefoot on the carpet. His filthy clothes and feet verified his life on the streets.

There was no way to ascertain how old he was—even he had no clue—but he had sprouted up a few inches of late despite his dubious health and lifestyle. Eleanora guessed he might be anywhere from thirteen to sixteen.

The lad's hungry gaze locked on the food on the table.

"Mrs. Bartle, please fetch a plate and utensils," Althea asked.

The housekeeper nudged Archie aside. "Have them right here, miss. I also made him wash his face and hands. My advice? Stay downwind." Mrs. Bartle bustled to the table and set the dish on it. "Go on, boy. Sit. There, opposite the young ladies. And behave, mind."

Archie grunted his thanks and rushed to the chair. "Cor, the food!"

"You may have as much as you like, but first, we talk. Thank you, Mrs. Bartle," Eleanora smiled.

The housekeeper departed, and Eleanora turned her attention to Archie. With his face washed, she could see a smattering of freckles trailing across his nose. She never knew he had them. He would be a handsome lad with his shock of sandy hair and piercing light brown eyes if he reached the age of twenty. Many children on the streets didn't.

"Your report?" she asked.

"Aye. Huxley left town this mornin', trunk and all. He took the train to the West Country, not sure where. The Brookton toff? I followed him to a brothel in Whitechapel. Were there hours he was. Then he nipped off to a music hall for a show. After he came out, I followed him home. He's been there since. The young duke? Also, stickin' close to his home. The spectacled one? Tolwood? Went to a fancy ball with a bunch of nobs, all respectable like." Archie's gaze kept wandering toward the food. "The old duke? Eats at fancy restaurants. Had that Knight fella with him. Only one gettin' action of late is the blond bugger."

Althea shook her head, her mouth curling in disgust. "Typical."

"Thank you." Eleanora slid a small sack full of shillings across the table, and Archie grabbed it and stuffed it under his worn coat with the swiftness of a practiced thief.

"I have another job for you. It's to follow a footman working in Brookton's house. His name is Aloysius Phillips. He is tall, lean, prominent nose, dark brown hair, about thirty."

"I'll find out who he is, and no mistake," Archie interjected.

"His surveillance may take some time. Being a footman, I doubt he ventures out much. But when he does, I want to know where and if he is meeting with anyone."

Archie was eyeing the food again, barely listening. "Right-o, miss."

"And what do you have on the ladies working at The Chrysalis?" Eleanora asked.

"Aye. Took me a bit to find the place as it's out of me territory. But that bunch meets up for lunch at the Rusty Anchor nearly every day. The pub be three doors from the brothel."

Eleanora nodded. "Good work. Now, Archie, I want you to consider another occupation. One that is legitimate."

That got the lad's attention; he looked at her as if she had grown a second head. "Leave off. I'm doin' all right."

"You have a real talent for this vocation, Archie. You could become a copper and work your way into the CID, the Criminal Investigative Division. You would no longer have to live on the streets. We will help you. Find a place to live, get an education—"

"Bollocks to that and all," he sneered. "Ain't interested."

"Archie, you don't have to be a copper. You could run your own detective agency as we do. Be your own boss," Althea interrupted. "You're a smart lad. You know time is up on your little criminal endeavors. We have it on good authority that the Metropolitan Police will soon move in to break up the gangs. You don't want to go to prison, do you? Or pressed into military service? Or die in some dark alley, rats nibbling on your corpse?"

"Althea!" Eleanora stated.

Her sister's shrewdness impressed her, for she had Archie's full attention. He was undoubtedly turning over what she had said.

"Already am me own boss," he muttered. "Ain't involved with the Sutton Gang. Aye, I do a little pickpocketin' and thievin' with the Blind Beggars when I need coin. I ain't no murderin' scum." He looked back and forth between them. "Run me own agency? As if."

"You can," Eleanora said, her voice firm with conviction. "We will aid you. But you will have to obtain an education first and foremost. We can help with that, too."

"Perhaps you can work and train with us. We could use the assistance," Althea exclaimed. "It would be a small salary, enough to pay for a room while you attend school. Think on it."

Althea laid out the plan off-hand, acting moderately enthusiastic when describing the proposal. It was the right tone to take with Archie, and Eleanora should have known it.

Well done, Althea.

He shrugged, but Eleanora could see the seeds had taken root.

"Aye, I'll think on it. Time to eat, yeah?"

"Go ahead," Eleanora replied.

Picking up the platter, Archie filled his plate with mounds of meat, mashed potatoes, and carrots and immediately tucked into his meal. His manners could have been better. They would have to work on those as well.

"Why do you want to know where the prossies meet?" Althea asked her.

"They might have further information on the names I showed you. I've been formulating a plan." Eleanora glanced at Archie, but he was too involved in his meal to give them any mind.

Regardless, she lowered her voice. "I aim to gain their trust. Prostitutes, on the whole, look out for each other. If I stage a certain scene that will gain their sympathy, I may be able to gather additional information."

"Be one of them?"

"Yes."

Eleanora hesitated. The duke was part of her plan, but she wouldn't discuss it with Archie nearby. Christian needs to be informed right away. She glanced at Archie shoveling part of a buttered roll into his mouth. And have the boy deliver the note.

"And the footman?" Althea asked quietly.

"There was something not quite right about him. I may be wrong. But it would not hurt to probe a little deeper," Eleanora replied in a low tone. "He acted, I don't know, twitchy. Shifty. Also, we will look into the drowning incident and see if there was an official coroner's inquest. Uncle Reece could discover it for us."

Althea turned her attention to her meal. "I noticed Phillips' behavior as well. Your instinct is rarely off. And I agree about the drowning. There may be more there. Or not."

Valid on all counts.

"Ignore Brookton's dismissal of your Addington hypothesis. Perhaps the heir to the baron *is* still alive. It is entirely possible; truth can be stranger than fiction," Eleanora stated.

Althea giggled. "I used a plot from a thriller novel I had just read. A potboiler indeed."

Eleanora laughed, then sobered. Regarding the footman, Eleanora's inner alarm had clanged with warning alacrity. She could not fathom why she experienced such forewarnings, but as her sister stated, it was rarely off. Same with the drowning incident.

That identical inner alarm was sparking for another reason: Allenby.

Relief covered her that he wasn't running the streets seeking out sin. Realistically, there could never be anything permanent between them. How foolish to even speculate on such an out-of-reach possibility.

Should she allow the attraction to take its course or shut it down before her emotions run away?

For once, she had no thought on which path to tread. And it was worrying as much as it was invigorating.

It would be best if she tried to tamp down her rampant desires and keep them hidden in the interim.

However difficult that may be to achieve.

Chapter 13

SITTING IN HIS STUDY waiting for Eleanora to contact him, Christan felt much like an anxious horse waiting for selection at Tattersall's at Knightsbridge Green. Or how he imagined one must feel. When he'd finally received word, his apprehension had turned to excitement. An indication that his life *had* been tedious of late.

But more than anything, he ached to see her.

Talk with her. Be *with* her.

Although he'd never expected a note delivered by a street lad. The youth, who claimed to work for Eleanora, had stood in the hall waiting for an immediate response.

ALLENBY,

I've decided to give you an assignment. Meet me at your club in four days at eleven in the morning. Do not shave. I will provide the garments and other accessories.

Eleanora

WHEN THE DAY ARRIVED, Christian made sure that he came early. He had left the door open to hear her knock. And she did, right at the stroke of eleven. The place was silent, except for the faint noises from the streets of people milling about and carriages moving past.

Christian rushed down the stairs, then halted. Overeager would not be wise. He arranged his features to show an air of calm he did not feel. He opened the door, and the sight of her nearly knocked him off his feet.

Eleanora was dressed provocatively—at least to him. She wore a low-cut faded red gown that had seen better days, fingerless lace gloves, a worn shawl that barely covered her ample cleavage and a black wig that finished the disguise. The sight of her stunned him. Blood rushed to Christian's shaft, stiffening it. Gulping, he stepped aside, reaching to take her carpetbag and hopefully use it as a shield to mask his arousal.

Once Eleanora stepped across the threshold and closed the door, she trailed the tips of her fingers along his whiskered jawline. Heat traveled to all points, not already sparking with sensual energy.

"Heavy whiskers for four days," she murmured.

"I sometimes have to shave twice a day."

Eleanora began to pull her fingers away, but Christian held her hand still, then moved it slowly across his chin until she cupped his cheek. He closed his eyes, reveling in her warmth, rubbing his cheek against the lace of her thin glove. The yearning moan that escaped him perhaps told more than he wished to reveal about what she did to him, but hang it all.

"Christian," she whispered.

"Hmm?"

"We should get ready."

Right.

He opened his eyes slowly. Eleanora stared at him as if trying to ascertain what exactly was going on between them. How tempting to explore that exact thing; he grasped her hand, then led her upstairs.

When they entered the large room, Eleanora pulled her hand away, then pointed at the carpetbag. "Dress quickly. You're to act as my procurer."

He couldn't have heard her correctly. "Beg pardon?"

"It's a role you will play. We will position ourselves outside the Rusty Anchor pub before noon. I have it on good authority that the ladies of The Chrysalis take lunch there every day. You're to grab my arm, shake me, threaten me, and demand that I make you more money. Growl in my ear, be menacing. Do you think you can do that?"

"Yes. Then what?"

"I will go into the pub and act like a beaten dog, scrambling to count my coins to buy a meat pie. If all goes well, they will take pity on me and invite me to their table."

Christian scoffed. "And why would they do that, perchance?"

"It has been my experience that the lower classes are welcoming and sympathetic to others in dire straits, especially prostitutes towards other prostitutes. Those ladies of The Chrysalis are lucky. They have a roof over their head and are well-fed and cared for. They are one step from the street and never forget that fact. Some of them were back-alley Sallys—their description, not mine—and will empathize with my plight. Which means you must be convincing."

"Be damned if I will hurt you!" he exclaimed.

Eleanora blew out an exasperated breath. "Squeeze my arm gently, but I'll yelp as if you're hurting me. Same with putting your hand around my neck. Act as if you're squeezing, and I will grimace—wasn't drama taught at your high-brow schools and universities?"

Christian smirked. "I never bothered with it. I wish now that I had." He opened the bag and peered in. "What a garish suit. Purple plaid?"

"It is what those criminal types wear. Quickly, get dressed. There are gloves in the bag. Keep them on. We have to hide your smooth aristocratic hands. I have a little makeup here to blacken a tooth or two."

"You enjoy dressing as another and playing a role, don't you?"

"Wait until you try it. It can be exhilarating. Hurry along, now."

"Yes, Miss Galway," he replied, his voice low and sensual.

By the deviled hell, he liked it when she ordered him about.

Slipping into the small storage room, he swiftly changed. The frayed suit could have been a better fit, too loose, and the sleeves too short, but it was no doubt what Eleanora wanted to convey. The scuffed boots at least fit comfortably. Christian placed the rumpled derby hat on his head.

Stepping out of the room, he held his arms out for inspection. "How do I look?"

She stepped in front of him. "Very convincing. Smile. Show your teeth."

He did as commanded, and Eleanora rubbed a black substance on his front teeth.

"I do hope that is easy to remove."

"We will see," Eleanora replied. "Your accent has to go. Try to say as little as possible. Drop your 'h's.' Mangle your syntax. If you're convincing, I will use you for other duties—if you wish."

Christian clasped her hand and kissed her knuckles. "I do wish. Cor, darlin', but yer a dazzler."

Eleanora laughed. "Close enough. I assume you heard such speech in your East End travels?"

"Perhaps. And I do want you—to use me—for other duties."

Suggestive talk, but he couldn't help it. Eleanora had captured and captivated him like no other.

Despite his vow to hide such emotions, he had the distinct feeling he showed more than intended, for her expression softened.

Gently, she brushed the back of her hand across his whiskered cheek. An affectionate motion that had his heart skipping several beats.

"We must leave." Taking his arm, Eleanora pulled him toward the stairs. Once outside, she pointed to his carriage. "We'll take a hansom instead."

"Why not make use of my carriage? It's a damned sight more comfortable."

"We cannot go traipsing about the streets of London in such a fancy conveyance. Your seal is on the door; it would draw attention."

"It was worth a try." Christian followed her to the front of Colosseum Terrace as she waved down a cab. The horse whinnied as it came to a stop next to them.

"Basinghall Street. I will tell you where exactly when we arrive," she told the driver.

The driver, wearing a crisp black livery, gave them a dubious look. "I'll need payment upfront," he grumbled disrespectfully.

Bravo, their disguises were convincing.

Eleanora slipped two shillings into the driver's gloved hand. "Be sharpish about it."

The journey lasted only a few minutes. Christian was excited about participating in and assisting with the investigation—and thoroughly stimulated.

Eleanora banged on the cab's ceiling, and it stopped. "We'll get out here as it is a short walk to the pub."

They strolled along the sidewalk.

"I do hope the police stay well clear. The coppers are a little more diligent in keeping these streets free of riffraff more than in the East End," Eleanora said, her voice low.

She slipped her arm through his, causing him to draw a sharp breath when her ample breasts brushed against him.

"There it is," she said, tugging on his arm.

Ahead was a Tudor-style building with a wooden sign swaying above the window by the large double doors. Eleanora leaned against the building, facing the length of the street. Christian stood in front of her and nuzzled her neck.

"What are you doing?" she asked.

"Playing the part. The procurer is staking his territory and ensuring everyone sees that you are mine to do with as I please."

His huskily spoken words caused his arousal to spring to life once again. He bit gently on her earlobe, causing a soft sigh to escape her lips. Yes, she was as affected as him. How gratifying.

"Don't knock my wig askew. I don't have it pinned on as firmly as I would like," Eleanora whispered.

"I will heed your warning. Best I face this way, in case any of them recognize me. I doubt it, but you never know." He nibbled again on her ear, and a breathy sigh escaped her lips. Not caring if anyone was watching, he briefly clasped her breast, and she moaned in response. Then he trailed his hand down her side, reveling in her curves.

By the deviled hell, he wanted her, as he wanted no other woman ever before.

Christian was falling for this magnificent woman—and fast.

ELEANORA'S INSIDES roiled with enough intense heat to singe them both. All her trepidations and rules of engagement?

It was gone in a flash.

Instead of pushing him away, she hauled him against her and rolled her hips. Even through their layers of clothes, she felt the hardness of his arousal.

Being impulsive again. Not going to fight it.

"Hell," he moaned.

Christian captured her lips with his, kissing her deeply and distracting her from her task. He swirled the inside of her mouth with his talented tongue, and she replied in kind.

Eleanora allowed it to linger and savored his hot, exciting taste before reluctantly pulling away.

"They're coming," she whispered in his ear.

That kiss, though brief, was more intense than the one in the alley.

Concentrate, Eleanora, on the task before me.

A congregation of about seven women strolled confidently toward them, laughing and talking. It's not as if the ladies dressed provocatively, but they certainly were not dressed in what society considers proper. They did not wear hats, shawls, or gloves, nor did they wear demure afternoon walking gowns buttoned up to the neck. A couple of them had their hair down, blatantly violating societal rules.

With a sudden move, Christian clasped her wrist and held it against the wall. "Listen to me, my girl," he growled rather loudly. "You'll be makin' me more coin, or you'll be more than sorry."

The women were within earshot.

"Leave me alone! I do what I can," she whimpered in reply.

His hand moved to her neck and gently squeezed, and Eleanora gave a performance worthy of The Gaiety Theater. Gasping, she gave a terrified look. The women slowed, watching the exchange as they headed toward the door. But they did not intervene. For they understood one did not step between a prossie and her pimp.

"Right, you are. I'll be back at supper. You better 'ave coin aplenty, or I'll be sellin' you to the traders; see that I won't," he said with menace and venom. The duke certainly had her convinced.

Well done, Your Grace, Eleanora thought admiringly.

She cringed as if he were going to strike her.

The women headed through the entrance, and one tsked and muttered, "Miserable bastard."

Once the door closed, Christian laid a gentle kiss on her neck.

"Did I hurt you?" he asked worriedly.

"No. Not at all."

With decided reluctance, she gently pushed him away. The solid warmth of him was intoxicating—and far too distracting.

But beyond such pleasurable sensations, too many men roughly treated women as if they were property. Eleanora was relieved to learn her trust in Christian was not misplaced. He would never physically hurt her; she knew it to the depths of her soul.

"Head toward where the carriage dropped us off. There is an alley near; wait for me there," Eleanora instructed.

Christian strode away, and with one last admiring gaze at his broad shoulders, Eleanora arranged her features into a fearful look of complete capitulation.

Stepping across the threshold of the Rusty Anchor, the odors of tobacco, beef, onions, and humanity inundated her senses. The pub was crowded, being noon, with laughter and clinking glasses drowning out all other noise. The wall and ceilings had large wood beams like the ones in the bowels of a ship. Nonchalantly she gazed about her surroundings, finding that the women had taken a large table in the back corner.

With a slow and hesitant meander, Eleanora made her way to the end of the bar, adjoining the women. She made a show of counting her insufficient coins.

"Here, what do you want?" the barman called out to her.

She looked up at the older man wearing a neat apron. He stared at her impatiently.

"How much will this buy?" Meekly, Eleanora held up her upturned palm with a few coins.

"Nothing. Get out; this ain't no charity soup kitchen," the barman snapped, moving away to his next customer.

"Charlie, a beefsteak pie for the lady and a pint of bitter. Have it brought to our table," a voice called out.

Eleanora turned to stare into the face of a beautiful woman with hair in the shade of fireplace flame. With a shaky smile, she murmured, "Thank you."

"Come and sit with us, ducks," another woman yelled.

The redhead slipped her arm through Eleanora's. "What's your name, love?"

"Bridget."

"I'm Sandra; that there who spoke is Annie."

Sandra introduced the others, and the ladies scrunched closer about the round table to make room for her.

Eleanora sat. "I cannot thank you enough; I'm that hungry."

Luckily, at The Chrysalis, she was whisked into Bathsheba's office and had not seen any prostitutes. They were no doubt busy with customers.

"We saw you with your man there. Bloody bastard," Annie said, shaking her head. "Ducks, you'd be better off on your own than with a man like that. His treatment of you will only get worse."

"He offers protection," Eleanora whispered.

"Aye, that's how they frame it. Then your so-called protector starts demanding more." Two barmen brought pies and pints, and Sandra laid a pound note on the tray. "Divide that with Charlie and the rest."

"Thanks, Sandra." The man smiled and moved away.

"I don't usually tip that much, but I wanted to show you what coin can be made if you find a good safe house to work out of," Sandra said. "You need to find one, my girl, and quick like. We're at The Chrysalis, a few doors down."

The beefsteak pie was delicious; she must inform Althea, for her sister enjoyed them. Eleanora cut into her pie and shoved two forkfuls in one after the other to show her faux hunger. "How can I find such a place?" she asked between mouthfuls.

"Our place ain't looking for new ones, but I know of a few," Sandra offered. She sipped her bitter, then took a bite of the pie.

Eleanora couldn't spend much time here. Last night she toyed with a particular line of inquiry but dismissed it as too obvious. But there was no other way to get to the point and procure the required information. Those who worked in brothels rarely ever shared their pasts. Or so Eleanora had been told.

She might as well plunge in. She shoved in another mouthful, a dribble of gravy trailing down the side of her mouth.

"There, ducks, easy now. Pace yourself," Annie purred as she wiped the gravy away with the tip of her finger. Then she sucked on it, giving Eleanora a seductive look.

Good God.

"Annie, leave it be. The poor girl is hungry for food, not for *you*," Sandra admonished.

"Wait, you said The Chrysalis? I knew one who works there, though it be a few years back," Eleanora said, then she gulped down a large swallow of bitter. Not her favorite beverage by any stretch. "Do you know her? Fiona Mapleton?"

The sensible move was to ask after the prossie who departed because of a protector instead of Lucinda/Emily.

Why?

Those who departed under suspicious circumstances became *persona non grata* and not discussed in any company. Another fact of street life Eleanora had learned through her years of investigating.

One of the ladies snorted.

"Oh, aye. That particular cat landed on her feet, and no mistake," Annie scoffed.

Eleanora looked questioningly between the women as she continued to eat.

"Fiona departed over a year ago and got herself a protector. The good kind. She services one as a paid paramour—a mistress. You don't have to worry about her. She's set up good and proper until the man tires of her. Hopefully, by then, she will have saved some money." Sandra patted her hand reassuringly.

"Do you know where she is set up? Perhaps she will see me, help me out," Eleanora asked.

"You don't want to be flouncin' around Half Moon Street; the coppers will run you off quick as spit," Annie stated. "She's too good for us and all, acting high and mighty with her toff banker, Gillis Mawles, and—"

"That's enough, Annie," Sandra cautioned.

Sandra glared at Eleanora with narrowed eyes. Suspicion was creeping in; Eleanora could sense it. She had all the information she needed.

Yes, time to depart.

Thank you, Annie.

Eleanora wiped her mouth with the serviette and placed it on the near-empty plate.

"I thank you again. I'd best be off. Got to earn coin, or he'll—anyway, thanks and all."

Eleanora moved to depart, but Sandra clasped her arm.

"You come here at noon in two days. I will have a list of safe places you can check out. Stay clear of Fiona. You know the rule. Fiona is out of our sphere, and good luck to her." Sandra slid a couple of shillings across the table. "Here, you give Mr. Misery Guts this coin toward your earnings today."

Eleanora nodded and scooped the money into her hand. Holding the fisted coins to her heart, she whispered, "Thank you. You are all that kind."

Without a backward look, she darted away. Once outside, she leaned against the pub wall and exhaled. Eleanora needed clarification on what the rule was that Sandra mentioned. Perhaps once someone was out of the life, there was no further contact, which boded well for her future inquiries.

Hurrying along the street, she ducked into a small chapel. Taking the shillings she had acquired from Sandra and adding a few of her own, she deposited them into the poor box.

Once she departed and entered the alley, strong arms pulled Eleanora into an embrace. The familiar warmth and enticing spicy scent had her toes curling in her well-worn boots.

"God, Eleanora. What you do to me," he growled. "Tell me that you feel it too."

The wise thing to do would be to deny the sizzling heat between them. But when Christian held her like this, Eleanora could not.

"I cannot deny it. I feel it."

He cupped her rear and brought her tight against him. "Feel this. I want you. We could have sex right here in the alley. No one would care."

The gruffly spoken words were eager and sensual. And it caused such a wave of desire to roll through Eleanora that it threatened to obliterate all common sense.

"You tempt me. Perhaps far too much," Eleanora replied huskily.

Christian swept her up into another devastating kiss. She knocked his hat to the cobbles and grabbed fistfuls of his hair, kissing him with the same hungry enthusiasm he showed. But that pesky common sense soon crept back in, and she pulled away. Eleanora clasped his hand and pulled him toward the street.

"We must go. I must return home and change, and then I'm off to find Miss Mapleton. I have the street and the name of the man keeping her." She turned to depart the alley, but Christian halted her.

He picked up his hat and brushed it off. "Wait, that's it? And where am I to go?"

Eleanora blinked. "Why, to your residence or your club."

"I thought we would spend time together—concerning this investigation?"

"We are. I've allowed you to assist me. That is a huge step on my part. I never, *ever* allow anyone to become involved in my investigations. I'm going against my sister's objections, let alone my rules on the subject."

Christian released her arm and leaned against the wall. "I also meant time together. *Alone.* With us sharing a meal—and more. Or am I being too blunt? Perhaps I am. I apologize for suggesting sex in the alley. I became lost in my role."

"Don't apologize. I liked your suggestion. But all in good time." Eleanora clapped her hands excitedly. "I have a lead; I must follow it up right away. I'm not sure if the ladies of The Chrysalis will contact Miss Mapleton, but I want to interview her immediately on the chance that they might."

He cocked an eyebrow. "Why would they contact Miss Mapleton?"

"To remind her to stay quiet about any doings at the brothel. Bathsheba would have told us nothing if you hadn't threatened her."

He gave her a quirky smile. "See? I *am* important to this case."

There was no denying it; the duke was quite adorable. Impulsively, she kissed his cheek.

"Come. We will return to your club, then you can drop me at Cleveland Street and continue on home, and I—"

"No." Christian shook off her hand and wouldn't budge. He stubbornly stood his ground.

"No?"

"I am going with you to Miss Mapleton. Introduce me as your assistant. I want all in, Eleanora. I must admit I enjoy your ordering me about, but not on this point. We travel this path together. The investigation—and whatever comes. I will brook no argument. What say you?"

His voice was firm. Confident.

Well, she had to admit it gave her a decided thrill to order him about as well, but she also found it arousing when he returned the sentiment and that he stood up to her.

Eleanora held out her hand. "Then let's shake on it. We travel together. All in."

He clasped her hand and pulled her beside him until her breasts mashed against his broad chest. Then Christian cupped her rear again and brought her in close until the apex of her thighs met his hard arousal.

"All in," he rasped hoarsely in her ear.

Oh. *Oh.*

The temptation was hard to resist. Eleanora rubbed against the tempting duke until they were both moaning. Only the approaching footsteps of conversing men broke them apart.

"We'd best be off." Eleanora took his arm, and they strolled out of the alley. Only Eleanora's legs were trembling.

These complicated emotions were uncharted territory.

While it was indeed thrilling, she also harbored nagging doubts about doing the right thing.

Chapter 14

"WHERE, EXACTLY, ARE we going?" Christian asked.

They had taken his carriage to Cleveland Street and stopped only long enough for Eleanora to change. He slipped his long black coat over the purple plaid suit and used his homburg hat. He then returned to his club for him to remove portions of his procurer disguise.

There was no time to delineate what had happened between them. There was no denying the sparks between them had ignited roaring flames of desire. But Christian realized no discussion would ensue beyond the investigation, not with Eleanora singularly focused. Hailing another hansom, they headed toward their destination.

"Fiona Mapleton is living on Half Moon Street. Her protector is Gillis Mawles, banker," Eleanora replied.

"Barclays Bank employs Gillis Mawles. I sit on the board, a primarily honorary position engrained with the family seat for over a century. My club meets in a building owned by Barclays. Mawles also sits on the board. A young and rising star within the Barclays sphere. A Director of Finance, he is married with two children."

Christian crossed his legs. "He is a serious sort. I am certainly amused to find he has a mistress, for he passed judgment on The Rakes more than once—damned hypocrite. Anyway, I know exactly where you will locate Miss Mapleton on Half Moon Street. Number 10. Do you see? I have proved to be useful once again." He gave

Eleanora a playful wink. "As I am certain you're aware, many prominent men house their paramours on this street."

"Yes, I'm aware. Well, that *is* useful information—my sincere thanks. Now we know exactly where to go. Have you ever had a mistress? One that you housed exclusively for your pleasure?"

Christian arched an eyebrow. Was there an edge to her voice? Disdain or, dare he hope—jealousy?

"No. I wanted no long-term entanglements or responsibilities. All my liaisons were of a brief duration."

Her bottom lip thrust out, but she said nothing.

"Sitting in judgment?" he ventured. "Isn't that what you want with me, or am I assuming too much?"

"A brief liaison," Eleanora mused. "I am not certain. I have to puzzle this out more. And no. I do not judge you or your friends on your activities. I never did. I always thought that whatever adults do in their private moments is no one's concern. Even though I make a living investigating them."

Before he had a chance to form a response about a liaison or anything else, she continued, "Speaking of judging, I'm often dismissed outright for merely being a woman. Insulted. Spat at for daring to venture in what is considered a man's domain."

"And yet you prevail," Christian said softly.

Eleanora's shoulders straightened. "Yes, and I always will."

A fierce wave of admiration moved through him. By God, she was fearless. Utterly brilliant.

"It astounds me that you, your sister, and your cousin move about this city without fear for your safety," he marveled.

"We protect ourselves. Althea carries a revolver, while Sybil and I prefer knives."

With a metallic click, a blade appeared from under the long sleeve of her jacket. "I also have one hidden in my boot. It has come in handy. I am also proficient at swordplay."

"I am impressed." Will she ever cease to surprise him?

"Have no worries, Your Grace. I will protect you." She gave him a delightful and teasing smile while moving the knife into its holder.

"I hardly need protecting. Like you, I'm more than able to defend myself." He said this straightforwardly. Although, having Eleanora close by in whatever capacity certainly appealed.

"You hired me. It is all part of the service from The Galway Agency. Caution is always practical. Now, as to your new role. I will introduce you as Mr. Christian, my assistant. I will ask the questions."

"Understood, Miss Galway," he acquiesced, and she chuckled in response.

Once they arrived, they dismissed the hansom as catching another on this street would be easy.

A maid wearing a crisp and starched uniform with a white apron and cap answered the door.

Eleanora handed the servant her business card. "I am Eleanora Galway; this is my assistant, Mr. Christian. We wish a few moments of Miss Mapleton's time in connection with a former acquaintance."

The maid took the card, gave it a cursory glance, then said, "Miss Mapleton is not receiving."

"It's all right, Hannah; show them in."

The maid stepped aside, and they entered the hall. There stood a stunningly attractive woman wearing a silk mauve tea gown. She was a proper English beauty with golden hair, flawless ivory skin, and sparkling blue eyes. No wonder Damon frequented The Chrysalis, for this woman was his friend's particular preference.

Christian searched his memory. Had he ever been with this woman the few times he had frequented the brothel? Damn it, he should have thought of that before insisting on attending this interview. She didn't look familiar. But who was to know? Nevertheless, he pulled the brim of his hat down over his eyes, then turned up the collar of his coat as if that wasn't obvious.

"What acquaintance?" Miss Mapleton asked.

"At your former place of employment. Emily McCarthy, known as Lucinda?" Eleanora responded.

"You had best come into the parlor."

"We will not take up much of your time," Eleanora assured her.

Banked coals simmered in the hearth, which made the room welcoming. It was balmy for early October, but Christian stood before it and warmed his hands. Miss Mapleton sat on a small settee and asked them to take the opposite. The residence was plush and luxuriant. Only the best for the men of Barclays Bank, Christian mused sardonically.

"Shall I ring for tea, Miss Galway, Mr. Christian?"

"Nay, lass. We thank ye, but as Miss Galway said, we won't be here long enough," Christian replied with a Scottish burr.

Miss Mapleton met his gaze, and no recognition registered in her eyes.

Dodged that.

Eleanora cast him aside glance as she pulled her notebook from the pocket of her cloak, surprised no doubt by his sham Scottish accent. Always a good mimic, Christian had picked up some of the vernacular and musical cadences. He and his mother had journeyed through Scotland during a few school holidays.

"Have you had contact with Miss McCarthy since you departed from The Chrysalis?" Eleanora asked, her fingers tightly gripping the pencil.

A furrow developed between Miss Mapleton's perfectly-shaped brows. "Is Emily in trouble?"

"A client wishes for us to locate her. They are worried about her safety. Any contact?"

Not a lie since he was the client, and remembering Eleanora's resolute warning about interrupting her questioning, he remained silent. Although it would be stimulating to do precisely that, only to have her reprimand him again.

"Yes, not three months past. Emily asked for a small loan and assured me she had a man who would soon set her up. Emily said the man was well off, but she could have been lying. I asked who he was, but she wouldn't say. I didn't have much money; I could only give her a handful of shillings."

Miss Mapleton sighed. "Emily did not look well. Her clothes were dirty and tattered. God only knows how she's been living since her dismissal. I know what she did. I told her it was wrong to cheat Bathsheba. She was good to us. Emily wouldn't listen."

Miss Mapleton pulled a lace handkerchief from her sleeve and dabbed her eyes. The concern appeared authentic, but Christian couldn't be sure.

"It's why she came to me. She couldn't seek out the others, for the brothel owners warned them to have no contact with her. Emily had no one. No family at all." Fiona continued, "I have no earthly idea where she went. I offered to take her in, even though my gentleman would be angry if I had. But Emily refused, thanked me for the money, and left. I never saw her again."

"Did you know if Emily had a venereal disease?"

Miss Mapleton was genuinely shocked at the question. "Not when we left. But now that you mention it, she wore no gloves when we spoke. There was a lesion on her thumb. She pulled her sleeve to cover it." Miss Mapleton's hand flew to her mouth. "Is that why she didn't look well? Oh, my dear Emily. I wish I had more money on me that day. I wish she had returned."

"She gave no indication where she was staying? Take a moment and recall the conversation," Eleanora asked gently.

"None. I assume a dosshouse."

"Had she ever discussed her past, where on the streets from whence she came?"

Miss Mapleton shook her head sadly. "None of us discussed our pasts; why would we? Best forgotten. Although she had mentioned once in passing, she'd moved from the workhouse to orphanages and back again until she was deemed old enough to look after herself."

After taking her notes, Eleanora stood, and so did Christian. "Thank you, Miss Mapleton." Eleanora held out her card. "Please contact us if Emily gets back in touch or you remember anything."

Miss Mapleton nodded. "I will. I promise. I wish I could have been of more assistance."

Once they stood on the sidewalk, Eleanora gave him another strange look.

"What is with that horrid Scottish accent?"

"It wasn't all *that* horrid."

A hansom cab approached, and Christian waved to gain the driver's attention.

Once settled inside, Christian said, "It sounds as if Emily may have met her end."

Eleanora sighed. "It may be a possibility."

"Is there a likelihood that whoever sent that macabre package has murdered Miss McCarthy and is cutting off bits and mailing them to us as a warning?" Christian asked.

Eleanora studied him. "What kind of warning? And for what?"

Christian wasn't sure. He crossed his legs and tried to think of every mystery or thriller novel he had ever read.

"The package was addressed to us all, even though Damon had more direct contact with Miss McCarthy than any of us. It could be someone who knows of us and that we are life-long friends. They know of the life we lead—or led—and where we meet."

"Like a former friend?" Eleanora asked.

"Or any acquaintance. Warning us to give up our vacuous and vile lifestyle? Had we inadvertently caused an insult to someone the perpetrator is fond of?"

"What about a former member?"

"I sent the list from Watford; have you looked into any of them?" Christian asked.

Eleanora shook her head. "Not as yet. That will be our third tier of investigation. What about a current friend or member?"

His eyes widened in shock. "Current? Like Tolwood or Huxley and the rest?"

It was not possible.

"Huxley left town. You said he was having problems. Perhaps the issues are with you all."

Christian was having difficulty processing this. "Wait, how did you know Warren had departed? Are you having us watched?"

Unbelievable.

She shrugged. "Everyone is a suspect."

"Including me?" he shouted. Taking a cleansing breath, he said, "I spoke to Warren. He suffered a breakdown and headed to a sanatorium in Standon, Hertfordshire. And I just broke strict confidence. Do not repeat this."

Eleanora pulled out her notebook and pencil and began writing. "The name of this place? It will be easy enough to check."

Christian rubbed his left temple. "The Bevan Sanatorium."

Now she had him wondering if Warren was behind all this.

Not possible.

He had known the man since they were ten. But Warren had been agitated last they met and had said: "We gravitated toward each other as children. What a privileged and carefree life we have all led. It is no wonder we became friends. The thread that held us together no longer exists. You know nothing about me."

Could it be true?

Warren also quickly agreed with Christian's assessment that they do not call the police. Coincidence?

"What *are* you thinking? Tell me, Christian. Share your thoughts with me."

Feeling like a damned traitor, he repeated what Warren had said at their meeting about deciding not to call the police.

Eleanora nodded as she wrote.

Warren is a suspect. He could not fathom such a dire possibility.

"And the other? Tolwood?" she asked.

"Harmless as a hedgehog. Merritt has distanced himself from the club, not that he was full-fledged. He wishes to find a suitable bride." Christian blew out an exasperated breath. "The club is fracturing. Brandon Knight will be leaving London in December, perhaps permanently. As to the rest? As far as I know, the club's members continue their carnal pursuits." Christian smiled. "No pun intended."

"Pun? Oh, *members*. I get it. How rakish of you."

"Forgive me. That sounded like something Damon would say."

He admonished himself for his crass behavior, for it was not like him. The delectable Miss Galway had him at sixes and sevens.

"You are forgiven." Eleanora continued to write. "Hedgehogs can inflict serious injury with their sharp quills. They can be aggressive. But we can rule out Tolwood for now; at least, I will place him at the bottom of the list. My report said he was attending various social events. No doubt seeking a bride, as you said."

"And me?"

She cocked her head as if studying him. "It would be deviously clever of you to act interested in joining the investigation in order to sabotage it from within. Flirt and act as if you were interested in me to appeal to my ego."

Act? He didn't have to bloody well act. "Then why allow me to assist you?"

"To ascertain if you are indeed a suspect. We haven't known each other all that long, but I *am* a good judge of character. I do not sense any sly machinations about you. So far as I'm aware, you've told the truth."

"Well, thank you for that, at least," Christian replied sardonically. "We can rule out the 'random body part from a hospital or graveyard' theory."

"Yes, I believe we can. Resurrectionists who sell dead bodies for research petered out in the Thirties with the Anatomy Act. Not to say there isn't a black market for such doings. The sender—let us call him Mr. X—for I assume it is a man, but who knows? Mr. X knew of this destitute woman's association with all of you. It has certainly moved beyond a macabre prank. Do you wish to involve the police at this juncture?"

Police? Should they? Not if one of his friends is involved.

"And what can they do? They would not have discovered as much as you have. They will toss it on the unsolved pile until the rest of Miss McCarthy surfaces. The thought this Mr. X is keeping the poor young woman on ice is rather disturbing. How long could she possibly stay preserved?" Christian paused. "And what about Ford Whitney? Shouldn't you also add Whitney to your suspect list if you consider Warren, Merritt, and the others as suspects?"

"First, I assume if the ice is changed regularly, a few weeks perhaps? I will have to ask Doctor Buchanan. As for Whitney, that will be our next line of inquiry. We will visit the baronet tomorrow and question him on his son's whereabouts." She waved her notebook before tucking it into her cloak pocket. "Thanks to Althea; I have his current address."

"And Hayes Addington?"

"Did you see a dead body?"

"Well, no. We assumed it swept out to sea. None of us attended the inquest. The story put forth was the one accepted. Such an outcome often occurs when peers are involved. Our fathers ensured no mention of our names, and we were never part of the official inquiry."

"The rest of you continued with your lives, believing him dead."

Christian gave Eleanora a dubious look. "Why would we believe otherwise? Especially as the years ticked by."

"My sister has a theory, and I concur. That perhaps Addington did *not* drown. Instead, he suffered from amnesia, regained his memory recently, and wishes to exact revenge on you all."

What could he say to such a hypothesis?

"At least you haven't scoffed at it as Brookton did," Eleanora stated.

"No, anything is possible. By all means, add Addington to the suspect list."

Eleanora gave him an admiring look, then scribbled in her notebook.

"As long as you take my name *off*," Christian added.

Eleanora met his gaze, smiled, and slashed a pencil stroke across the page. "Done."

"There is a chance you will never find out who is behind this, isn't there?" Christian asked.

"There is that likelihood. However, as you stated, we have already discovered more than the police would have."

"Where to next, Miss Galway?"

"Me? I'm going home. I need time to think and to do that; I need to bake."

Christian nodded, giving her a dazzling smile. "Brilliant. I will accompany you."

"Whatever for? To sit in my parlor while I toil in the kitchen? Why would you do such?"

Christian leaned forward, giving her his full attention along with a heated look for good measure. Just in case she had forgotten the attraction simmering between them. It was bubbling at full force—at least on his part. He didn't want to leave her. Not yet.

"As I said, if you allow me, I want to be in your company. And I'm not acting in a devious manner for any reason. It's because I am interested in everything you do. And in everything you say."

Because, my dear El, you have caught my attention as no woman has done before.

Chapter 15

A DUKE? SOMEONE FROM the peerage interested in her?

Perhaps she seized his attention because she was distinctly different from young ladies within his privileged sphere. There was no denying it; he had caught her interest as well. Easy to talk to—and easy on the eyes—loyal to his friends, honorable. Clever. Intelligent. Interested in the world around him and investing in the future.

For a brief moment, she allowed a daydream: the two of them living happily as a couple—while she continued to live her independent life as owner-operator of The Galway Agency.

The bubble burst as swiftly as it formed.

It could *never* happen.

Dukes made marriageable alliances with daughters of peers, not with a middle-class miss who lived life her way. She could never conform to his stuffy upper-crust existence.

Good God, marriage?

Since when did she indulge in sentimental claptrap like a happily-ever-after?

Never.

Or hardly ever.

Her gaze met his. He was vastly alluring, not only physically, but in how he held himself aloof to others, not with her. Christian was upfront and honest. They genuinely liked and respected each other, even though they had hardly known each other for two weeks.

Factor in the simmering but sizzling heat between them; he was everything she ever wanted in a man.

"We cannot become distracted from the task at hand, solving this case," she said. Eleanora could hear the regret in her voice.

"I completely agree, but there is something *there*, there—and it would be a damned shame if we did not explore it. Why not take this a day at a time?"

Smiling, she said, "Come with me to my house. You can assist me in preparing the scones. Have you ever been in a kitchen?"

Christian had been correct when he said there was something—*there*.

Her two previous brief encounters with men were empty. Meaningless. She did not want such with Christian. If what lay between them even advanced that far. By chance, it did; Eleanora wanted it to be a memory she cherished for the rest of her life.

"I used to make regular journeys to the kitchen," he replied, his pale blue eyes sparkling with amusement. "Granted, I was eight years of age and hoping to charm a biscuit or two from the cook, Mrs. Tallmadge."

Eleanora chuckled. "It will be a new experience for you. Domestic work."

He gave her his quirky but arresting smile. "I am a quick learner. I'm doing well as your assistant, am I not? And yes, I'm looking for a compliment. My ego needs the boost."

His intense but heated gaze gave her heart a jolt. All he had to do was smile, and she was utterly lost.

"You're doing well. So far," Eleanora smiled.

"Thank you. I appreciate that."

Thirty minutes later, after Christian changed his clothes at the club and gathered up his carriage and driver, they arrived at Cleveland Street. Christian gave Michaels some money to seek his lunch at the George and Dragon Pub next door and to pay to have the carriage watched as he did so.

They entered the front hall, and Christian automatically removed his greatcoat and hat and hung it on the hall tree as if he had done it every day.

"No one home?" he asked.

"Althea is off doing follow-up work for me, and my housekeeper is at the market. Here." Eleanora helped him remove his suit coat. "You cannot wear such finery in a kitchen."

After hanging it on an empty hook, she trailed her fingers down his shirt sleeve, marveling at the solid muscle underneath. Reaching his cuff, she slipped the pearl buttons through the holes and slowly but purposely folded the shirtsleeve upward, exposing his forearm. Then she did the other.

Eleanora blushed, her body reacting to the nearness of him. Every feminine part of her was alive. Her fingers absently caressed the exposed skin on his arm. So warm.

"We had best head to the kitchen."

"Lead on." His voice was gruff, his look heated.

Impulsively, she kissed his cheek, then turned swiftly and headed toward the kitchen.

It would be difficult to concentrate on the case, let alone bake with Christian nearby. Eleanora moved about gathering earthenware bowls, utensils, and ingredients.

"I know many upper-class cooks make round scones; I like to cut them into wedges," Eleanora said as she opened the icebox. "First, the butter must be cold."

She turned to face Christian and held up the dish. He leaned against the counter, arms crossed, giving her that sensual half-smile that made her heart beat faster.

"Next is buttermilk. It heightens the scones due to the acidity reacting to the baking powder." Eleanora cocked her head. "How can you be the least bit interested in this?"

"I am all attention, I assure you. What is baking powder?"

She brightened at the subject. "A British chemist, Alfred Bird, was the first to develop it in 1843 because his wife was allergic to yeast. It is a mixture of several things, including baking soda and cornstarch. It's a fascinating invention. The carbon dioxide causes the baked goods to rise. First, though, we want to light the oven. I have a gas cooker, how modern of me. Helen Louise Johnson introduced a working electric cooker at the World's Fair in Chicago. She is an editor of a home economics magazine in America. I read she cooked steaks and baked bread as a demonstration. It will be years before it catches on, but imagine!"

"Fascinating," he smiled.

"It is! Corbett told me a Canadian developed the electric cooker. Anyway, on to the baking." She lit the cooker, then faced him. "Next, we need to mix the dry ingredients. That will be your chore. It would be best if you mix the butter with the dry until it has the consistency of small peas. You will be using your hands. It's why I rolled up your sleeves."

Eleanora opened a drawer and pulled out an apron. "Here, wear this to protect your fine waistcoat." Without waiting for a reply, she looped the strap around his neck, then stood behind him.

My, how shameless that she admired his fine arse. How tempting it would be to slide her hands over the muscled globes. Would he give that combination of a growl and a moan that caused her heart to stutter? Lingering momentarily, she grasped the apron ties and secured them at his back.

With a swift turn, Christian faced her. Cupping her cheeks, he leaned in to kiss her. This one was different from the others. It was gentle, tender, and soul-stirring. Reverent. And absolutely stunning. He ended it by softly nibbling on her lower lip.

"If the scones taste as sweet as you, they will be amazing," he crooned.

Eleanora took a moment to savor the kiss and his flirting. Oh, she could kiss this man forever.

"Now," she said briskly, focusing on the task at hand. "We measure the flour, baking powder, and sugar."

With quick efficiency, she had all the ingredients in the large bowl. Taking Christian's hands, she admired them, her thumbs stroking them from his wrist to his long fingers and manicured nails. A reckless part of her—more impetuous than she was acting now—wanted to drag him to her bedroom, tear his clothes off, and have her wicked way with him. No man had ever caused her ordered mind even to consider such.

"Here, time to mix the ingredients," she muttered, trying to keep her voice from shaking.

Who knew baking could be so blasted sensual?

Eleanora guided his hands into the bowl, demonstrating how to fold in the butter. Their fingers entwined as they moved through the flour blend. Good lord, if she was overheated before, now she was ready to burst into flame.

For a moment, they stood hip-to-hip, hands covered with flour. Christian squeezed her hand, his thumb caressing that sensitive area between her thumb and index finger. A soft sigh escaped her throat before she could stop it.

"I'd better prepare the pan." Eleanora couldn't tear her eyes from him. Reluctantly, she moved away but kept giving him clandestine glances.

A duke is mixing scones in her kitchen. It beggared belief.

"This is quite relaxing," Christian stated while blending the flour.

"Yes, exactly why I love it." The bell clanged. "Oh, blast it all. I will get the door. Continue, assistant."

"Understood, Miss Galway," he replied in his low, gravelly voice.

She chuckled. After wiping her hands on the tea towel, she headed into the hall. Opening the door, she found no one there, only a tiny box on the stoop.

Eleanora glanced at the brown paper-wrapped package, and as soon as she saw the word "Rakes" scrawled on it, she yelled, "Christian!"

The George and Dragon Pub was one of those places with two entrances. The other entry at the rear alley led to an intersection of three streets.

Stepping onto the sidewalk, she looked up the street, then down, and caught a glimpse of someone with a long cloak and a floppy hat duck into the pub.

Eleanora didn't hesitate; she lifted her skirts, tucked them under her waistband, and started running in pursuit of the mystery person.

Eleanora raced through the pub, shoving her way through the crowd. The pub was crowded enough that she couldn't immediately locate Christian's driver, but the man with the cloak was near the rear exit. Once he ran into the crowded convergence on the streets, he could be lost easily, particularly if he tossed the hat and cape.

"Eleanora!" Christian yelled as he was right on her heels.

"This way!" she replied, not looking back.

They must look a pair, her with her skirt tucked up and Christian, wearing an apron and with his flour-covered hands.

Once she reached Clipstone Street, she stopped dead in her tracks. Three men, at least she assumed they were men, judging by their height and build, stood at the intersection. All were dressed similarly in floppy hats, dark spectacles, a handkerchief tied about the lower part of their face, and a long cloak.

Like illustrations of villain pirates, only without the sword and the parrot perched on his shoulder. Behind them were three similar carriages in different directions of the three streets. These were not hansom cabs but actual Clarence carriages with two horses. The men each climbed into their conveyances. The coachmen, dressed the same as the caped men, all snapped their reins departing in different directions.

Which one to chase?

Christian came up behind her, slightly out of breath. "Michaels is right behind me—"

"We can't wait! Pick one, quick!" Eleanora took off as if shot out of a cannon.

"Wait, El!"

Eleanora headed toward the slowest carriage, which was finding navigating the busy streets difficult. But she didn't stop. She'd always been a fast runner, thanks to her long legs.

She was almost to the door and was relieved to see the windows were not glassed in. Taking a giant leap, Eleanora landed on the metal step, her hands clasping the handle. She pulled, but Cloaked Pirate held it closed.

"Eleanora!"

Why was Christian pursuing her?

She distinctly told him to chase one of the other carriages. Why wouldn't he listen? The one time he didn't follow her orders, stubborn man!

The carriage went over a bump, and she nearly lost her footing. While she struggled with the handle, the carriage picked up speed.

Without warning, the door flew open. Acting swiftly, Eleanora looped her arm through the open window and held tight since she lost her footing on the metal step. Grunting, she swung the door forward, her booted foot desperately feeling for the stair.

There!

If she managed to lean in far enough to pull the handkerchief off the face of Cloaked Pirate, they would have a lead or clue.

If only she had her wrist knife on her, she could at least make a threat, enough of one that she could halt the carriage. Trying to dig the one out of her boot would give the man advantage, and she would lose her footing.

About to step inside, the pirate's leg shot forward. The motion caused her to lose her grip. The heel of his boot caught her square in the chest, knocking the wind out of her.

Eleanora's arms flailed as she fell to the cobbles with such force; she rolled at least three times, her head banging against cobblestones with enough impact that she saw stars.

Oh, hell.

Everything went dark.

Chapter 16

CHRISTIAN'S HEART CEASED to beat when Eleanora was kicked clear from the carriage. Instinctively, he wanted to chase the masked bastard, tear him from the carriage, and beat him to a bloody pulp—even murder.

But—El. Oh, Jesus, El.

He came out of shock when Michaels finally caught up to him and exclaimed, "My God!"

Christian ran to her side, dropping to his knees. There was blood pooling behind her head.

"The carriages are getting away, Your Grace!" Michaels cried.

"To hell with them." He hooked his arms under Eleanora's knees and tried to lift her.

"You won't be able to carry me," Eleanora said weakly. "I'm no featherweight."

Thank Christ, she's awake.

Christian tore off his apron and bunched it up. "Here, are you able to hold this behind your head? Apply pressure; it will stem the bleeding."

She took it and did as instructed.

He would transport her in another position if Christian couldn't carry her this way. He sat her upright, leaned in, and heaved her over his shoulder. With shaky legs, he stood and distributed her weight.

"Stop!" Eleanora protested. "You and Michaels can assist me home by acting as crutches—"

"It will take too long. Michaels, with me. Eleanora, keep the pressure on your injury."

He made his way toward the alley with long strides and as swiftly as he dared.

"This is humiliating, carried like a sack of potatoes," Eleanora stated. "Wait, you are not going through the pub?"

"It's the quickest way."

Eleanora groaned.

Christian stepped across the threshold. "Make way! Injured lady coming through!" he bellowed. The crowd parted, leaving a clear path to the opposite door.

"Miss Galway," the barman called out. "Are you well?"

Before she could reply, Christian said, "She fell on the cobbles. Just taking her home so we can call in the doctor."

"I will never live this down," Eleanora sputtered. "The entire street will be talking."

Christian patted her rear. "Your safety takes precedence over any potential embarrassment."

Eleanora didn't reply.

"El, answer me. Are you awake?"

They were almost to the Cleveland Street entrance.

"I feel woozy," she said, her voice nearly inaudible.

Christian burst through the pub door with Michaels on his heels. Once on the sidewalk, he found Althea outside the Galway home, holding the parcel.

"My God, what's happened? I arrived to find the door wide open. Ellie!" Althea's hand flew to her mouth in shock.

"We need a doctor immediately," Christian yelled.

"I want—Buchanan," Eleanora whispered.

Of course, her Canadian.

Not an appropriate time for him to feel any protectiveness. He entered the house and strode into the parlor.

"Give Michaels the directions," he said to Althea.

"He lives on the top floor of Mollie's, Upper Wimpole Street. Number 49."

Christian snorted. A brothel. Typical.

"I'll go straight away, miss," Michaels replied, heading for the door.

"Don't come back without him," Christian called out.

"I won't, Your Grace."

Michaels departed, and Christian laid Eleanora gently on the sofa, taking care to keep the bloody apron against the back of her head. Her face was white as a sheet, her eyelids fluttering. As he crouched next to her, genuine fear clutched his insides. Christian knew next to nothing about head injuries. However, he figured letting her slip into unconsciousness might not be a good idea.

He tapped her cheek none too gently. "Stay awake, El. You hear me?"

"So commanding," she murmured, her words slurring. "I like you calling me El." The letter 'l' trailed out for several seconds.

Then she leaned forward and promptly vomited on his boots.

"Sweet Mother. Beefsteak pie. How horrid. So sorry." Eleanora fainted.

Christian tapped her cheeks again. "Stay awake, El!"

A moment passed, then another. At last, Eleanora's eyelids fluttered.

"Oh, thank God," Althea exhaled. "I'll fetch water."

"Yes, and anything else you think Buchanan will need."

Althea rushed from the room as Christian took Eleanora's hand. "The doctor will be here directly. He's not all that far away."

"The parcel," she rasped.

"Althea has secured it for now."

"The carriages, the costumes," she swallowed. "That cost money."

Althea returned with a tray with various items. She dipped a cloth in the water and handed it to Christian.

As he gently wiped Eleanora's mouth, he said, "Do not focus on the case now, El."

"Have to. It keeps me awake."

Althea passed him a glass of water.

"Here, take a sip." He tilted Eleanora's head up slightly enough for her to drink. She did.

"Your boots—" she whispered.

"They do not matter. Only *you* matter."

"My head aches."

He tenderly kissed her forehead. "If I could take away the pain, I would."

"This is a game," she whispered. "Whoever is doing this, it's all a game to them."

"Hush now," Christian answered as he stroked her brow.

"What does she mean? What happened?" Althea asked.

Christian gave her a quick synopsis of the events.

"You should have followed one of the other carriages. Michaels could have followed the other," Eleanora interjected.

"And leave you bleeding on the cobbles? I think not."

Christian heard the carriage pull up to the door, and a tall bearded man burst into the room.

"Doctor!" Althea cried. "Ellie's had a nasty fall. Kicked from a moving carriage. The injury is to the back of her head."

Buchanan shoved Christian. "Move aside," he barked.

"This is the Duke of Allenby," Althea said.

"Then move aside, *Your Grace.*" Buchanan sat his bag on the nearby table.

Annoyed, Christian stood next to Althea. The doctor did a cursory exam, checking her eyes and feeling her head.

"Your pupils are not dilated, a good sign. Who am I?"

"Dr. Corbett Buchanan."

"What day is it?"

"Thursday, October seventh."

"Very good. You answered correctly and with no hesitation. Where were you kicked?"

"The chest."

When Buchanan started to trail his hands across Eleanora's torso, Christian could not keep the possessive animal growl from escaping his throat.

Buchanan looked up at him with his eyebrows arched in question. Then he turned his attention to Eleanora.

"No broken ribs, but your chest will be sore and bruised. Now, turn slightly so that I may examine your injury."

Eleanora did, and the doctor tossed aside the apron.

"Head wounds bleed something fierce. It's always worse than it looks."

How gratifying to hear that.

"You will need a few stitches. Althea, I will need scissors—and hot water. I believe Eleanora has a mild concussion. Eleanora, on a scale of one to ten, how would you rate the ache in your head?"

"Five, maybe six."

"Good, not overly severe." The doctor glanced at Christian's boots. "I see you vomited, expected with a concussed head." He looked about the room. "Where is Miss Sybil?"

"Gone," Althea answered.

"What?" The doctor's eyes widened. "For good?"

The man sounded distressed over the prospect.

"No, she should return soon. Her father was ill, nothing serious, but she wanted to be with him," Althea replied.

The look of relief that crossed the doctor's face was palpable. Was there something between Eleanora's cousin and Buchanan?

Althea touched Christian's sleeve. "Come with me. We will gather what the doctor needs and clean off your boots."

Christian was not eager to leave Eleanora but followed Althea into the kitchen.

"Did I smell gin on that sorry excuse for a doctor?" he snarled.

Althea waved for him to sit at the table as she moved to the sink.

"Yes, he drinks, but you've seen him in action; he knows what he is about." Althea handed him a wet tissue, and he wiped his boots. Then she took the cloth from him and passed him another. "For your hands."

Yes, hands covered with a blend of flour and blood made for quite the mixture.

"We were making scones when the bell rang."

"Were you? I agree with Eleanora that whoever is orchestrating this, to them, it's a game. Could there be more than one? Possibly, since there were three masked men. Or they could have all been hired. Regardless, they knew Ellie was home, and you were with her."

"Are you saying we are all under surveillance?"

Althea nodded. "It *is* possible. Even probable. Stay and finish cleaning up. I will take in what the doctor needs. I'm glad you were here, Christian. Ellie can be—impulsive. Despite her well-ordered and analytical mind, there are times she acts impetuously. Anyway, thank you." Althea picked up the tray and departed.

Christian slowly wiped the grime from his hands. The scene of Eleanora kicked from the carriage repeatedly played in his mind. Impulsive indeed. Never had he known such a moment of stark terror. The horrible thought that she could be seriously injured—that he could lose her—was a bleakness he had never experienced.

What in the deviled hell?

There was no use denying it; he was indeed falling for Eleanora Galway. All plans of finding a society-suitable wife dissipated into the air.

He wanted Eleanora.

The difficult part? Trying to convince her they could have much more than a temporary affair.

They could have it *all*.

DARKNESS HAD SHROUDED the room when Eleanora next opened her eyes. Sitting next to her bed was a prominent figure in silhouette. Her heart leaped with joy.

"Da?" Her confused brain tried to make sense of what was occurring.

Her father—here.

"I've missed you so much." Her eyes filled with tears.

"El, it's Christian."

"Oh. Of course. I was dreaming."

"Understandable. Your father was a large part of your life."

"Da was all we had. I used to sit by that window," she pointed at the one facing Cleveland Street, "every late afternoon, waiting for Da to come home. Terrified that some crazed criminal would murder him. But he always came home."

"But not anymore," Christian interjected softly.

"No. Not anymore," Eleanora sniffled.

He sat next to her on the bed. Gently, he gathered her into his arms. Christian took her hand, lacing his fingers through hers. Eleanora swung her legs across him and laid her head against his chest, basking in his warmth and the strong beat of his heart.

"Give sorrow words; the grief that does not speak whispers the o'er-fraught heart and bids it break."

His voice. How sensual yet soothing.

A lump formed in her throat. She may have just fallen for this enigmatic duke. So remote with others, but all genuine warmth with her.

"Shakespeare?" she ventured.

"Yes, from Macbeth."

"How true. When Da passed, I made a vow. I would never give my love to anyone ever again. Not my sister, uncles, cousins—no one. For if you do not love, you will never be hurt. Or so I foolishly thought. The vow didn't last; it was my family, after all. It was the grief speaking. But that pain and anguish linger, hiding in dark corners, popping out when I least expect it."

"Like now."

Those gathering tears spilled over her cheeks. Her father was not here, and the misery cut through as deep as it had the night he died.

Christian held her close in a rocking motion and smoothed her tangled hair. "There, love. It's all right. Cry as much as you like."

"W-w-why does it still hurt so much? He's been gone over three years!" she sobbed piteously into his shoulder.

"You loved him very much," he murmured.

"Yes. My father was my hero, my whole world."

"I wish I could have said the same. I hardly knew my father. He rarely came to Bamford Park when I was a young child."

"At least you had your mother. I don't remember mine at all," Eleanora sniffled.

"I did. The Duchess was—and still is—a constant in my life. My mother just informed me she has received an offer of marriage from the Duke of Coldbridge."

"Will she accept?"

"I believe so. My mother is quite besotted."

"You will have to share her affections with another man."

"Yes. But I won't begrudge it. My mother's happiness means more to me than my emotional needs."

What an altruistic thing to say. Christian loved his mother and wanted her happiness. It spoke well of his character, and it moved her.

Eleanora couldn't say anything else; the pain of losing her father and the lingering grief was still too acute. She definitely didn't want to reveal that her deep-seated fright extended to her growing feelings for him.

Instead, she allowed Christian's comfort to flow through her until she quieted. Incredible that he was still here by her side. Drat it all for showing her vulnerable side. Yes, she could be sensitive but kept it well hidden. Why had she allowed it to surface with him?

"Chris, thank you for listening. For comforting me," she whispered.

"Ah. Chris. I like that, El. Call me that when we're alone." He trailed the tip of his finger gently across her cheek.

"And I like that you call me El. We shouldn't be alone, though."

"Who cares what anyone thinks? If you knew how much I have longed to hold you in my arms like this. I can stay here all night. For the rest of my life, even. Just say the word."

What is he saying?

"You don't mean that."

"You believe there can be nothing between us? And don't start with the 'but you are a duke' nonsense. I won't have it. I would never smother you or tell you how to live your life. Think about that. What is growing between us is powerful, El. It will only grow stronger."

A future with a duke?

After only knowing each other for a matter of a few weeks? Her head started to ache, and she could not speak or think of this anymore tonight. Instead, she nuzzled in closer, and Christian kissed the top of her head, holding her as if she were precious cargo.

How much time passed; Eleanora wasn't sure. "What time is it?"

"Nine o'clock at night. Buchanan gave you a pinch of laudanum for the pain and sleep. He said you're to be watched closely for the next thirty-six hours. I informed Althea I would stay and assist."

"Oh. There is no need—"

He cupped her cheek and gently stroked it with the pad of his thumb. "There is *every* need. Every two hours, I check if your mental capabilities have deteriorated. And you're to get as much sleep as you can. Your Canadian doctor claims it will aid in your recovery. You must stay abed twenty-four hours. No leaving the house for thirty-six. I am afraid I must insist."

Eleanora bristled and pushed his hand away. Every two hours?

"I do *not* require a keeper or a nursemaid," she tried to swing her legs around, but Christian halted her movements by gripping her lower leg.

"If it means your complete recovery, then I *will* be your keeper. Bed rest and fluids, the doctor said. Althea and I will make certain you follow his implicit instructions."

"But the case. The parcel! What—"

Christian laid a finger gently against her lips. "Calm. If you drink water and lie down, I will tell you."

Frowning, she took the offered cup and drank it all. Then she lay flat. Christian pulled the covers up before he took his seat.

"There was a severed hand in the box."

"What?" Eleanora cried, motioning to sit upright, but Christian held up his hand. Frustrated, she lay flat once again. "Continue."

"Doctor Buchanan has taken it to your uncle's precinct to perform blood analysis. Althea compared the writing on the brown paper of both parcels. It matches."

"I've been thinking," Eleanora mused. "Do you recognize the writing? Does it match any of the rakes?"

"No, I don't believe so."

"Or perhaps Ford Whitney. Do you still have the letters he sent?"

Christian shook his head. "That was years ago; they're long gone. Besides, I don't study a person's handwriting. My analysis is useless in that regard."

Well, it had been worth a try.

"You observed no distinguishing features on the masked men? The drivers? The carriages themselves?" Christian asked.

"My, you sound like a seasoned investigator. Answer me this, why didn't you and Michaels chase the other carriages?" she demanded.

"We're not getting into this. Try to sleep. Recover. There is plenty of time for the case later."

Eleanora turned away from him, annoyed at his high-handedness. But it dissipated when she recalled how he had comforted her. Not many men would have offered such compassion.

Exhaling, she turned and met his gaze.

"You are a caring and intelligent man, Christian Bamford. Do not allow anyone to tell you any different."

"Thank you."

"When I said it was a game? I believe it started that way with the person or persons involved. But I have this feeling here," she balled her fist and laid it in her middle. "That it will take a dangerous turn. This stunt this afternoon took careful planning and money. They left the box here. They no doubt knew that you were with me. You had best inform your friends to take precautions. It's more imperative than ever that we follow up on other leads."

Christian took her fist. After kissing it, he laced his fingers through hers, then gently kissed her hand again.

"I will pass on the warnings. We will talk more tomorrow. Althea received a telegram a few hours past. Miss Sybil will be returning immediately. You will have even more assistance. Sleep."

Christian once again tucked the blankets about her as her eyelids fluttered. Lord, she was tired, and she ached all over. As sleep overtook her, she couldn't shake the thought that one of Christian's friends had a hand in this.

But above all that? What filled her thoughts even more than the case was Christian.

How he held her soothed her pain and spoke openly about his feelings opened her guarded heart.

Eleanora was more than falling for him—and it scared her sick.

Chapter 17

DAYLIGHT WASHED THE room in warm illumination. Eleanora cracked open her eyes. Sitting next to her was Sybil and Althea, smiling encouragingly.

"What day is it?" Eleanora croaked.

Sybil immediately reached for the glass of water as Althea assisted her in sitting upright, far enough to take a drink.

"Friday, the eighth, three in the afternoon. You've slept around the clock," Sybil replied, holding the glass.

Eleanora leaned forward and drank generously. Finished, she lay against the pillows.

"When did you arrive?"

"About an hour ago. The trains actually ran on time for once."

"Uncle James?"

"Much better," Sybil replied. "Father improves by the day. And now I arrive to find you an invalid."

"I'm getting out of this bed tonight." Eleanora looked about. "Christian?"

"I insisted that he go home," Althea stated. "The man was exhausted. He stayed up all night with you."

"Oh," Eleanora replied in a small voice. "He did?"

It was hard to know if he had been there wiping her brow, speaking in low, comforting tones, or if it all had been a dream.

Sybil placed the near-empty glass on the table.

"Spill, Eleanora. What is transpiring that you have a duke seeing to your every need? What has developed since I left? Althea filled me in on the case. But bringing Allenby in on the particulars? Making him your assistant? Making scones together? Since when do you allow anyone in your kitchen when you're baking, let alone join an investigation?"

"Don't admonish me," Eleanora pouted. "I'm attracted to him. What is the harm?"

Sybil and Althea exchanged looks of astonishment.

"Do you not remember what happened the last time?" Sybil asked, her voice soft.

"With whom?"

"The second dalliance. With Sir Roger Fletcher?"

Eleanora was not ashamed of her involvement with men. She readily shared the details with Althea and Sybil.

She folded her arms defiantly. "I don't know what you mean."

But she had an idea. Roger Fletcher, a knight of the realm, was someone she'd met while inquiring about another client. He had flattered her, praised her confidence, and took her to dinner and his bed. Then he rejected her for the very reasons he had complimented her.

"My heart did not break; it never came into play with Fletcher."

Eleanora spoke the truth. She had been relieved when he summarily rejected her. No, what stung was that he'd looked down upon her profession. Stating that if there were to be anything between them, she would have to forgo her independence and take her "proper place in society."

And what was *that* exactly? Whatever a man dictated it to be—under his thumb.

If a knight acted this way, what would a duke do?

A duke would be even more insistent that a woman "fall in line" despite his declaration that he would never do that. Was Christian like Roger? All compliments and admiration until he got what he wanted? Blast it; her head started aching once again.

"You were hurt for different reasons, not to do with your heart," Althea interjected. "You were frustrated more than anything."

Frustrated was correct: that men would always treat women as second-class citizens. Women didn't even have the right to vote, though many brave ladies in suffrage societies were fighting for that very thing.

"We do not wish you to go down that path once again. To find yourself disappointed in yet another man. They always let us down," Sybil stated. "No man will take any of us seriously. We are outsiders. Doing a man's job."

"You sound bitter, Cousin," Eleanora said.

"I am. So should you be."

"I must admit that Christian was genuinely concerned for Ellie after her carriage adventure," Althea interjected. "Sybil, if you could have seen his expression. Stark worry. Ellie vomited on his boots, and he didn't turn a hair. The man stayed all night. He will return before dinner, he said."

Sybil snorted. "Sounds as if the duke has won you over, Althea."

Her sister shrugged. "He's not what I expected. Now Brookton? He lives up to every stereotype of an arrogant peer. But I believe Allenby is a different sort of man. One worthy of our respect."

"There has to be something wrong with him," Eleanora muttered. "Some dark secret or a disgusting quirk of his personality he keeps well hidden."

"If anyone can get to the bottom of it, it's you, Cousin," Sybil teased.

"The case." Eleanora brightened at the subject and sat up straighter.

Althea dutifully fluffed the pillows behind her.

"Thank you, Sister. Now, I will need one of you to travel to Hertfordshire and make a visual check that Huxley is actually at the Bevan Sanatorium receiving treatment; and if he was there when this carriage incident took place."

Althea was about to speak, but Eleanora flapped her hand to silence her. "I am well aware he could have made all these arrangements before he departed, but we need confirmation nonetheless. The rest home is in Standon."

"How far away is that?" Althea asked.

"North of here, about forty-five miles. There is no use in writing as these places have strict rules of confidentiality. Best we get a visual on him. Going by train, you could be there and back in less than two days. It will require an overnight stay."

"Me?" Althea questioned.

"Yes, you."

"I can go with her," Sybil interrupted.

"I need you here. Sybil, Uncle Reece offered his network of coppers should we require assistance. I also need a follow-up from Doctor Buchanan. I am also waiting on a report from Archie concerning the footman."

Eleanora took a breath and exhaled, then continued.

"Sybil, go to Uncle Reece and ask for anything he can find on the coroner's inquest on Hayes Addington, age sixteen. He was heir to a baron. The reported and supposed death took place fourteen years past. We also need the name of the distant cousin who inherited the barony. Also, inquire if Buchanan has completed his inspection of the severed hand. When he does, I want him here, giving me his report as soon as possible."

"Very well," Sybil replied.

"We have a list of former members of The Rakes. We will have to investigate the men soon," Eleanora added.

Sybil smiled and pulled the list from the pocket of her skirt. "Althea already gave it to me. What are these names crossed out?"

"Watford said they are happily married, like the baron listed there, Simon Wolstenholme. Set those names aside now, and concentrate on current friends and members."

Yes, she was feeling more like herself. No time to wallow in sentimental sensitivity. Something she should remember when next with the duke.

"Tomorrow, I will pay a visit to the baronet, Sir Howard Whitney," Eleanora continued. "And yes, Allenby will be coming with me. I will not be able to gain an audience otherwise. I will question the man about the drowning incident and the whereabouts of his son, Ford Whitney."

Eleanora doubted the man had anything to do with this. According to Christian, Whitney's letters were all friendship and good cheer. However, she must explore all avenues.

EIGHTEEN HOURS EARLIER...
   An abandoned warehouse in the East End

"HOW LONG DO WE HAVE to wait? I want my pay for the job done," one of the men groused. He tossed the floppy hat and cape aside.

"Momentarily," Jeffrey Mason crooned. "I'm to have your assurances that you will not speak of this to anyone. If you do, there will be consequences. We know where you all live and work. I do not like making threats, rather poor business in my mind."

Jeffrey looked at the six men standing before him, hired as carriage drivers and masked passengers. "But a threat it is. Do I have that assurance?"

"Yes, Aye," the men answered in unison.

Nodding, Jeffrey moved behind a stack of empty wooden crates and brought out a small valise. Taking out bundles of pounds notes, he passed them to each man.

"Leave the disguises on the table by the door. You are to send word to the barkeep at The Ten Bells if anyone comes around asking questions. Leave the message for Mr. Mangle."

Jeffrey had hired actual carriage drivers that worked for various wealthy families in London instead of renting traceable carriages.

The men gathered up their money and departed.

However, the last disguised man lingered as if waiting until the others left before doffing his hat and scarf. Closing the door, he turned to face Jeffery as he tossed the bills into the valise.

"Honestly, Ford, what possessed you to act as one of the hired men?" Jeffery admonished.

Ford Whitney smiled. "It was quite thrilling, especially when that beast of a woman made chase."

Jeffrey shook his head. "You could have killed her. The driver told me what happened."

"I watched out the rear window; she was moving about on the cobbles. Not dead." He removed the cape and threw it on top of the other garments. "We'll have to burn all of this."

"What is next? We have accomplished our goal of breaking up that club of rakes. Huxley has tucked his tail and left town. Tolwood is off pursuing rich heiresses. We rattled them good and proper, according to your man, Phillips. The game has reached its conclusion."

Ford shook his head. "No. They haven't suffered enough."

"This has already gone too far. Keeping a dead prossie on ice? It's beyond macabre. And the circumstances of her death are murky at best. You never explained the particulars."

Ford took a step closer to Jeffrey. "What are you implying?"

Ford had gathered a few men, Jeffrey included, with one common theme: they all detested The Rakes of St. Regent's Park. All of them had their reasons, but none as significant as Ford's, at least in his mind.

Jeffery must have seen the dangerous look in his eyes, for he took several steps in reverse.

"N-n-nothing. You found the prossie dead, I-I believe you."

Emily McCarthy had been in the final stages of her debilitating illness; Ford merely assisted her with a pillow over her face.

It would not be the last time he ended a life. He had it in him. Look at what had occurred that night so long ago with Hayes. Although with McCarthy, he looked upon it as a mercy, for she had suffered immensely.

He initially discovered her sleeping in an alley. Ford knew of every brothel his former friends frequented. When Emily mentioned her place of previous employment, he enticed her with the promise of a roof over her head, food, and comfort. She took it gladly, filling him in on the doings of his reprobate former friends.

"Besides," Jeffrey mewled, "As you know, Allenby has hired an investigative agency and is keeping company with 'the beast of a woman,' as you called her. The next step they will take is reporting all this to the police. I say end this before we place ourselves in danger of discovery."

Ford grabbed a fistful of Jeffrey's shirt, pulling him close. "This concludes when I say it does. You are in this to the bitter end, as are the others."

"What others? I only know of Phillips."

Ford tightened his grip. "And that is all you need to know."

"Yes. Fine. Release me at once," Jeffrey said, his voice shaking. "I cannot abide aggressive behavior. It's rather unsettling."

Ford released him and snorted with disgust.

Damned sniveling coward.

But the man had proved useful—and stupid. If any of the hired men were found and asked to make a description, they would only know of Mason, not him. And as dumb as Mason was, he innately understood that his life would not be worth a farthing if he pointed any blame in Ford's direction.

Jeffrey straightened the collar of his shirt. "What is next, then?"

"Allow me to mull it over. I will call a meeting soon enough. Meanwhile, I have to deal with my father."

"Right, he doesn't know you have returned to London."

He damned well knew Ford had left Switzerland, however. The owners of that wretched asylum no doubt informed his father of Ford's escape and the fact that he had cleaned out the safe. They probably demanded recompense for the twenty-odd thousand pounds he had stolen. *Good.*

After that horrible summer night fourteen years ago, Ford had returned to his father, begging for his assistance, only to be beaten within an inch of his life. His father had used a heavy brass candlestick to thrash him. Ford believed his father would have killed him had the butler not intervened. Ford trailed the tip of his finger along the jagged scar that ran from his left temple to his jaw.

At times over the next several years, Ford wished that he had.

Instead, his father sent him to that remote school in the Alps of Switzerland.

School. More like a military prison. There he suffered unspeakable torture and abuse, physical and emotional.

Not one word from his father in all those years. Letters went unanswered. He even sent letters to Damon and Christian. They, too, went unanswered.

No one cared.

Ford tried to escape more than once, only to be dragged back through the snow and thrown into a windowless locked room no better than a prison cell.

Then to be transferred to an asylum?

Ford played the part of a madman, biding his time, planning his escape.

He rubbed his temple as his head ached, as it often did when recalling those haunted memories.

No more ruminating on the past. Not today.

He had to think clearly about what to do next.

Revenge is what kept him going.

Only when he exacted his revenge on those who had wronged him could he start to live. Only then would the nightmarish images fade. Only then would his head stop aching.

What next? Financial ruin? Public disgrace?

Murder?

The thought took root. Murder was a messy business but one not to be completely ruled out. What Ford's former friends had done was mild compared to what his father perpetrated. The plan would need further reflection.

"Grab the valise and let us depart," Ford commanded.

Ford gathered up all the garments on the table and followed Jeffery out the door. It was dark outside; the gaslight illuminations cast eerie shadows on the coal fog rolling past. They passed an unattended burning barrel, often used by anyone who wished to stop and warm his hands or cook a potato over it. Ford dropped the garments in it and kept walking.

Yes, revenge is indeed—sweet.

Chapter 18

THREE DAYS HAD PASSED, and Christian had spent most of that time caring for Eleanora. Initially, she had bristled but soon settled in and allowed him to serve her meals, gauge her temperature, and keep her company.

They spoke on all subjects and found they had more in common than he had thought.

But at the foremost of Eleanora's mind was the investigation. He admired her work ethic and desire to get to the truth. She was resolute in her purpose.

How to turn that passion toward him?

He may have revealed too much that night he held her in his arms, but he was intelligent enough to know not to bring the subject up again. Not as yet. The fact that she didn't reply gave him a spark of hope. At least she hadn't dismissed him outright.

As for a possible future together?

Christian had thought of nothing else. No other woman had caught his interest like this or engaged his heart. How could he ask her to give up her investigative agency?

And why should she? To please society? To please him?

He would *never* ask it of her.

He glanced at her sitting across from him in his carriage as they headed toward Sir Howard Whitney's residence. Christian had sent word two days ago that he wished for an audience, and Sir Howard had reluctantly complied.

"So, am I to remain quiet during his interview," he teased.

Eleanora gave him an alluring smile. "Not completely silent. I may need your assistance prying information out of him."

The carriage pulled up in front of a rather dingy set of flats. The address was in a respectable section of Lambeth, but this particular building had seen better days. Michaels opened the door and assisted Eleanora out of the carriage, with Christian following.

Christian pulled the bell, and a stooped older man answered.

He handed his card to him. "Christian Bamford, Duke of Allenby. Sir Howard is expecting us."

The man took the card with a trembling hand. "This way, Your Grace."

The lighting was nonexistent, and the place had not had a good dusting or airing out in years. The air was stale and oppressive. Christan heard barking off in the distance.

"Sir Howard will join you directly." The butler pointed to a room with double doors, turned, and left. There was no taking of their coats, no offer of tea.

Entering the parlor, Christian made a quick inspection of his surroundings. Cobwebs were visible in every crevice. Tattered draperies hung on slanted rods, and moths had made a meal of the tapestries and furniture. The room looked to belong to a villain in a Dickens novel.

"Has Sir Howard fallen on hard times?" Eleanora whispered.

"It appears so unless he doesn't care. I've never met the man. Ford never invited us here; he had been adamant about it. I see why."

The door flung open, and a man in his sixties entered. He wore slippers and a dirty robe along with his shirt and trousers. Two yapping beagles ran around him in circles.

"You mangy curs! Sit by the fire!" Sir Howard roared.

"I hope you are speaking to the dogs and not to us," Christian said sardonically.

Sir Howard adjusted his glasses. "Of course, I'm talking to the dogs, but sit yourselves at any rate. There, on the sofa."

The older man coughed and spat into the fire. "Allenby, eh? What is this about, eh? Why is a duke coming to see me? Better not be to give to charity. The great unwashed get enough from government, be damned if I will throw them a crumb."

The dogs had settled by the fire, giving the baronet frightened glances. The man probably beat the poor animals.

"This is Miss Eleanora Galway of The Galway Investigative Agency. We are here to talk to you about Ford."

Sir Howard didn't look Eleanora's way nor acknowledge her. "Talk about who, now?"

"Your son, Ford," Eleanora interjected.

Finally, he looked at her. The baronet gave her such a contemptuous glare that Christian was about to say something. Eleanora must have sensed it because she briefly laid her hand on his arm.

"I have no son," Sir Howard spat venomously.

"You do," Christian replied, "because he was friends with me when we were lads."

Sir Howard's eyes narrowed. "You're *that* Allenby? One of the brats at the drowning?"

"Yes. That is what we want to talk about. What happened that night? Ford must have told you," Christian said.

"Why ask me? You were there. It seems to me you should have stopped the tragedy from occurring, I warrant," he bellowed. "Coming here stirring up trouble, it's over and done. Best to let it lay."

"I have no idea what occurred, so I couldn't very well prevent it. Ford came home and told you, I'd wager to guess. Then you sent him away. Why?" Christian asked. "We received letters from Ford—"

The baronet laughed cruelly. "Oh, he sent letters, only you never got them; I saw to that. I had them at the school make a pretense of mailing them to the parties involved, but the correspondence came to me. Pathetic those letters were, imploring you all to come and rescue him. Sniveling coward. He never had any sense or a backbone."

Eleanora retrieved her notebook and pencil from her coat. "You wrote the letters the friends received, saying all was well. He wasn't with his uncle in India at all."

"No, missy, he wasn't. It's no one's business." Sir Howard ran his hand through his dirty gray hair.

What a thoroughly disagreeable man.

"And the letters we wrote, the ones delivered to you to send to Ford?" Christian asked.

The baronet snorted. "Burned them."

"We believe that Ford is back in England," Eleanora said.

Sir Howard scratched his whiskered chin. "Maybe. He escaped three months ago. The idiot stole money from the asylum safe and—"

"Wait, did you say asylum?" Christian interrupted. He couldn't believe this.

"He's mad as a hatter! And a murderer to boot. Of course, I put him away," Sir Howard snapped. "He is a danger to society!"

The clock chimed. The time was fifteen minutes off. Everything was off about this man, but Christian believed his story. A spark of pity for Ford took hold. His former friend had been sent away to school and ended up in an asylum. What a horrid fate.

"Murderer? Do you mean the drowning?" Eleanora said, her voice soft.

"Might as well have been a murder," Sir Howard grumbled. "He fought with the lad, held his head underwater, and held it a bit too long. He says he didn't mean it. Anyway, I beat Ford within an inch of his life. I sent him away to a special school in Switzerland. What if the coppers came looking for him? But then, those at the inquiry told me there were no witnesses. I thought they were covering up for you pampered lot."

Christian shook his head. "We were drunk and fell asleep. We didn't hear or see anything."

"Why didn't you send for Ford after he was safe from being accused of the accidental death?" Eleanora asked.

"Mouthy little missy, aren't you? First off, I'm not certain that it was accidental. He brought shame to the family. To me. I disowned him. Besides, he was out of control at school. He finally had to be put away in an institution. And before you ask, I haven't heard from him. Why are you looking for him?"

"We had a body part sent to our private club. We wondered if Ford was behind it," Christian replied.

"Wouldn't put it past him. In one of his last letters, he ranted and raved about getting revenge on all those who abandoned him. It's all talk." Sir Howard flapped his hand dismissively.

"Do you still have that letter?" Eleanora asked.

"Burned like all the others. My son is mad, I tell you. It is best to ignore him. And don't go repeating about the drowning. I'll deny it all."

"Sir Howard, you should take precautions concerning your safety. Your son is unpredictable, capable of causing you harm," Eleanora stated.

"Bah, stuff and nonsense," the baronet barked, flapping his hand again.

"Miss Galway is correct. Take her advice. Now, concerning the letter. If we bring you a handwriting sample, could you identify it as Ford's?" Christian asked. "None of us could remember it. But you would."

Whitney stood. "Be off with you. I no longer wish to speak about this. And don't come here again."

He shuffled out of the room, the dogs following close behind.

Christian and Eleanora exchanged looks of astonishment.

"Well," she said, stuffing her notebook into her coat.

Christian stood and held out his hand. "I believe we will have to see ourselves out. Come, I need the fresh air. In more ways than one."

Once in the carriage, Christian asked, "Come to my place for tea. We can discuss what we've learned. I'm famished."

Eleanora hesitated. "Althea is expected home today. I should greet her."

"Come for an hour; then we will go to Cleveland Street." He took her hand and gently squeezed it. "Spend time with me. Share a biscuit and a cup of tea," he coaxed.

"What are you doing? There can be nothing between us. Surely you see that," she murmured. Then she pulled her hand from his.

"I don't accept that. Already we are friends. We're attracted to one another. Why not see where it goes?"

Eleanora shook her head. "I have already decided that I will never marry. And because of it, I have no interest in any dalliance with a promise of 'more' attached to it. I'm sorry, but it's how I feel."

She had spoken flatly as if coldly discussing one of her cases. Christian felt as if his insides had been kicked clear out of him and stomped on for good measure.

"I could lie to you and say I have no interest beyond a brief affair while secretly planning to get you to agree to more, but that is not me. I cannot pretend. Nor will I deny my feelings. I would never try to dictate your life and make you give up yours to accommodate mine. I've told you that before, and I mean it."

Eleanora gave him a dubious look. "You want to have this conversation now, sitting in a carriage on the street?"

"Why not?" Christian sat back and crossed his arms.

"Very well. You will need to marry and have an heir. I am most decidedly *not* duchess material. I've dismissed having children as they would interfere with my ambitions. How could I still run my agency? Oh, this discussion is absurd."

"Since we are speaking hypothetically, why can't we have it all?" he replied softly.

Eleanora's lower lip trembled, the first show of emotion. "Oh, damn you for making me feel."

"You care for me; admit it. More than any man you have ever met. That is not arrogance on my part; I have seen it in your eyes. I see it now. Perhaps, you more than care. Trying to push me away will not rid you of those feelings."

"Fine. I care. It doesn't change the fact that we are impossible as a couple." Eleanora sighed wistfully.

"Hear me out. If we were to fall in love and marry, I would never ask you to give up your agency. Do you want us to live in London all year round? Done. Think of what you can do with my money. You can expand, hire more people, even that street lad, Archie, you told me about. I'll pay for his upkeep and education. You can continue to work and run your business. Keep your own money. Make your own decisions."

He meant every word.

Christian watched Eleanora closely. Confusion and uncertainty crossed her lovely features.

"As far as children, yes, I would like one or two, but only if you agree," he continued. "The good news is I am wealthy; we can afford nannies and nurses. You can balance your career with motherhood in any way you wish. Again, I am speaking hypothetically."

Perhaps he was crafting a possible theory, but he also spoke straight from his heart. His emotions were laid bare.

"You have an answer for everything. It sounds too good to be true. I can't leave my family. Althea—"

"Move her and your cousin in with us. Or I can move into Cleveland Street." Christian sat forward, taking her hands. "My dear, nothing is impossible. Surely you know that I am falling for you. You *must* know it."

"Chris, I-I—"

He pulled her across the carriage until she straddled him, her shapely legs fitted against his thighs. He brought her in tighter until her feminine core rubbed against his erection.

Eleanora moaned softly.

"See what you do to me? God, I want you. To hell with tea and biscuits. Come home with me. To my bed. I want to make love to you, El."

She rocked back and forth, causing a delicious friction that had him moaning.

"Why not right here in the carriage, like this?" she whispered in his ear.

THIS SITUATION WAS entirely naughty. A quick tup in the carriage? What possessed her? But more importantly, Christian was falling in love with her. What else could falling mean? Her heart had soared at the declaration. Though she hadn't spoken it aloud, she more than cared. For she was falling, too—how far and how fast, she couldn't make out.

As for right now, she couldn't think about all he said; it was too much to process.

But this? Oh, how she wanted him. Deep inside her.

"Here?" he growled, nuzzling her neck.

"I will tell you; I have been with two other men."

"At the same time?" Christian teased playfully, nibbling on her earlobe.

"Silly man, of course not. I just wanted you to know that I'm not a virgin."

"I don't care if you are or not," he replied firmly.

"I know what will happen between us is my point. Do you have any sheaths?"

Christian pulled back and met her gaze. "Not on me."

"I trust you. So, when you're close, tell me, and make certain that you don't come inside me," Eleanora said.

He growled. "I won't come inside you; I promise. You can trust me on this and anything else."

In a flurry, they rucked her skirt, pulled down her underdrawers, and unbuttoned his trousers. Eleanora pulled out his erect shaft, giving it a couple of strokes.

"Oh, sweet Mother," he hissed through clenched teeth, using her expression.

She giggled. "We will have to be quiet; Michaels might hear."

Eleanora rose and positioned herself over his erection, and plunged downward. She smothered Christian's shout with a passionate kiss.

"Hold still a moment," he gasped. "I want to savor this."

Eleanora sat still, reveling in how he filled and stretched her. "I have to move."

"A minute more." He thrust upward with his hands on either side of her hips, causing them to moan.

"We must be quiet," Eleanora whispered.

"I don't give a good damn if Michaels hears. I pay him enough to be discreet. Ride me, El. Take your pleasure."

"I believe you have done this in a carriage before, Your Grace," she teased.

"Once, maybe twice. Now, move."

A thrill shot along her spine at his commanding tone. Eleanora started slowly, rocking back and forth, her hands resting on his shoulders. Then she rose and plunged downward as Christian thrust upward with his hips—the frantic rhythm hit with a sensual synchronicity, with Eleanora's nerve endings sparking with desire.

Christian banged on the roof, and the carriage lurched forward.

"What are you doing?" she squeaked.

"It's even better when in motion." Christian kissed her hungrily. "Ride with the rocking of the carriage," he crooned. "That's it."

It took no time at all. Christian was right.

Moaning, Eleanora grabbed fistfuls of his silky hair, returning his fierce kiss as she moved faster. The swaying motion was indeed a bonus to an already heated and passionate encounter. Christian's hips propelled upward, meeting her frantic movements. This was nothing like what she experienced with the other men. Not at all. It was so much—more. Intense. Passionate.

Eleanora's peak reached its crest within minutes, and she cried out, burying her face in his shoulder.

"Oh, Jesus. I'm close," he groaned. "Off, quickly, love."

Tired but completely sated, Eleanora scrambled backward as Christian grasped his cock. His entire body shook with his release. Pulling a handkerchief from his pocket, he swiftly cleaned up and tucked his semi-hard erection into his trousers.

"I could go again. But we are almost there if I miss my guess." He looked up and caught her gaze, giving her such a sultry smile; her insides trembled. "Are you sure you won't come up to my bed?" Christian's deep voice rumbled throatily.

"As you said, tea and biscuits. And discuss the case." Eleanora gave him a teasing wink as she swiftly righted herself.

"But you don't rule it out? At another time?"

She cupped his cheek and stroked it affectionately. "No, Chris, I will not rule it out."

Heavens, no, she wanted more. As for the rest?

The future was unknown.

Perhaps she was not quite as adamant about nothing being between them. But how much was still a muddle.

It *should* be impossible.

There was no denying the swell of emotion rising in her. Feelings she had not experienced the other two times she experienced sex. Not even close. This heated physical aspect only deepened her—call it what it is.

Love.

For the first time, Eleanora allowed herself to have hope.

Perhaps—she could have it all.

Chapter 19

"HUNTINGTON, THIS IS Miss Eleanora Galway. El, my venerable butler, Huntington."

"Good day, Miss Galway."

Before she could reply to the older man, Christian took her hand and pulled her along the hallway.

"Afternoon tea, Huntington, with whatever Mrs. Tallmadge can scrape up. We are famished," Christian called out as he marched down the hall.

"At once, Your Grace."

Eleanora stepped into what must be the parlor. It struck her that Christian was wealthy—and a duke. Their previous conversation and her glint of hope were more fanciful than ever. She could never fit into this life. Pretending to belong to the upper crust for a few hours at a ball was mildly amusing. But to do this the rest of her days?

Oh, why did I allow emotions to sweep me away?

But the emotions were not only swept but fully engaged, and there was no going back now. What a dilemma.

The room is bespoke of money and title with its velvet curtains and gold wallpaper garnished with dragons and peacocks. The expensive furniture was in the neoclassical style.

Christian pointed to the far wall. "See? Electricity courtesy of the City of London Electric Lighting Company Limited."

Curious, Eleanora followed him across the room. He turned the button, and bright light washed over the room from the chandeliers above.

"Oh, how wondrous," Eleanora exclaimed.

"You should see it at night. No more squinting to read by candlelight, firelight, or a gas lamp. I will be expanding to other rooms in the future. Although, Mrs. Tallmadge is adamant that she will not have an electric cooker in her kitchen. Come, I want to show you my study. It also has electric light."

Christian crooked his arm, and Eleanora took it. As they wandered along the hall, she marveled at the artwork.

"No family portraits?"

"Not here, but there are several at Bamford Park. Our country seat, in Essex."

Again, Christian's wealth and title caused her insides to knot. That spark of hope, which allowed her to believe something could be permanent between them—started to dim. In all aspects of her life, she had complete control.

Except for Christian.

He caused a maelstrom of confusion and unrest. And blast it all; it was damned exhilarating.

The study was as opulently appointed as the parlor. All that was missing was a shield and a suit of armor. The stone fireplace looked from another age, and the sword on display above it caught Eleanora's attention. There were faint etchings along the blade.

"What a beautiful sword; is it a family heirloom?"

Christian removed it from its display holder. "As a matter of fact, it is. Many Bamfords have fought in battles through the centuries. The most recent was my grandfather, Duncan Bamford. Before he inherited the title, he fought in the War of 1812. When the Americans set fire to the government buildings in Upper Canada, my grandfather was trapped in the fire and badly scarred."

"How terrible. Wait, 1812? Wouldn't he be your great-grandfather?"

"No. Duncan Bamford never married until the age of forty. My father never married until he was fifty-six."

"Good Lord. Do you intend to wait that long?" Eleanora asked.

"Not if I can help it. Every Duke of Allenby has displayed this sword for centuries. Since its usage in the Battle of Agincourt—or so the story goes."

His family went back to Henry VIII?

That unease percolating inside her just increased.

"This is a knightly or arming sword," he continued, oblivious to her inner turmoil. "This sword is more of a sidearm since the two-handed, long sword had gained popularity as the main battle weapon. Here, see how lightweight it is."

. Christian handed the sword to her. She grasped the leather pommel, swung about, and thrust at the air. Eleanora was having so much fun that her uneasiness dissipated.

Taking two steps back, she lunged forward in a stabbing motion. "I like the feel of it."

"Where did you learn, by the way?"

Eleanora smiled as she handed the sword to Christian. "Some girls have piano lessons. I wanted to learn how to handle a sword and a knife. My father arranged instructions for me. I enjoyed the strategy involved; it challenged me."

Christian encircled her waist, bringing her against him. "Can I say it's damned arousing to see you parry and thrust about? I have imagined you as a warrior goddess leading an attack. Glad to see I was not wrong."

He nuzzled her neck, sending sparks through her, igniting that flickering flame to a roaring blaze. The warrior goddess's remark pleased her to no end.

"Actually," she said, her voice husky, "A parry is when you deflect your opponent's blow."

"And a thrust?" Christian rolled his hips and demonstrated precisely that as his erection ground against her.

Going to his bed for the rest of the afternoon was indeed tempting. To hell with tea and the case. She was about to suggest that when a clearing of the throat interrupted her heated thoughts.

"My pardon, Your Grace."

Eleanora squeaked and turned away from Christian.

"Yes, Huntington?" Christian placed the sword on the holder, then gave Eleanora a sly grin only she could see.

"Tea is served in the parlor."

"We will be along directly," Christian replied.

When the butler departed, they both burst out laughing.

He offered his arm. "Shall we take tea, my lady?"

"Of course, Your Grace."

Once in the parlor and seated on the sofa, she reached for her notebook.

"Right to business, then? Tell me your hunch of what is happening here." He gave her a teasing but warm smile, her toes curled in her boots.

Yes, concentrate. Business.

"I believe that Ford Whitney—is that his full name?"

"His name is Stafford, but he's always gone by Ford," Christian replied.

"Right. I believe Ford is behind this gruesome game. Whether he meant to drown Hayes Addington or not is a moot point. The fact is that he was beaten, disowned, and sent away. He suffered mentally, but who knows what further torture he endured at this school and later in the asylum? It could have twisted him further."

"Do you think he murdered Emily McCarthy?"

Eleanora tapped her pencil against her chin. "I think not, but I don't rule it out. Emily was already suffering from her affliction. And, by all accounts living on the street. She told Fiona that a man was going to look after her. What if it was Ford? He no doubt has been having you all followed and asked questions. When he found out about Emily's past employment and her connection to your group, he could have found her a room while getting information from her. Then, when she died, he found another use for her."

Christian curled his lip. "This is beyond macabre; that is insane."

"Yes, perhaps his father has the right of it; he could be mentally unstable, which makes him unpredictable and treacherous. And the money he stole from the asylum could be financing his schemes."

"The carriage rentals and drivers."

"Yes. I asked Sybil to dig into it, but the carriage companies she has spoken to have not had a large rental. I believe he hired independent drivers or those already employed by the upper classes. It will be next to impossible to trace. There was a covering on the carriage door. Hiding a crest, perhaps?"

Christian sat back. "My God."

"You said a baronet is not part of the peerage, but would Ford inherit when his father passed?"

"Yes, he would have to be placed on the Official Roll by providing proof of succession. Ford can hardly do that locked away in an asylum. Which was probably Sir Howard's plan, having the baronetcy die with him."

Huntington entered, with a maid carrying a three-tiered silver stand following directly behind him. The butler placed the silver tea service on the table, and the maid set the tiered stand upon another table nearby. Sandwiches, biscuits, cheese, and frosted cakes filled the silver rack.

"That will be all, Huntington. We are not to be disturbed."

The servants bowed and departed the room, closing the double doors.

"Will you pour, El?"

"Right, milk, no sugar, correct?"

"Correct," Christian replied.

Eleanora sat forward and reached for the teapot. Her hand shook slightly, which surprised her. Because she was out of her element, or that flicker of hope that this could be her life?

Or perhaps it was dread.

The last thing she wanted to do with her life was sit in a parlor pouring tea all day; nothing was wrong with that; it just wasn't for her. She put the thoughts right out of her head. After serving the tea, they both filled their plates and ate heartily.

"So, what *is* Ford's end game here?" Christian asked as he sipped his tea.

"To cause mischief. To break up your group. Perhaps Ford doesn't even know. Maybe it was enough to see you all flustered. Or perhaps this is just the beginning of his plan. The sooner we find him, the better."

"How do we flush him out?"

Eleanora nibbled absently on a sugar biscuit. "Let me think on it."

"I want to talk about what happened in the carriage—and how much I want it to happen again. I told you I am falling for you, El, and I am. I've never felt this way toward any other woman. You have captured me, heart and soul."

Although her heart soared at his emotionally spoken words, she shook her head. "We've only known each other a few weeks. It's not possible."

Or so she told herself.

"Stuff and nonsense, as the baronet says. It *is* possible, and you know it. When shall we be together again? Will you come to me here late one night? Will I let you in the back entrance and sneak you up the stairs? Or shall we rent a room somewhere?"

"You *are* serious? You want an affair?"

Christian set his teacup on the table. "Have you not heard a word I've said on this subject? I want you in all ways. I want to know what it feels like to have my breath feather across your bare skin. I want to explore every curve, taste every part of you, and be inside you until I take my last gasp on this earth."

Eleanora's eyes welled with tears. His words resonated in a voice so full of feeling yet gruff with passion. It sent her heart beating double time and heat pooling between her thighs.

"I am making you feel again, aren't I? I do apologize," he said lightly, passing her a handkerchief.

She dabbed her eyes. "You are going to break my heart; I know it," she whispered. How could there be anything between them?

"Not if you give it into my care," he answered, moving closer to her. Christian took the handkerchief and gently wiped away the couple of wayward tears that had snaked down her flushed cheeks.

"I will ensure the safekeeping of it. I will never smother it or deny it its true ambitions and desires. I will do my utmost to protect it from any possible hurt or breakage. It would be my most prized and precious—I don't want to say possession, for I would never possess any part of you. But it would be my honor to be the caretaker of it."

Christian leaned in and kissed her gently on the lips.

The feelings swelling through Eleanora were overwhelming, and the loss of control had her in knots. But beyond that, his emotionally spoken words were seared into her heart.

Christian ended the kiss and stood, holding out his hand. "Now that we have eaten everything, are you ready to travel to Cleveland Street? You will think about what I said?"

She slipped her hand in his. "Yes, and yes."

And Eleanora had much to reflect on.

How she adored his forthrightness. The ease with which he expressed his feelings. So different from her. Christian didn't flinch from expressing his feelings, regardless of whether he was revealing vulnerabilities or not. Eleanora should take a page from Christian's book.

Puzzling this out would take time, but she would not dismiss his emotional revelations.

Yes, she was falling for him, indeed.

Chapter 20

AS SOON AS THEY ARRIVED at Cleveland Street, Althea and Sybil greeted them at the door, and the ladies chattered as they moved toward the parlor. Christian smiled at their enthusiasm as they took their seats.

Sybil cast him a dubious look. "No offense, Your Grace, but Eleanora, should he be here?"

"Christian is part of the investigation, Sybil. I'll tell you later on how he has assisted us. He has a natural talent for this work," Eleanora replied.

Christian swelled under the praise.

"Thank you, and please, Miss Norton, call me Allenby, or Christian, whatever you prefer. Let us forgo the 'your graces.'"

"Allenby will do for me, and you may call me Sybil."

"How was your trip, Althea?" Eleanora asked.

"Well, Huxley is indeed at the sanitorium in Hertfordshire. I observed him occasionally walking about the grounds or sitting outside. He looked troubled and in need of care."

Christian couldn't believe this.

"Wait, you traveled to Hertfordshire to check on Warren?"

"It wasn't that far," Althea replied. "And we had to rule him out."

"And I have," Eleanora said.

She filled in her sister and cousin on what they had discovered. She no sooner finished when the housekeeper entered.

"Miss Eleanora, that street urchin is at the door again."

Eleanora clapped her hands together. "Brilliant! I've been waiting for his report. Bring him a plate of food, Mrs. Bartle. And his name is Archie."

"Aye," she said. "And I'll have Archie wash before he makes his appearance."

Once Mrs. Bartle departed, she turned to Christian.

"I've had Archie following the footman, Phillips."

This was a surprise. "I don't care for the man, but I cannot imagine why you would suspect him."

"He's disrespectful, arrogant," Eleanora counted on her fingers. "And I've seen how he glares at you all when you're not looking. Disgust, disdain, a true dislike. He could have lied about the boy delivering the package. What if *he* brought it? If Ford is our main suspect, how has he discovered certain information on your group unless he had someone on the inside? Whitney couldn't have found out everything from Emily McCarthy. Like where you are living, your comings and goings. The rake club itself at St. Regent's Park."

Again, Eleanora's deduction and reasoning skills were to be admired. "Allow me to interject here. I know it is a cliché that men—particularly young men—in the peerage are profligate and useless, and at various times in our lives, that may have been the case. Deep down, I believe much of the bluster arises from boredom and loneliness."

Christian looked about the room. He had the ladies' attention.

"Not even Damon is as licentious as before. Many of his trips to the East End are to take in a show. But we allow him to brag of his conquests, knowing that some are fictitious."

"What of Huxley?" Althea asked.

"Well, there is an example of going off the cliff. Warren has cloistered himself away to get help. Asher confided in me last month that although he occasionally indulges, it's not near as often as in the past. So have the others. Even Watford has slowed his activities somewhat. I do not understand why this person is singling us out. Believe me; there are far worse out there than The Rakes."

Eleanora gave him an indulgent smile. "They are your friends. Of course, you would stand up for them; I admire that. It is likely that anything done by the group that may have offended others—was in the past, not recently. Why would Phillips allow himself to be recruited? Money is an enticing incentive. But what if something in your club's past caused resentment, not only to Phillips but to others? What if Ford has gathered together a club of his own?"

Deviled hell. A conspiracy?

He was about to comment when a towhead lad entered the room. He wore frayed clothes; his eyes focused on the plate of food Mrs. Bramble carried to a small table near where they sat. Christian had never seen hunger like that, and it reminded him how lucky he was.

"Sit, Archie. You know how we do this, report first, then food," Eleanora motioned for the youth to sit at the table. "Mrs. Bartle, if you could bring lemonade and glasses for us, it would be appreciated."

The housekeeper nodded and departed.

"What's the toff doin' here? Takin' him to the coppers, yeah?" Archie questioned. "I knew he were guilty; he has those shifty eyes, he does."

Sybil snorted. "Not quite, Archie. The duke has been assisting us."

Archie gave him a skeptical look, then turned to face Eleanora. "The footman, Aloysius Phillips, workin' at the place of the Blond bugger—"

Christian bit back a grin, for he'd often thought of Damon the same way.

"Didn't go out much," Archie continued. "But he received a few messages at the back entrance. I saw him open and read them, then tuck them in his coat. Unless he ain't delivering messages to his nibs. He went out twice while we watched. We couldn't watch all the time, so he might have gone out when we weren't there."

"Where did he go?" Eleanora asked.

"The East End. The Ten Bells pub. He met two men there. I have never seen them afore. Three days later, he met them again. Same place."

It sounded just as Eleanora described. Ford had formed a club of his own, one steeped in revenge.

"Can you describe the men?" Christian asked.

"Who's he think he is?" Archie gibed while pointing his thumb at him.

"You like this work, Archie?" Christian asked. "I know the Galway sisters have mentioned you will be acquiring some schooling and training, then working for them. Is it what you want? Because if it is, I'll sponsor you. Here's the golden opportunity. Get off the streets, boy, and make something of yourself. Take it."

"Cor, blimey, he's off his nut, he is," Archie snorted.

"No, I'm speaking the truth. Answer me here and now. Do you want this?" Christian demanded.

Archie blinked, then nodded. "Aye."

"Good lad," Christian nodded. "We'll work out the particulars after you eat. But first, the description of the men."

"The men all looked to one who acted like a toff. He had a long scar, runnin' here." Archie traced the tip of his finger from his temple down to his jaw. "It's a bad one, like someone had torn his face open. The toff has dark brown hair, a long nose, and thin lips, shorter than his nibs there, but not by much. He was skinny like."

Sybil was furiously taking notes.

"It's Ford. I'll lay coin on it," Christian said. "Though last I saw him, he wasn't exactly thin." Chills curled about his spine at the revelation.

Archie described the other man, and Sybil took further notes as he spoke.

"Well done, go ahead and eat," Eleanora said.

She motioned for Christian to join her across the room. "You don't have to do that, sponsor Archie," she murmured.

"You have faith in him, and that's good enough for me. It is about time I did some good with my title. I assume we will be doing surveillance on The Ten Bells? And on Phillips again?"

"We?" Eleanora chuckled. Then she sobered. "As you heard Archie say, doing a 'twenty-four-hour observation' is difficult and expensive. We should watch Sir Howard's place as well."

"Difficult and expensive? Not for us, not for me." Christian turned and walked toward the table. "Archie, are there people you trust willing to work around the clock? I have plenty of coins to pay."

Archie looked up from his plate, gravy dribbling down his chin. "Aye, I do. I've about eight, I trust."

"Finish up, lad. You're coming with me."

A wary shadow crossed Archie's face. "Where?"

"You're staying with me."

"What? Cor. Bollocks to that," Archie sneered.

"If you want this opportunity, you will do what I say. Learn to take orders; then, you can give them."

"Pshaw. I do that now."

Everyone laughed.

"I believe we are on the right track," Althea said.

"I believe it's time to let the others know about Ford and tell them to be even more vigilant," Christian said.

"I agree. Bring your friends up to date," Eleanora replied.

Christian felt waves of excitement move through him. Despite his title and friends, boredom, idleness, and loneliness had ruled his life for years.

But now, he had a purpose, a goal—a sense of achievement.

Though what possessed him to take in a street lad, he may soon regret.

Being with Eleanora and becoming part of her life had him feeling more alive than he had in years.

Christian wanted that to continue—for the rest of his life.

How to convince Eleanora that, deep down, she felt the same way was indeed a puzzle.

Just looking at her sent his insides tumbling. Oh, he was utterly besotted. He was falling in love even more with each passing hour.

And Christian reveled in it.

Chapter 21

ELEANORA, ALTHEA, AND Sybil sat in the parlor, drinking what remained of the lemonade. Christian and Archie had just departed.

"I cannot believe Allenby taking in Archie like that; does he mean it? To sponsor the boy until he comes to work with us?" Sybil marveled.

A small smile curved about Eleanora's lips as she sipped her drink.

"He means everything he says."

"Oh, does he?" Althea said, one eyebrow raised. "Do tell. What has happened between you? Something is sparking. It could have lit the lights in this house. Every house on the street, in fact."

There was no one she trusted more than her sister and cousin. Did she want to discuss this when she didn't completely understand what was happening between them? Who else was there to discuss such a sensitive subject?

"Christian says he is falling for me. And the thing is, I'm falling for him," Eleanora confided.

"Well, don't look so miserable about it," Sybil smiled.

"I don't want this," Eleanora said dejectedly. "I had my life planned, the agency—"

"Oh, what drivel," Althea dismissed with a wave. "Life never goes as planned. Life is, indeed—messy. A duke in love with you? Such a problem to have."

"He claims that we can have it all," Eleanora sighed.

She then proceeded to tell them, in general terms, about his declarations. Eleanora kept most of the conversation with Christian to herself, as it was private. And, drat it all, she wanted those emotional attestations to stay close to her heart.

Sybil and Althea exchanged astonished looks.

"Do you believe him? Well, evidently, since you just said he means everything he says. I think you're more than falling. You are in love with him. Deeply and irrevocably. You don't want to admit it," Althea stated.

"I don't know what to do," Eleanora wailed.

"What's this? The confident Eleanora Galway having doubts?" Sybil teased.

"You both say I'm impulsive, act without thinking. What if this is one of those times?"

Eleanora didn't dare mention that she had initiated the sex in the carriage. Talk about impulsiveness. But it had been ultimately satisfying and utterly enjoyable.

"What you do is embrace it. Reach out for it with both hands and hold tight. See where it goes. Christian is right; why can't you have it all?" Althea said.

"But it might mean—I don't want to lose you both!"

Sybil laughed. "His house is minutes away by carriage. It's not as if you're moving to Northern Scotland. If it ever comes to that. I agree with Althea. See where it goes. Savor it."

Mrs. Bartle entered the room. "Sorry to interrupt, Dr. Corbett Buchanan is here."

Sybil immediately flushed.

"Perhaps," Eleanora whispered to her cousin. "You should take your own advice. See where it goes."

"With Buchanan? He's a drunkard," Sybil hissed through her clenched teeth.

"Corbett is troubled, haunted. A little compassion would not go amiss. You don't have to marry the man."

The doctor strode into the room, wearing a proper afternoon suit and not looking as disheveled as he had of late.

"He's quite handsome, Sybil. Underneath that is a good man." In a louder voice, Eleanora said, "Do come in and sit, Corbett. We have lemonade."

He sat in the chair. "Ladies, I've examined the hand and done blood analysis. The markers are the same as the leg. They are from the same person."

Eleanora passed him a glass of lemonade. Corbett frowned and placed it on the table.

"We have concluded an old friend of the peers is behind these disturbing deliveries. At least, he is our number one suspect," Eleanora said.

"I've no doubt you will bring this case to a swift conclusion," Corbett replied. "I've been thinking over your uncle's offer. Working for him on salary. I might give it a go." Eleanora clapped her hands together. "Brilliant! You won't regret it, Corbett. Speaking of which, Althea, will you fetch Corbett's fee?"

Althea rose and exited the room.

Corbett faced Sybil. "I've come with another purpose. Miss Sybil, I would like you to join me for dinner and a show anytime you say."

Eleanora gave Sybil a soft nudge under the table.

But she said nothing.

"I admit I've been in a bad place," Corbett continued. "But I want to climb out of the pit. I've started to make improvements in my life already. Give me a chance, Sybil. One chance, please."

His words were soft and sincere, and his gaze never left Sybil. His look was hopeful, and it was clear to Eleanora that he had been smitten for quite some time.

"Corbett, I-I—," Sybil sighed.

"Perhaps I should give you privacy," Eleanora said.

"No, stay." Corbett stood, then dropped to one knee before Sybil, taking her hand. "I've stopped drinking and ceased all other vices. This last week's been difficult, but I'm making an effort. I care for you very much. Give me a chance."

Sybil looked up at Eleanora and smiled shakily. "And see where it goes?"

"Yes, exactly that," Corbett replied eagerly.

"Yes, dinner and a show. After this case concludes, but know this, I cannot be with a faithless man, a liar, who has no honor or respect for himself or others."

Corbett kissed her hand tenderly. "I understand."

Althea bounded into the room. "What did I miss?"

Eleanora snatched the pound notes from her sister's hand, laid them on the table, then spun Althea about. "Come, help me in the kitchen. I'll explain everything."

As Eleanora slid the parlor door closed, she caught of glimpse of Sybil leaning in to kiss Corbett.

Well, they had a chance at happiness. Eleanora hoped it all worked out.

It may work out for her as well.

"YOU'RE DOIN' THIS FOR Miss Eleanora, ain't you?" Archie stated as he gave Christian another of those narrow-eyed gazes. "You like her."

Christian moved aside the curtain and stared at the street. He had asked Michaels to take a circuitous route to the town house so he could talk to the lad.

"I more than like her. I'd do anything for her. Eleanora sees something in you, they all do, and I have the means to give them what they desire." He released the curtain. "I want to know why you haven't been entirely honest with them."

"Cor. Give over. You're talkin' out of your arse."

"How long have you been on the street?" Christian asked.

"Don't know, don't care," Archie sulked.

"I think you know *exactly* how long you've been on the streets, and you know your age, even though you told Eleanora you had no idea. I believe you're playing a role. You're not the complete street waif you pretend to be, though you *are* homeless. You did it to fit in. Am I correct?"

An uncomfortable silence filled the carriage. The only sound was the clip-clopping of the horse's hooves against the cobbles.

"How did you know?" Archie's voice changed, a tone deeper, no cockney accent.

"I didn't, not completely. It was a hunch."

"Miss Galway's right; you *are* good at investigating. I've been on the street for two years, since age twelve. I ran away from an orphanage, the one I was placed in after my father passed. He was a clerk at a bank; we had a comfortable enough life. Then, when he died, there was no one I could go to, or at least, no one claimed me. What little savings my father had, paid for my upkeep. That's what they told me."

"Why run away?" Christian asked, completely fascinated.

"Who's going to adopt an older boy? No one. The only interest was from a fisherman who wanted me for cheap labor. He had a cruel look about him. I decided to look out for myself and earn my keep—on my terms. So, I ran." Archie shrugged. "I soon learned to fit in."

"Why not confide in Eleanora? And why admit it to me?"

"I'm making good coin with her—and on the street. I'm making more than if I got a job in a factory. I've had schooling up to age twelve; I can read and write. As for Miss Galway, I wasn't ready to tell her. I'm still not."

"You've had different schooling these past two years," Christian said softly.

"You don't want to know. And I don't want to talk about it."

"Fair enough. So, again, why tell me?"

"Since you're going to pay for my upkeep and education, I thought I'd better come clean. In another year or two, I was going to tell Miss Galway. Until then, I wanted to make as much money as I could; however, I could. I've got money stashed away. But then the Galway sisters offered me a job. I wasn't expecting that."

"You're wise beyond your years, Archie."

"You have to be on the streets."

"What's next?" Christian sat back and folded his arms.

Archie sat back and folded his arms, too. "Let's be honest; I can't stay with you. It's folly."

"I own a large town house. In the rear is a small outer building with two good-sized rooms. I'll turn it into a guesthouse, just for you. You can come and go as you please. Take your meals and use the facilities in my place, but you will have privacy. Once you're earning your keep legitimately, you can pay a small stipend in rent. Be your own man and take control of your future."

"It's that easy for you?" Archie said, his voice quiet.

"Yes, things come easy for me. I'm a duke, after all."

"All right, then. I'll make the break after this case. I'll need a bag of coins to hire the ones I trust. We'll watch The Ten Bells, and that Blond Bugger's place. And the baronet's flat. I'll report to Miss Eleanora—"

"You'll report to me. I'll introduce you to the staff. Once the servants know who you are, I get the message quicker." Christian banged on the carriage's roof, and Michaels picked up the pace. "While at my place, I'll fetch the coin and show you the outer building. We'll discuss the rest after the case, as you say."

"Miss Eleanora won't like it, me reporting to you."

Christian smiled. "No, she won't. I'll explain it. We'll change the arrangements if she insists that you report to her. Until then, report to me, day or night, whether I'm at home or not. My staff will know how to get a message to me."

Archie sighed wistfully. "I'm really getting out, away from the filth."

"You are. Take this opportunity, and make it a success."

He nodded, his eyes glistening—the first show of emotion from the lad. "I will, and thanks. To you and the ladies."

"You can thank them properly later. Are you still hungry?"

"I hate to admit it, but aye—I mean, yes."

"Good. My cook, Mrs. Tallmadge, is amazing. She will get meat on your bones in no time at all."

A genuine smile from the boy.

A curl of warmth moved through Christian. Yes, he was doing this to please Eleanora. But he also wanted to do a good deed for once in his life. Why not sponsor the lad? How many diamonds in the rough were out there, only needing a chance to allow them to shine?

Once Christian returned to Parliament, he would make damned sure those stuffy lords looked into the plight of those less fortunate. A few peers genuinely cared about those experiencing poverty, like Aidan Wollstonecraft, the Earl of Carnstone. The man was closing in on eighty, but still a vibrant man with a cause, like his father and grandfather before him.

Then there was Harrison Hornsby, the Duke of Gransford, and his brother, Tremain Hornsby, Viscount Hawkestone. Viscount Hawkestone was an extinct title on the maternal side of the family, resurrected by letters patent and bestowed on Tremain for his service during the Zulu War. Having two brothers serving in the House of Lords was rare.

Didn't he hear that the Wollstonecrafts and Hornsbys had collaborated on various causes, including a home for those with special needs?

Yes, there were enough well-meaning men he could approach.

And if any of them turned him down, nothing stopped Christian from investigating and developing an opportunity on his own. A place for young boys, and another for young girls, to learn a trade. Get proper schooling, and give them a chance in this often-harsh life.

Christian had been bored, adrift, and lonely.

All that changed with meeting the splendid Eleanora Galway.

Chapter 22

WHILE CHRISTIAN SHARED another afternoon tea with Archie, Eleanora had sent word to Christian that the doctor had reported that the hand and the leg had matching blood properties.

Ford must be mentally disturbed to keep a dead woman on ice, sawing off appendages to spook their group. Christian was off again in his carriage when they finished their beefsteak sandwiches, and he had introduced the lad to the staff.

Christian had to meet with the rakes at the club. He had sent word yesterday that they needed to show up. Now he had even more urgent news to tell them.

Before that, Christian had to drop Archie off near the East End. Before saying goodbye to Archie, he handed him a wool scarf and gloves he had fetched from his room.

"Tell your compatriots that you stole them from a rich and foolish toff," he had said to the boy.

Archie had taken the items and saluted him as he stepped from the carriage.

It was already past six, and the sun had started to set. A chill was in the air, hinting that winter was close at hand. He pulled his scarf tighter about his neck to ward off the cold. Christian kept glancing out the rear window. Deviled hell, he was acting paranoid.

Once he arrived at Albany Street, he instructed Michaels to seek a bite to eat below stairs. There was always food on hand. Christian had also clarified that Phillips's services were most decidedly *not* required tonight. Nor was Damon—or any of them—to mention the meeting to anyone.

"You expect me to wait on myself?" Damon boomed as Christian strolled into the room.

"Yes, for once, be self-sufficient. Pour your own drink."

"I saw your man go below, have him wait on us," Damon replied.

"Michaels is my coachman, not a footman." Christian tore off his cloak, scarf, and gloves and sat at the head of the table. "Please, sit, all of you. I have news. A good deal of it."

Once the men poured their drinks, Christian told them everything he had learned. The delivery of the hand. The carriage chase and the attack concerning Eleanora. The visit to Ford's father. Phillips meeting with what was, in all likelihood—Ford and another man. The fact Ford was their prime suspect.

"You mean to say that initially, we were suspects? That Althea Galway traveled to Hertfordshire to check on Warren?" Damon said, his voice incredulous. "She journeyed alone?"

"I said at the beginning that these ladies were up to the task, and I have been proven right," Christian replied as he sipped his drink. "I believe this is beyond a prank. Ford wrote to his father that he would seek revenge on all those that abandoned him."

"How were we to know that the baronet burned the letters? It's not our fault Ford was locked away!" Merritt whined.

"We were all suspects, incredible," Asher marveled. "But Ford? I never would have guessed at that. But God knows what he has been through. Horrid places, asylums."

Gideon downed his drink and stood. "This has nothing to do with Knight and me, as we were not part of your schoolboy clique, so forgive me if I take my leave. Brandon? Are you coming?"

"So, you're going to swan off instead of assisting us with this plight?" Christian asked. He couldn't believe this, but on the one hand, he could. Gideon looked out for himself, not much of an "all for one" sort of chap when it came down to it.

"Correct. No insult meant, but you've all made this chaos," Gideon replied.

Brandon stood, grabbing his cloak. "Sorry. Watford's right. Until next time."

The two men departed.

"Blasted selfish sods, the both of them. Knight follows Watford around like an obedient puppy," Damon growled.

"Well, I wasn't there that night of the drowning, but I will stick by you," Merritt said, his head bobbing.

"Speaking of obedient puppies," Damon muttered. Then louder, he said, "The thing of it is, I just remembered something about that night. I awoke briefly and heard arguing. It must have been Ford and Hayes. I don't remember what was said; I thought it was a dream. Christ, I could have stopped it before it went too far."

"How were we to know?" Christian said. "Ford didn't wake us for assistance. He went home, confessed to his father, and was beaten and sent away for his trouble."

"But what could we have done?" Asher exclaimed. "We were sixteen years of age and kept out of the inquiries. We returned to school and got on with our lives. I'm sorry to say that I soon put the incident out of my mind."

"As did we all. What chills me is that this was no accidental drowning. Ford held Hayes underwater. Perhaps not premeditated murder, but provocation resulting in the ending of a life. And he was punished for it. The baron saw to that," Christian interjected.

"That is not on any of us here," Merritt stated.

"In Ford's mind, it is," Christian replied. "I suggest you all forego all social situations until the agency's case reaches a resolution. Stay by the hearth."

"And you will be the hero?" Damon interjected drolly.

"No. But allow me to continue to represent the group in this venture. We all can't blunder into this. We hired The Galway Agency to handle the situation; we should let them finish it. If they require my assistance, I will give it."

Damon whispered, "You are infatuated with the older sister. That's why you're doing this."

"Well, I hear *you* are fascinated by Althea," Christian hissed between clenched teeth.

Damon sat back; his cheeks flushed a deep crimson. An actual reaction from the man, how riveting.

"Who told you that—of course, the older sister. Even if Galway the Younger caught my interest briefly, I, at least, have the prudent judgment to realize nothing can come of it. Can't say the same for you, you besotted bastard." Damon crossed his arms, giving Christian a smug look.

Though tempted, Christian would not give Damon the expected and desired reaction. Christian understood that his friend often did this for attention, saying something provocative to gain a response and drive people away.

Just how much danger were they in?

Ford was unpredictable, and the fact that he may have placed Eleanora and her agency in harm's way did not sit well with him.

"YOUR GRACE, A YOUNG lady is at the rear entrance, insisting on seeing you. I know you wish to be informed immediately of anyone asking for you."

"A young lady?" Christian placed his scotch on the table. He had returned from the club four hours ago.

"I believe it to be a young lady, although the voice is deep. The person is wearing a cloak with a hood, Your Grace," Huntington replied. "Difficult to see the face."

Excitement tore through Christian, sparking his nerve endings. It couldn't be Eleanora, could it? It was past eleven. Or it could be a ruse. Ford in disguise or an assassin he had hired. My, how his imagination had run wild since meeting Eleanora Galway.

Christian stood, walked over to his desk, opened the drawer, and slipped his Webley revolver into his trousers pocket. He had purchased it a few years past, never believing he would ever have a use for it.

"You can retire for the night. I'll see to the person at the door," he said. "Also, inform the rest of the staff, Barrett included."

His valet. Christian had never liked having a valet underfoot, but a duke cannot be without one. So the rules state.

"Very well, Your Grace."

Making his way to the rear entrance as quietly as possible, Christian reached into his pocket and grasped the pistol pulling it out partway as he flung open the door.

"Your Grace." The figure curtseyed and held up a basket. "I bring apple scones and apple jelly." The hood lowered. "And I bring myself. 'Will I let you in the back entrance and sneak you up the stairs?' I believe you said. Well, here I am. Sneak away."

"El. You came to me." Christian pulled her across the threshold and swept her into a fierce kiss. He then stepped back, gripping her arms.

She leaned in and whispered, "I couldn't stay away."

He kissed her again, all but devouring her.

Eleanora trailed her hand past the waistband of his wool trousers.

"My, Your Grace, is that a revolver in your pocket, or are you just happy to see me?" she teased playfully. Then she stood back. "My God, that really is a revolver."

He grasped her hand and laid it across his aching cock. "Oh, I am *very* happy to see you," he growled as he nuzzled her soft neck. "But I was also prepared for anything."

Eleanora grasped his aching shaft and squeezed. "Can I say that has me quite excited?"

Enough of teasing stimulation.

Christian grasped her hand and ran up the backstairs, hurrying toward his room.

"What about the scones?" Eleanora laughed.

"We'll eat them later. I'm certain we will build up an appetite."

Once inside his room, he released her, spun about, and kicked the door shut with his booted foot. "Be certain this is what you want," Christian said, his voice gravelly with need. "A quick tup in a carriage is one thing, but to me, *this* means *everything*. It tells me that you want more. That you accept that we could have a future. Am I delusional?"

Christian's insides were in knots waiting for her reply. What if Eleanora didn't want what he wanted?

A companion and lover, a partner in life—for life.

Eleanora placed the basket on the floor, grabbed his shirt collar, and pulled him close. Her eyes bore into his, capturing him with the intensity of her stare. "Did you mean everything you said in the carriage? All of it? Especially about respecting my independence and my ability to make my own decisions? That you will never smother me?"

Christian cleared his throat. "I have a confession—"

"Oh, no. Please don't tell me you didn't mean any of it. I couldn't bear it." She whispered as her head lowered. "It would break me in two."

Christian cupped her cheeks, lifting her head to meet his gaze.

"And that is quite the confession from *you*—a vulnerability. I would never have thought it," Christian said softly.

"Only when it comes to you," Eleanora replied shakily.

"As for what I said in the carriage, I meant every word. You are the most glorious woman I have ever met; why would I want to stifle your brilliance? I want to encourage it, support it, and applaud your successes." He laid a gentle kiss on her forehead.

"My confession," he continued, "Is that I am a needy bastard. I long for the touch of another. I cannot explain it. Some of those past trips to brothels? It didn't involve sex. I just wanted someone to hold me."

Eleanora blinked. "Oh, Chris."

Her look was sympathetic, not pitying. Christian couldn't abide it if she pitied him.

"I cannot explain why. The father I barely knew? My mother's absences after my father died? Or perhaps I am trying to fill an emptiness I have had my whole life. I have never felt complete—until you."

Christian stroked her cheeks with the pads of his thumbs. "While I support you, I will need something in return. Attention. Affection. I want to be part of your life. I don't expect to be the center of your world, but I require that you do not neglect or leave me behind."

He touched his forehead to hers, still cupping her cheeks. "I am not ashamed of my needs, nor does it make me any less a man. Not in my mind," Christian concluded, his voice unwavering.

"And not in my mind, either. Never. If we have a future, I will never disregard you in any way," Eleanora replied.

Christian stared at her. "If? I thought that you coming here meant we were moving forward together. I said so."

Eleanora took two steps in reverse. "Oh," she whispered. "It appears you're a step or two ahead of me. I'm still at the 'let's see where this goes' step. Have I made an error?"

Was he moving too fast?

It took all Christian had not to declare his abiding love here and now. He wouldn't act petulant. Instead, he brought her into his embrace once again. "You said your vulnerability is because of me. Perhaps. I believe it is also what you told me that night in your room after your injury. You're afraid to love *anyone* because the heartache is too much to bear. You are more sensitive than you let on or admit to yourself."

Christian hugged her closer. "My dearest El, loving someone means taking a chance, throwing caution to the wind, and grabbing happiness. Live and love in the here and now, and face the future—together. Whatever it brings."

Eleanora rested her head on his shoulder. "You're right, of course. I *am* terrified and far more sensitive than I realized. And because of it, I'm trying to keep you at arm's length—even though I cannot stay away."

Christian nuzzled her neck. "Then the only thing for it is to accept our susceptibilities and do all in our power to support each other. And we can, El, I know it. We make a perfect team in all ways."

Eleanora flung her arms about his neck and kissed him hard. Her fingers trailed through his hair, and she grabbed fistfuls of it as she took the kiss deeper.

"Enough talk," she whispered huskily. "I need you inside me, now."

"Now?"

With a growl, he spun her about until her back rested against the wall. Once he retrieved sheaths from the table by his bed, Christian wasted no time releasing his erection from his trousers and slipping on the condom.

He stood in front of her, watching her. Her brown eyes shimmered, her breathing deep and shallow. Christian pulled her skirt upward, reveling in the softness of her inner thigh. Then he groaned.

"Deviled hell. No undergarments. You are indeed glorious—and wet."

Since there was only a few inches difference in their heights, having her against the wall would not need any outlandish contortions.

Christian didn't hesitate. Reaching behind and clasping her rear, he lifted her just a fraction, enough to thrust into her.

And he did, burying himself deep. They moaned in unison.

Christian held still, savoring the tight fit, the glorious feel of her. Her inner muscles clutched him intimately.

Then he moved. He started slow, then built to a rising crescendo. Sweat trickled down his temple with the ferocity of his exertions.

"Oh, sweet Mother," Eleanora gasped, her breath coming in short bursts. "Yes, right there. Oh, perfect."

And it was absolutely *perfect*.

He pounded hard, her back hitting the wall with each forceful thrust. Eleanora kissed him, her tongue dancing with his. The passionate kiss spurred him on, his desire taking over all rational thought. All he wanted was to be buried deep in her hot wetness.

Moaning loudly, Eleanora wrapped her long legs around his waist, pulling him in closer, if possible.

"Harder. Give me more," Eleanora gasped.

Growling, Christian did precisely that. He moved faster; all control had left him.

As in the carriage, it didn't take long, and Eleanora cried out, her head thrown back.

He was close, oh so very close.

His climax hit with one final thrust, washing him in waves of utter and complete ecstasy.

They stayed joined, their breathing slowing.

Eleanora nibbled affectionately on his earlobe.

"My. You are still hard. My turn. Get on the bed, now."

How commanding she was.

There was no doubt of it. Christian had died and gone to heaven. And he had fallen intensely and irretrievably in love.

Chapter 23

ELEANORA SMILED, REVELING in Christian's darkly erotic look with her demand that he lay on the bed.

Withdrawing, he turned and strode toward the bed, pulling off the sheath. He dropped it in the bin, opened the night table drawer, and pulled out several envelopes.

"I plan for us to continue this through the night," he said.

"Good. So do I," Eleanora replied.

Eleanora had no idea how he could walk straight, for her legs had turned to jelly. Tossing her cloak aside, she pointed to the bed.

"There will be time enough for removing clothes and further exploration. For now, I want you to lay on the bed, and I will climb on top."

"As you wish, Miss Galway."

After he grabbed another sheath, he laid flat, then lowered his trousers enough to free his erection and slip the condom on. Christian gave his shaft a couple of strokes, showing Eleanora such a sultry look that her insides turned into custard.

He was a magnificent specimen—what she had seen so far. Eleanora couldn't wait to see the rest of him.

But, patience.

The leisurely lovemaking would come later in the night. All she wanted, all she desired—and had dreamt about since first meeting him—was to ride him into oblivion.

The quick tup in the carriage was a taste. As was the wild against-the-wall encounter.

Eleanora wanted the entire meal, along with the dessert.

Lifting her skirts, she sat astride him.

"What next, Miss Galway?" Christian murmured.

"You are to lie perfectly still and allow me to have my way with you."

He groaned, grasped his erection, and stroked it again.

Eleanora laid her hand over his. "No pleasuring yourself unless I say you can."

"Do you want me to come right here and now? If so, continue to order me about," he growled.

Eleanora laughed as she undid a couple of the buttons on his shirt. There were too many of them for her liking. Taking hold of the bottom of the shirt with both hands, she jerked it apart, and the delicate silk tore right up to the collar. Buttons pinged across the room, landing on the wood floor.

"Oh, Christ," Christian moaned.

Separating the sections of the torn shirt, Eleanora admired his impressive chest, lightly dusted with black hair. Christan was as leanly muscled as she thought he would be.

With a contented sigh, she laid her hands flat against his torso and started to explore. Across his muscled pectorals, his hardened nipples lower to the knot of muscles across his stomach.

"As I observed on many occasions, you are finely made in all ways," she murmured.

Touching him like this sent her desire clear off the cliff. In her two previous encounters with other men, never had she been this aroused.

It was the deep emotions in play. Eleanora understood it. They were engaged as they never were the other times.

The tips of her fingers explored every curve of sinew and bone, then she rose and made a slow descent until she buried his shaft deep inside.

Eleanora rocked back and forth, rising and plunging downward with each motion. The leisurely stroking grew by increments. Christian placed his hands on her hips but stayed still, allowing her to set the pace for her maximum enjoyment.

How she reveled in this.

Her hardened nub rubbed against Christian's thick hardness, and wonderous sensations tore through her.

Eleanora picked up the pace.

"Take your hair down—please," Christian rasped.

Considering the wild sex against the wall, it had partly come unpinned.

"I like that you said *please*," Eleanora teased as she reached up to release the rest of her locks.

"It's beautiful, like chestnut waves of silk."

Shaking her hair loose, she threw back her head and moaned softly.

"Come for me, my love." She met his gaze. "Please," Christian added with a sultry smile.

"Oh, yes."

Eleanora completely lost herself in the moment. The crescendo built as she moved faster, exploding in what resembled fireworks she had seen once at the parliament buildings years ago. Eleanora cried out, holding still, allowing wave after wave to roll over her.

"Yes," Christian growled. He then moved, thrusting his hips upward. Though she still tried to catch her breath, she met Christian's rhythm until he grew taut and groaned with his release.

Intense. Otherworldly.

Gasping, she leaned in and kissed Christian deeply, and their tongues clashed, fighting for domination.

Eleanora couldn't stay upright, she collapsed next to him, and Christian pulled her in tight, laying her head against his shoulder.

"Rest, my love. We have hours yet," he whispered.

Eleanora yawned as her fingertips trailed through the hair on his chest.

They slept.

WHEN SHE AWOKE, ELEANORA found a shirtless Christian standing before the bed, holding a tray.

"Oh, how long did I sleep?" she asked sleepily.

"About an hour, as did I." He held up the tray. "I have the scones, butter, jelly, and cold milk. Sorry, I can't make tea or coffee. I found a few biscuits in the larder as well."

He sat beside her on the bed and placed the tray between them.

"Oh, I am famished." Eleanora reached for a frosted sugar biscuit.

"El."

"Hmm?" she replied, her mouth full of biscuits.

"I am in love with you."

Eleanora stopped chewing. It was hard to swallow anyway, considering a lump had lodged in her throat at the emotionally spoken words.

"I do not expect you to reply in kind, not yet, anyway," Christian said, his voice low. "Many would say this could not be tangible, for we have only known each other a few weeks. But it is most decidedly real for *me*: intense, soul-stirring, and my heart is yours for as long as we draw breath."

Tears threatened, but she remained silent, unsure of what to say. Or too frightened to put her own powerful emotions into words. In nearly every aspect of her life, confidence ruled her actions.

But this?

Her well-hidden sensitivity roared to the surface.

Christian took her hand. "El, swallow your biscuit before you choke, my love."

With an audible gulp, she did as a lone tear trickled down her flushed cheek.

"I've come to know you quite well. As with every aspect of your life, you must ponder it and come to a logical conclusion. Even where your emotions are concerned. It is one of the many, many things I love about you. Your bold confidence, mixed with a heart-breaking sensitivity, vastly appeals to me."

"Chris—"

"Let me finish. You said you would protect me from physical harm. It turns out I need protection from my confessed vulnerabilities. Know that I will do the same for you. Protect you with my very life—in all ways. And when you're ready, share your life with me. I. Love. You. I'm all in, El. Forever." He kissed her hand, then released it. "Butter me a scone, will you, love?"

What did he say?

Scone?

Her head swam, with all manners of emotions firing her nerve endings. Where was that intermittent impulsivity when she needed it? Instead of throwing herself in his arms and returning his deeply affecting words of love, she buttered a scone and passed it to him.

Christian smiled as he took it from her trembling fingers. How can he be so understanding? Why is he not angry at her for not being capable of returning his honest declaration?

"A little jelly won't go amiss," he whispered.

A gasping sob left her throat.

"Everything is all right, El. I understand."

And she loved him all the more for it.

PROTECTING THE DUKE 237

"I meant to ask, why were you dressed as a laborer that night you came to the club?" Christian asked as he spread jelly on another piece of scone.

Eleanora could hug the stuffing out of him right now. Christian had observed her turmoil and changed the subject to focus her mind on something else. He knew and understood her, after all.

Grateful for the change in topic, she told the narrative of Mr. Kitchener (without mentioning his name or occupation) and how she followed him to the molly house. The agreement they came to, and his giving his wife the divorce.

"Everything worked out for all concerned. You handled it well, with sensitivity and compassion," Christian said. "But how did you know of The Sportsman Club? I assumed it was a well-kept secret among the upper echelons."

"When I started my investigative agency, my father and uncle took Althea and me on tour. Of 'Underbelly London' as they called it. I know the location of the more prominent brothels, opium dens, and gambling establishments throughout the city."

"You continue to surprise me, Miss Galway," Christian teased. Then he sobered. "Had enough to eat?"

"Yes, for now."

"Good, because I need to make love to you." Christian removed the tray, then held out his hand. She stood, and he slowly undressed her. "Your beauty astounds me. El, you take my breath away." He gently laid his hand against her chest, and his brows knotted with concern. "The bruises, do they still hurt?"

"The color is fading. The bruises were purple yesterday. Now they're yellowish-brown. I am fine. The days spent in bed hastened my recovery. I don't ache nearly as much."

"To mar such perfection. If I ever find who kicked you, I will rip the villain to shreds."

"I appreciate that. And I am far from perfect. I'm too tall—"

He gently laid the tip of his finger against her lips. "I will not have you run down a list of supposed flaws. I see none. You're tall enough for me."

Eleanora chuckled, then kissed his finger. "My height was the only supposed flaw I was going to mention, and others see it so, not I."

"Exactly right."

He deftly removed her blouse, skirt, and chemise, tossing them aside. Then he knelt and placed her boot on his thigh. Slowly, Christian unlaced and removed them. Then her stockings.

Standing, he admired her. "Stunning."

He divested himself of his remaining clothes, and they lay on the bed. He fitted on another sheath. Christian made a deliberate study of her body. He was kissing, nipping, and licking along the way and paying particular attention to the most feminine part of her, using his mouth and tongue to heighten her desire.

He brought her to a rapid and intense climax, then entered her before she could catch her breath. Christian's thrusts were deep but slow, building to a faster pace in increments.

Eleanora wrapped her long legs around him, lifting her hips to meet him. They weren't quiet; they moaned and urged each other onto a higher plane. Their peak hit at nearly the exact moment. Taking their pleasure and taking their time, but freely giving.

Christian collapsed on top of her, and she held him close, swiping his damp hair from his brow and kissing him. Eleanora had shown in action how she truly felt about him.

There was no doubt of it. Eleanora loved him with every fiber of her being. Now she had to gather the courage to put those actions into words.

A life together? Could they achieve it? On the surface, it seemed impossible.

A duke and a lady detective?

But in her heart, she knew they belonged together.
If only her mind would agree.

Chapter 24

AT FIVE IN THE MORNING, Christian escorted Eleanora home by a hansom cab. As for sleep? She had tried to nap but couldn't. The night played over and over in her head on a never-ending loop: the intimate acts and Christian's emotional words. There were things about herself she would never confess to anyone, but she had admitted her vulnerabilities to Christian, and he had accepted them.

The give and take, in bed and out of it, astounded her.

Sweet Mother, we could *have it all.*

No matter how wonderful their wild yet tender lovemaking, his declaration of love won her. He innately understood her need for independence yet also accepted her susceptibilities. And to admit that he also had them?

Christian Bamford was the man she had yearned for. His need for affection and attention? Oh, she would give it gladly, anything he wanted.

She had already given him her heart.

Althea entered the parlor, rubbing her eyes. "When did you get in?"

Eleanora whirled around and faced her sister. "How did you know I went out?"

"Deduction, my dear. You made apple scones, which, I remember, is a certain duke's favorite. So, I watched from my bedroom window and saw you hailing a hansom at a quarter to eleven. You stayed with him all night, didn't you?"

Althea was not admonishing her, or judging, just laying the facts before her.

Eleanora sighed. "Yes, I haven't had a wink of sleep, except short naps in between—er, well, you can imagine."

Althea smiled and sat on the sofa. "That's all I can do—is imagine. Was it wonderful?"

Eleanora sat next to her sister. "Beyond wonderful. I'm in love with him so much it hurts. I'm frightened and exhilarated all at once. My emotions are in a whirl; he has captivated me completely."

Althea took her hands and squeezed them affectionately. "I am so very happy for you."

"He loves me, he told me so, but I couldn't say it in return. What does that say about me?"

"That you need time to process it, as you do every aspect of your life," Althea replied as she released Eleanora's hands.

"Christian said the same, that he understands. That he will wait. What have I done to deserve him?"

"You deserve every happiness. Do you know who would have approved? Da. He would have liked Christian as I do. He is a fine man in all ways. Tell him so as soon as possible."

The bell at the front door sounded.

"Who can that be? It's barely seven, and I'm still in my dressing gown," Althea stated.

"Well, I'm dressed. I'll answer the door and get rid of this early riser. You stay put." Eleanora rushed into the hall and opened the door.

"Uncle Reece!" She stood aside to allow him to enter. "This is a pleasant surprise."

He leaned in to kiss her cheek. "I wish it were under better circumstances."

"Come into the parlor; Althea is up. Althea!" Eleanora called out. "It's Uncle Reece."

Althea ran to their uncle and gave him a warm embrace. "Excuse my mode of dress, dear uncle."

"I've called far too early, but when the police report of the previous night's doings crossed my desk, I had to come to you at once. It's concerning Sir Howard Whitney." He sat in the wing chair opposite the sofa. "He's been murdered. The man was found late last night by his butler."

Althea covered her mouth in shock. "How?"

"Beaten to death. I remembered the name when you made inquiries about the drowning inquest. It took ages, But I've located the summary." Uncle Reece pulled out a folded paper and handed it to Eleanora. "There's not much there."

She took the paper but didn't look at it. "First, I want to hear of the baronet."

"It was a brutal thrashing," Uncle Reece continued gravely. "Beaten to a pulp, a frenzied attack. There was a terrible gash down the side of Sir Howard's face. The weapon was a large, brass candlestick."

"It was the son, Ford Whitney. I'm sure of it," Eleanora declared. "That was how Sir Howard had beaten his son after the drowning incident. Ford is my main suspect in the body parts case."

Eleanora told her uncle about her meeting with the baronet and the revealing facts. "We cautioned him that his son may be in town and that Ford was dangerous. He dismissed our warnings."

Uncle Reece stood. "This is not my jurisdiction, but I will go at once to Rory Kerrigan at the Lambeth Division. He and his partner, Cian O'Connor, are fine detectives."

Eleanora had met Detective Sergeant Kerrigan a few months past. The detective was a fine figure of a man and as tall as her uncle. For a brief moment, Eleanora entertained the idea that a detective with the Metropolitan Police would make a fine partner—in life and business.

But no sooner introductions were made when Uncle Reece mentioned that Rory had recently married. It was no matter, as Eleanora congratulated the handsome copper and continued her life without further thought.

And yet, a duke had filled that empty part of her heart.

It was still unbelievable to contemplate.

Eleanora unfolded the paper and scanned the details. "You're right, Uncle; not much here. It was ruled accidental due to Addington's supposed drunkenness. The baronet told a different story."

"Unfortunately, the baronet is dead, but we have your and the duke's account of the conversation. More on that later. I must make haste. Goodbye, my dears."

After Uncle Reece departed, Althea wasted no time dressing and rejoining Eleanora in the parlor. Before they could even speak, the bell sounded again.

"Good Lord, what now? I'll get it this time." Althea hurried along the hall. Eleanora tried to make out who it was, but Althea reemerged with Archie before she could investigate.

"I'm right sorry, miss," Archie said to Eleanora in a low voice. "The one who took me place in watchin' the baronet's home lost Whitney in the dark. Don't know where he be now."

"You'd best take and seat and tell us everything," Eleanora said.

"I watched the baron's place for hours because you said that Ford bloke may show up at his father's. My relief arrived at midnight. It was after I left that Whitney showed up. My relief waited, and when Whitney came out, my relief followed him but lost him in the fog. I failed you, should've done it meself." Archie banged his fist in frustration on the table.

"You had to take a break, Archie. It's no one's fault. He would've slipped away regardless of who watched the place."

"Well, we have proof that Ford Whitney was at his father's residence about the time of the murder," Althea interjected.

Archie's eyes went as round as saucers. "Cor! Murder?"

"We had best get word to The Rakes that they could be in immediate danger. Ford is unpredictable." Eleanora's inner alarm started to clang.

"His nibs wanted me to come and tell him anything first, but I came to you instead," Archie said. "I did, right, yeah?"

"His nibs? You mean, Allenby?" Anger boiled Eleanora's blood. After she had warned him, and more than once, how dare he interfere in her investigation?

Archie must have seen the fury rising, for he said, "His nibs said it were only because he were easier to find. He'd do whatever you want if you didn't like it."

"Don't stick up for him, Archie. How dare he?" Eleanora seethed.

"Ellie, Allenby may have been trying to help—"

"Oh, aye, 'help.' 'Tis all it is," Archie interjected.

Eleanora jumped to her feet. "Archie, you know my uncle by sight?"

"Aye, the big copper?"

"Yes. My uncle left here not five minutes ago in the police carriage, heading to Kennington Lane, the Lambeth Police Division. Find him and tell him about Whitney being at his father's."

Archie touched his forelock. "Aye. I'll find him, and no mistake."

"Ellie, where are you going?" Althea asked.

"She be going to his nibs to tear a strip off him. I am right, yeah?" Archie said, smiling.

"Yes, you are correct. After I tear Allenby into little strips, I'll warn him about Whitney," Eleanora muttered crossly.

"Do you want me to bring your uncle along to the toff's place after he be done with the other coppers?" Archie asked.

"Yes, thank you, Archie. Nip along now."

Archie was gone in a flash, and Eleanora stormed into the hall to grab her coat.

"Perhaps I should come along as this is shaping into one of your reckless actions. You may say or do something you will regret. Christian is the man who captured your heart, remember? The man you love? I don't believe he interfered on purpose. Archie said it was because he believed his staff could find him quickly."

Already a good deal of her swift bout of anger had dissipated. Althea, as always, no doubt had the right of it. Still, Eleanora must see him as she must tell Christian about the baronet's murder. Maybe she will bring up his highhandedness. Tear one or two of those strips.

"No, I'll go. You stay and rouse Sybil out of bed, and the two of you must inform the other men of the developments. I'll rely on you both to handle that."

"Allow Allenby to explain before you excoriate and eviscerate him, my dear," Althea teased.

She kissed her sister on the cheek. "Sound advice."

As Eleanora stepped onto the sidewalk to hail a hansom cab, doubt started seeping into her thoughts.

Why couldn't she be firm in her convictions concerning Christian? She loved him deeply, yet she had no idea what a true partnership with a man should entail.

Would she be capable of the give and take needed for such a relationship? And how to even verbalize her deep feelings?

Shaking her doubts from her mind, she waved down a hansom and turned her thoughts to Ford Whitney.

He had murdered his father: a horrible act, no matter the circumstances.

What would his next move be?

Eleanora shuddered to think.

THIRTY MINUTES EARLIER...

Ford stood watching Christian Bamford's residence. After wandering the streets until the sun rose, he reasoned it was time to confront those who wronged him. And Christian was the leader; he always had been.

Ford had always liked Christian—when they were children. They had all looked up to him since they were children. Was it the fact he became a duke at age nine? Perhaps.

Christian had held out his hand in friendship and stepped in and stopped a particularly fraught situation that could have turned into a sexual violation by older boys at school.

It had all been for naught.

Sexual and physiological abuse had been the total of his life for years at that military-type school in Switzerland and later at the asylum.

Christian had rescued him for nothing.

And then for Christian to invite him into his group of friends? Ford had thought he had died and gone to heaven. To interact and be accepted by people who cared for him, shared things, and protected him.

The other boys eventually accepted him into their tight clique, even Brookton.

But that all ended on that damned beach in Kent.

The argument had been silly over who would drink the last of the whiskey they had stolen from Brookton's father's study. Then Addington made fun of Ford's weight and other cutting remarks, calling him a mollycoddle.

The exact name those older boys at school had called him when they had accused him of liking boys.

Ford had gone white-hot with rage at hearing that slang word. He barely remembered holding Addington underwater. When he came to his senses, it was too late.

What to do? He had been scared stiff. How could he wake the others and tell them? They would never forgive him. They would cast him out. Then he would have no one.

Ford located rocks large enough to fit in Addington's pockets so he would sink below the surface. The current did the rest by sweeping Hayes away from the beach and out to sea.

There was only one person Ford could turn to—his loathsome, abusive father.

It turned out to be a gross miscalculation.

Well, the tides had turned now, no pun intended.

Ford looked down at his hands.

He had scrubbed off his father's blood, changed his clothes, and burned the ones soaked with the evidence of the beating. But to him, the blood was still there, engrained into his skin.

His wretched father had been the predominant cause of all Ford's troubles, and he thought removing his father from the equation would give him a modicum of peace and set his mind to rights.

But it hadn't. Not at all.

His father's death left him even more detached and removed from reality.

There had been one kindly doctor at the asylum who spoke of motivations crafted in past experiences. He stated that mental events could mold one's future self.

In other words, none of this was Ford's fault.

Everyone else was to blame.

Before his father succumbed to his injuries, he spewed poison, which had taken root. His father said the duke and his sycophant friends had laughed at Ford behind his back. They burned his letters, mocking him, spreading the lie that he had killed Hayes Addington, and because of it, Ford was wanted by the Metropolitan Police for questioning.

He had to hear it from Christian.

And if it turned out to be true?

Then he would take his revenge on Christian. And then see to it that the others in the group paid as well.

There was no putting it off.

If not a wanted man before, he would be now.

It wouldn't take long for the coppers to become suspicious, especially when they contacted the asylum and found that Ford had escaped and had stolen their cash reserves.

Ford looked at his hands again, then rubbed them to clean off the imaginary blood. He hadn't meant to kill his father; he merely wanted him to suffer as Ford had suffered that night long ago when he had beaten Ford and sent him away.

But a mind-numbing fury had taken over, and he had lost all control.

Like that night on the beach.

Enough.

He had to know the truth.

And Christian had better answer honestly, or the duke would be heartily sorry.

Crossing the street, Ford headed for the rear entrance.

He had learned to pick locks at the miserable school since his jailers often sealed him away in the damp cellar, so entry into this house would be easy.

A cruel smile curved about his mouth.

Time for a reckoning.

Chapter 25

CHRISTIAN USUALLY WAS not an early riser, but since he returned from escorting Eleanora home, he had been in his study, deep in thought. A person would think his appetite would be ravenous after a passionate night. Huntington had brought him a tray with coffee, eggs, toast, and bacon to accompany the remaining scones. Some of the food still sat on the platters.

But Christian was only hungry for Eleanora.

His declaration of deep and abiding love had not been returned, at least not in words.

The more time he spent with Eleanora, the more he understood the workings of her mind. Yes, she could be impulsive. But Eleanora had to go through a definitive process regarding previously unknown emotions. Her ordered brain would not allow any other way.

So, Christian had to be patient.

Eleanora reciprocated his intense feelings; he did not doubt it. Not after the night they had shared. Eleanora would get there; he felt deep in his bones. And as far as Eleanora was concerned, he would wait forever.

Restless, he pushed the tray away and stood. Pacing back and forth, he decided to head to the parlor to sit by the fire. He had told Huntington not to bother with one in the study, and he wished now he had, considering the chill in the air.

Opening the door, Huntington greeted him. "Is there anything else, Your Grace?"

"If you would please take the food away. And bring a tea tray to the parlor. I'm in no particular rush for it—just a couple of McVities digestive biscuits. I know Mrs. Tallmadge abhors mass-produced biscuits, but it's all I wish for the moment. Tell her the breakfast was delicious, but I wasn't all that hungry."

"Of course, Your Grace." Huntington snapped his fingers toward Thomas, the footman, then they both entered the study to collect the dishes and trays.

Striding down the hall, Christian entered the parlor and closed the door. A figure stepped out of the early morning shadows.

"Good morning, *Your Grace*."

Christian reeled. There was no mistaking the disfiguring scar on the man's face. The words dripped with venom.

Ford Whitney.

"Do not call out or yell or scream." Ford held up a hunter's knife. "Or I will use this to silence you." Ford made a slicing motion across his throat to punctuate the point.

Christian's mind raced. What tack to take? Compassionate? Or Uncompromising? Perhaps a blend of both.

"Here for revenge?" Christian asked, keeping his tone as apathetic as possible. "Your father told me that your last letters stated nothing else."

"Ah," Ford said. "You've seen my storied father. Quite the character, wasn't he? He was a miserable bastard."

Christian arched an eyebrow. "Was? As in past tense?"

"He is *very* past tense; I saw to that last night."

A chill curled around Christian's spine. As Eleanora had said, Ford was dangerous and unpredictable.

What to say?

He certainly didn't want to anger him, considering the circumstances. All he could do was keep him talking until Huntington returned with the tea tray.

"Your father has been lying to you for years. Are you aware?" Christian said softly.

Damn, he had left his revolver in the bedroom. What could he use as a weapon? The fireplace poker, but it was on the opposite side of the room. Ford would gut him before he could retrieve it.

"We answered your letters," Christian continued. "Your father burned them instead of sending them on to you. He told me so a couple of days ago."

"Here's the thing, old boy," Ford laconically said as he moved closer. "I am not here to discuss my motivations or explain what happened to me over the past years. I know there is always a place in novels or in a drama play where the villain elucidates why he is doing dreadful things to others. I'm here for something else."

"Revenge? For not replying to your letters? The letters that your father sent us were from *his* hand and filled with lies. We thought you were with your uncle in India."

"How convenient."

Christian took one step toward the fireplace. "What *do* you want?"

"Do not make another move. Or I will spill your blood on your fine Abyssinian rug. I've decided to hold you to your promise, the one you made me twenty years ago."

Christ, what is he talking about?

"We were children—"

"You said you would protect me, be my friend," Ford hissed through clenched teeth. "You lied; you haven't done *any* of it. Not when I needed it most. Now, I am giving you a chance to finally fulfill your vow. Unless your word means nothing."

"My word means everything. And I *did* protect you through school. And I was your friend; I still can be. You should have come to us after what transpired on the beach instead of going to your despicable father."

So much for not making him angry as Ford's face turned purple with rage.

"Me?" he cried, but not loud enough to attract attention. His look was a mixture of fury and suspicion. "You blame all this on *me*?" Then he quieted. "My father told you what happened when you saw him a few days ago, not before."

"No, not before. I had no idea—none of us knew what truly transpired."

"If the police weren't after me for that, they will now. Protect me, fulfill your promise of defending me, and help me leave the country."

"You have money that you stole from the asylum. You don't need me; buy a ticket on a steamer."

Ford looked gaunt. He must have been half-starved in that institution. A spark of pity flared to life—but only a spark. Ford stood now as a murderer—of multiple people.

"You will send your butler to buy me the ticket on that steamer; while you stay here with me. Know this; if he goes to the police, I'll kill you," Ford said.

Yes, a murderer with murderous intent. And Ford ignored the comment about the money. Did he even have it anymore?

"And what destination have you in mind?" Christian asked, keeping his voice steady.

"Any place far from here. Far enough that no one can come after me," Ford snapped. "Far enough away from the horror and memories tied with it."

"Where is Emily McCarthy?" Christian asked.

Ford gave him a cruel smile. "That beast of a woman, Galway, is a top-notch detective. I'll give her that. I have Emily neatly tucked away. How *is* the lady investigator? Recovered from her injury? It was a nasty fall." Ford tsked with phony concern.

Christian growled and moved closer, but Ford held his knife before him.

"Yes, it was me that kicked her from the carriage. I'll do worse to her if you don't do as I ask. You care for her, I can tell. I know where she lives, with her sister and cousin on Cleveland Street. Now, stand there, and we will wait for your butler to return. I can wait all day."

Christian's mind swam with possible scenarios. He could rush Ford and take a chance at getting sliced. Or wait until Huntington returns, and they both subdue him. Would his butler be up to such doings?

After Ford got his travel voucher, then what?

He could easily murder Christian and his butler and make his escape. Or bash them insensibly and tie them up.

Christian had to do something to stop this, and soon.

ELEANORA KNOCKED ON the front door instead of ringing the bell, in case Christian was still abed. Thomas, the footman, answered.

"Miss Galway."

As she stepped across the threshold, she noticed Huntington carrying a tea tray toward the parlor. She sprinted to catch up with the venerable butler. Christian must be up, after all.

"He's the in the parlor, then? The duke?" she asked brightly.

"Yes, miss. Allow me to deliver the tea, and I will announce you," Huntington replied.

"No need for that, I will just—"

She held her hand up to halt the butler. With her hand gripping the doorknob, she paused. Raised voices wafted from inside the room.

She heard Emily's name mentioned. And hers. Eleanora's eyes widened. She grabbed Huntington's arm and tugged him along the hall away from the door. He almost lost his balance, and the tea dishes clinked together.

Blast it. All Eleanora had was a small knife in her boot.

What could she use—of course!

The sword.

She ran into Christian's study, stood on the tips of her toes, and snatched the blade from above the fireplace.

"Put down the tray, Huntington. The duke is in danger. I came to inform him that Sir Howard Whitney was murdered last night, and his son is undoubtedly the perpetrator. I believe he is in the study now with Christian."

Huntington laid the tray on the desk. "I remember Stafford Whitney. How did he get in?"

"No doubt slipped in the rear entrance or through a window. Come with me. I may need your assistance. I have no idea if Whitney has a weapon, so we must rush in and overwhelm him. Are you with me?" She tucked the hem of her skirt into her waistband, reading herself for battle.

"Of course, Miss Galway. You may count on me."

The butler, probably in his early fifties, looked fit enough. With Huntington hot on her heels, Eleanora returned to the parlor door. There was nothing else for it; rushing in and catching Whitney by surprise was all she could do. Eleanora could only hope that an effortless entry awaited. As she turned to whisper to Huntington, he held up a ring of keys, indicating he was already one step ahead of her.

Grasping the knob, she turned it slowly.

Christian did not lock it.

Eleanora stormed into the room with the sword held in front of her. Whitney was near Christian but not near enough to cause immediate injury. Seeing him brandish a knife toward Christian simultaneously angered and frightened her. How tempting it would be to run Whitney through.

Instead, she ran up behind the man, shouting, using the various swinging slices and thrusts she had learned in her sword fighting classes.

Snarling and recovered from her rushed entry into the room, Whitney faced her, ready to lash out.

They exchanged a few thrusts and parries. Even though the hunter's knife was large, it was no match for the sword. Eleanora smacked Whitney across the backs of his legs with the flat of her blade, causing him to cry out and nearly lose his balance.

Out of nowhere, Christian tackled Whitney from behind, and they rolled about on the floor, fighting. Waiting until Whitney moved back toward her, Eleanora laid the point of her blade against Whitney's neck.

"Enough. Drop your knife," Eleanora demanded.

"Go ahead, do it," Ford spat. "End it."

"I think not. Yield."

She had always wanted to say that. It wasn't much of a fight, like in books she had read of medieval times, but she had bested him nonetheless with Christian's assistance.

Christian stood and gave her an admiring smile.

"I said I would protect you," she said, returning his smile.

"That you have," he murmured silkily.

"Your Grace! You're injured," Huntington exclaimed as he rushed to Christian's side. Blood dripped from a gash on his arm.

Christian immediately covered it with his hand. "It's not serious."

At that moment, Uncle Reece, Archie, and Detective Sergeant Rory Kerrigan burst into the room with the footman, Thomas, close behind.

"Good God," Reece cried out. "What's all this?"

"It appears your niece has this well in hand, Galway," Kerrigan said. The detective strode toward her, then laid his hand on her back.

A possessive growl emitted from Christian.

"I'll take the sword, lass. And I will take Whitney into custody," Kerrigan said. "Well done."

"Thank you, DS Kerrigan."

As soon as she handed the sword to the sergeant, she vaulted into Christian's arms, kissing his cheeks frantically. "Are you sure you're not seriously injured?" she cried.

"It's just a scratch," he whispered, nuzzling her neck.

"Seeing you in peril—oh, Chris. Forgive me for not saying what I was too frightened to say last night. I am not making any sense. Except in this, I love you with my whole heart. It doesn't beat without you. I don't care who hears me say it."

A gasping sob escaped her at the confession. Seeing Christian in danger erased all lingering doubt regarding her feelings and how to vocalize them.

Christian embraced her tight. "Change this lonely life, my darling. I want to feel you in my arms for all time. Be with me. Marry me. When, where, and how, we will work out later. Just love me."

"Oh, I do, most desperately. Yes, marry. We will. And soon."

"A lovely scene, Niece, and may I offer my congratulations? But we should send for a doctor. His Grace's wound is bleeding profusely now." Reece interjected gently.

Eleanora squeaked and jumped back. Blood had pooled on the floor near Christian's boot. She immediately ripped away the rest of the sliced-to-ribbons shirt sleeve, then tore off a piece of her petticoat and wrapped it tightly around Christian's forearm.

"Archie, fetch Doctor Buchanan at once," she ordered.

"Wait," Christian said. "I have my own doctor. Huntington, send for Doctor Forester."

Eleanora put her hands on her hips. "I think we should send for Buchanan—"

"Niece, you have a lifetime to argue; allow the man to send for his doctor," Uncle Reece interposed. "Meanwhile, Kerrigan and I will escort Whitney to Lambeth Station. We will talk later."

Yanking Whitney to his feet, the men took each arm. Ford looked down, defeated, a broken man. But, Eleanora mused, he'd been broken for a long time.

Kerrigan tipped his hat. "Always a pleasure to see you, Miss Galway."

Christian growled again, shooting Kerrigan a threatening look.

Eleanora had to admit that having Christian act territorial sent a decided thrill through her.

Kerrigan laughed. "Your Grace. Nice to meet you. Detective Sergeant Kerrigan at your service."

Huntington bowed. "I will ensure the doctor is here directly. Thomas, fetch a fresh tea tray. I will bring hot water and antiseptic. Archie, come with me. Mrs. Tallmadge will have food for you, no doubt."

They were left alone.

Eleanora escorted Christian to the sofa and sat beside him. Worry furrowed her brows.

"It *is* bleeding most profusely." She laid her hand on the cloth and squeezed his arm. "That should help stem the bleeding until the doctor arrives."

"It appears it is deeper than I thought. I will need stitches."

"Seeing you in danger—Sweet Mother, I pray I never experience that again. All my lingering doubts broke away. Again, I apologize for not returning your most heartfelt feelings last night. It was the fright, as you said."

"I understand more than you know. And I knew you reciprocated those emotions; all I had to do was look into your beautiful eyes."

With his free hand, he laced his fingers through hers and squeezed. "We are one, El, and everything I have said holds. I will never, *ever* control you. Except occasionally in bed. If you promise to reciprocate, I do so love it, you know."

She laughed. "Absolutely. We will share it all. My dearest love."

Christian sat back and pulled her close, and she rested her head against his chest. She listened to the warm and welcoming cadence of his heart.

Her life was about to change.

Eleanora couldn't wait.

Chapter 26

TWO DAYS LATER, ELEANORA and Christian traveled to a location given to them by her uncle. He would be giving them an update on the case. The address turned out to be an abandoned warehouse in the East End.

Christian rubbed his arm as the carriage navigated the busy London streets. He would have a scar, but it would remind him of how he and Eleanora met and fell in love.

"Is it paining you, love?" Eleanora asked, concern in her voice.

"Not while you're near," he whispered as he pulled her closer.

"We are going to do this, aren't we?" she said.

"All the way. I want us to be upfront with each other—always. But let us discuss one issue. Children. What is your feeling on this?"

Eleanora sighed. "I suppose one, or possibly two—at some point. But not right away if it is achievable. As I said, I want to keep my business and keep a hand in."

"If we make an heir, fine. If we have a girl, and you want to stop there, I am fine with that. Whatever you want, my love."

"Thank you. That's if we can even have children at all."

"There is that. If not, then we find our happiness elsewhere, my darling."

"That won't be difficult."

As she kissed his cheek, the carriage stopped in front of a dilapidated warehouse by the docks. Eleanora's uncle stood outside the double doors, waiting for them.

"Is Kerrigan with him? Christian questioned. "Do you have past involvement with him? I meant to ask."

"No, not at all. The sergeant is recently and happily married."

Kerrigan was too tall and good-looking for his own good. Even if there had been something between them, it was all in the past. All Christian wanted to focus on was his future with Eleanora.

Before they could disembark, the carriage door flew open, and Reece Galway stepped in, though it was not an easy fit considering his height. He closed the door.

"A bit of privacy, as the CID is inside the building. Ford Whitney has not said much at all. However, we brought in that twitchy footman, Phillips, who spilled all sorts. He named the third man seen at the pub: Jeffery Mason. I'll get to him in a moment. Phillips states there may be one or two more, but he isn't certain. He said this warehouse was a meeting place, along with The Ten Bells."

"Has he said why these scurrilous men formed such a group?" Christian asked.

"To cause mischief more than anything. Phillips has a sister, one of the rakes dallied with her and broke her heart. She never told Phillips the name, but he narrowed it down to Huxley or Brookton. Phillips was stealing from Brookton. We found a stash of goods and money in a rented room. He claimed he was doling out portions to his sister for her upkeep."

Christian rubbed his temple. "Robert Southey said in a poem: "Curses are like young chickens; they always come home to roost."

Come home to roost, indeed.

He will obtain the name of the sister later and make a settlement. All the rakes would contribute; Christian would see to that.

"We've made a discovery in the warehouse. I believe it is—or was—Emily McCarthy," Reece said. "The ice had melted days ago. You may wish to forego coming inside as there is an unpleasant odor, to say the least."

Eleanora took Christian's hand. "That poor young woman. Was she murdered?"

Reece shrugged. "Hard to know. Doctor Buchanan is at the station house, further examining the body. There is no violent evidence of murder. She could have succumbed to her disorder. It will be hard to prove. This is my district, so I will handle the investigation on this end."

"We would like to see Emily McCarthy properly buried, not in a pauper's grave," Christian stated.

"Thank you, Your Grace. Now, I will need the name of the young lady that worked with Emily at the brothel. We do need an identification."

"First, please call me Christian. We are to be family, Reece."

"Of course. Christian." Reece gave him a friendly smile.

"Fiona Mapleton, 10 Half Moon Street," Eleanora interjected.

"Thank you. Concerning Mason, he's another sniveling toad. He arranged the carriage incident. He won't speak of Whitney directly or of Whitney's role in all this; he lives in fear of the man. However, we'll get him to talk. A few nights in prison loosen many tongues."

"And how have the rakes injured Mason?" Christian asked though he loathed knowing.

"I'm afraid it is Brookton, once again, but indirectly. Mason's younger sister, he discovered recently, was sired by Brookton's father, the duke. When he approached the Duke of Chellenham, the staff sent him packing. He had hoped to humiliate his son, the marquess, to gain revenge and perhaps do a little blackmail."

"My God," Christian muttered. What had Damon said about half-siblings spread about London? Well, there was a possible half-sister for him. "Can it be proved?"

"Mason claims so, but that would be for the duke or the marquess to explore. This case is in its early days; there is much to investigate. But this brings your case to a close, Eleanora."

"Yes. It does, Uncle."

"Whitney is a disturbed individual and the son of a baronet; even if we prove murder in the case of Emily, his father, or even Addington, I doubt he will dangle from the noose. Shut away for life, either in prison or asylum, will be the outcome. Well, back to work." Reece's look softened. "Congratulations again to you both. I know you will be exceedingly happy. You make quite the formidable team."

The men shook hands, and Reece Galway departed.

Christian reached into his pocket and pulled out a roll of pound notes. "Payment for a job well done, Miss Galway." He passed her the money. "Fifty pounds as agreed."

"You already paid me fifty pounds," Eleanora chuckled.

"Consider this a bonus and an investment in the future of your agency. I am so proud of you, El. You are a top-rate investigator."

Eleanora took the notes and tucked them in the pocket of her cape. "Thank you, Your Grace. You are not bad, yourself. As my uncle said, we are a team. A formidable one."

Christian laughed, then sobered. "Considering Archie."

"Oh, heavens, what?"

"Nothing serious."

Christian told her of the boy's street life and playing the role of a lifelong street child to stay alive and earn coins.

"He is heartily sorry that he deceived you and your family, but he wishes to take you up on your offer of joining your agency. In due time."

Eleanora was silent.

"Well, he had me completely fooled," she said with awe. "Which proves he is perfect for the job. What a cunning lad."

"He is that. I will turn the outbuilding behind my home into a guesthouse for Archie. He's agreed to my sponsorship, and I will engage a tutor to catch him up on his studies before continuing his education at a school. I thought, perhaps, Charterhouse. We will see where he goes from there and how he applies himself. He's clever and intelligent."

"I'm so glad you are giving him this opportunity. Thank you."

Christian gave her a dazzling smile. "I have a surprise for you. Our next stop is the Daimler Motor Company assembly plant. As I promised, a tour of the facilities. It is only a small operation, but we plan on building bigger and better facilities soon."

Eleanora jumped in his lap and kissed him, stirring his passion in no time at all.

"If you wish to pin me to the cushions and have your way with me, I won't object," Christian growled in-between kisses.

"I am so tempted."

"How impetuous are you feeling today?" he asked.

Eleanora stopped kissing and stared at him. "Why?"

"We can go to the Registrar's Office today, take out a license, and be married as soon as possible. Or we can be married by year's end in any fashion you wish."

Eleanora stroked his cheek affectionately. "I always thought, if I ever married, I would like a Christmas wedding. A small ceremony, mind, with close friends and family. A huge decorated tree and all the trimmings. Mince pies and mulled wine served to the guests. And Uncle Reece walking me down the aisle."

"Consider it done," Christian whispered huskily. "Loving you has opened the world for me, where anything is possible. I am your devoted servant—in all ways."

"Oh, Chris," she said, her voice soft with emotion. "You are the center of my world. I will never neglect you; how could I? You fill my waking thoughts and my nighttime dreams. You are mine; I am yours."

"I love you to distraction, with the entirety of my being. I am yours, body, heart, and soul. Let's continue this adventure—together."

"Together—always."
Loneliness? Boredom?
Banished forever.
With Eleanora, life would never be dull.
Christian couldn't wait.

Epilogue

Summer 1907
Bamford Park, Essex

IN THE ENSUING DECADE, as Christian had surmised, life with Eleanora was always exciting. After the Christmas wedding, Eleanora moved into the town house, and the next five years were filled with laughter, adventure, and an overabundance of passion. Christian often assisted in her various assignments, big or small.

After the arrest of Ford Whitney, word traveled fast about The Galway Agency. While prejudices remained regarding women running an investigative concern, the cases had increased. Divorce cases still made up most of the assignments, but more intriguing cases concerning murder and fraud had also cropped up.

As Reece Galway had predicted, Ford did not stand trial for the murder of Addington or Emily McCarthy; they couldn't prove either. But fingerprints on the murder weapon proved his guilt in the murder of the baronet.

After a well-publicized trial, the verdict was life in prison. When Newgate Prison closed in 1902, the authorities transferred Ford to an asylum. Christian had gone to visit him, but Ford didn't know him. His former friend had withdrawn into his own world.

Changes have occurred with the birth of Christian and Eleanora's son more than four years ago. While Eleanora, Althea, and their cousin, Sybil, still kept a hand in, Archie Fitzgerald, now twenty-four, ran the day-to-day operations. Although a few men were on the payroll, most investigators were women.

Every summer for the past several years, Eleanora and Christian came to Bamford Park in July and hosted a summer party by inviting friends and family. They would start arriving in the next couple of days.

His mother and her husband of nine years, The Duke of Coldbridge, were already here, as were Reece Galway, his wife Wilhelmina, and their six-year-old daughter, Roisin. Arriving tomorrow would be Sybil and her husband, Doctor Corbett Buchanan.

The rest of The Rakes and their families would be arriving after that. The manor house would be full to bursting, but Christian and Eleanora enjoyed the noise and activity—and seeing everyone.

The next few weeks would see various picnics, outdoor games, sports, and concerts, as Christian invited musicians to perform.

Hollis Duncan Richard Galway Bamford, age four and a half, ran toward his father. Christian scooped him up and tousled his mop of black hair.

"Mama says it's going to be a girl, but I want a brother," Hollis declared.

Eleanora came into the room, her arm resting on her large middle. Last year Eleanora miscarried. It had been a devastating experience for them both. But this one was tucked away safe as Eleanora was due in a matter of weeks.

Christian opened his arm and brought his darling wife in close. "Mama is usually right, Hollis, so a girl it will be." Christian leaned in and whispered to Eleanora, "Just like her mother, she will be beautiful and confident, passionate about all things."

"And be a lady detective?" Eleanora interjected.

"She can be anything she wishes. We will see to it."

Family life had cut into the investigative exploits, but their mutual love and desire had not diminished. They were on a new adventure as a family.

Christian once predicted that they could have it all.

And so they did.

Look ahead for a sneak peek of The Baron and the Mistress (Revised Edition) book #2 in The Rakes of St. Regent's Park

Author Biography

A MULTI-PUBLISHED AUTHOR from Eastern Canada, Karyn Gerrard loves to write sensual historical and contemporary romances. Tortured heroes are an absolute must.

Karyn's been happily married for a long time to her own hero. His encouragement and loving support keep her moving forward.

To learn more about Karyn and her books, visit www.karyngerrard.com[1]

Also visit her on Facebook, Twitter, Pinterest, Instagram, and Bookbub.

"Looking for a swoon-worthy read? You can't go wrong with the lovely and emotional romances from Karyn Gerrard." ~**Vanessa Kelly, USA Today Bestselling author**

"Karyn Gerrard writes very enjoyable, richly textured historical romances." ~**Kate Pearce, New York Times and USA Today Bestselling author**

---

1.   http://www.karyngerrard.com/

More Books by Karyn Gerrard

~HISTORICAL~

The Spinster and Mr. Glover (Book #1 Blind Cupid Series)

The Governess and the Beast (Book #2 Blind Cupid Series)

The Copper and the Madam (Book #3 Blind Cupid Series)

Protecting the Duke (The Rakes of St. Regent's Park #1)

The Baron and the Mistress (The Rakes of St. Regent's Park #2)

Bold Seduction (of Professor Hornsby) (Book #1 Hornsby Brothers Series)

The Vicar's Frozen Heart (Book #2 Hornsby Brothers Series)

Marquess of Secrets (Book #3 Hornsby Brothers Series)

Beloved Monster (Book #1 The Ravenswood Chronicles)

Beloved Beast (Book #2 The Ravenswood Chronicles)

Marriage with a Proper Stranger (Book #1 Men of Wollstonecraft Hall Series)

Scandal with a Sinful Scot (Book #2 Men of Wollstonecraft Hall Series)

Love with a Notorious Rake (Book #3 Men of Wollstonecraft Hall Series)

Knight of Christmas (The Rakes of St. Regent's Park #3)

The Duke of Pain (The Rakes of St. Regent's Park #4)

The Not So Perfect Duke (The Rakes of St. Regent's Park #5)

The Viscount of Shadows (The Rakes of St. Regent's Park #6) is Coming Soon!

~**Contemporary**~

My Highlander Cover Model (Heroes of Time Travel Anthology Series #1)

Timeless Heart (Heroes of Time Travel Anthology Series #2)

My Wicked Soul (It's Never too Late for Love Anthology Series #1)

That Christmas Feeling (It's Never too Late for Love Anthology Series #2)

Wild Pitch

He's the Wicked Bad (Wicked Men of Rockland City #1)

His Wicked Celtic Kiss (Wicked Men of Rockland City #2)

His Wicked Cold Heart (Wicked Men of Rockland City #3) is coming soon!

Sneak peek of The Baron and the Mistress
(The Rakes of St. Regent's Park #2)

Prologue

LONDON
  Late November 1897

IF THERE WAS ONE THING the Rakes of St. Regent's Park understood, it was how to have a rousing good time.

Asher Colborne, Baron Wenlock, was out on the town with his fellow 'rakes.'

He sat at a table with the remaining members of their small and private association. Over the past fifteen years, the membership ebbed and flowed. Some went to war, others married, and they moved on to a less profligate life. Part of the current group had formed a close bond in school, all the way to Cambridge University, until today.

Not just anyone was allowed within this privileged circle. First and foremost, the other members had genuinely to like the fellow, and these formidable men did not give their friendship, trust, or reveal their emotions.

The recently engaged Christian Bamford, Duke of Allenby and former group leader attended tonight as a sort of farewell.

Not only was he leaving their club, but they had gathered to also say their goodbyes to Brandon Knight, who would depart for Herne Bay in a few weeks.

These past months much had happened with the Rakes of St. Regent's Park. One could argue that their organization neared its end. At its peak, there were twenty-one members.

Recently, they were down to seven.

Now?

Their numbers were about to deplete even further. It was rather depressing when Asher thought about it. He had recently made an invitation to Oliver Wollstonecraft, grandson to Aidan Wollstonecraft, Earl of Carnstone. The twenty-seven-year-old heir to the earl had earned a bit of a notorious reputation, one that came close to his grandfather Aidan's scandalous younger years. Oliver had said he would think it over, but that was weeks passed.

Asher glanced around the table. Next to him was the elder statesman, as they called him, Gideon Broyles, Duke of Watford, one of the original founding members. About to turn forty, Gideon outpaced them all for casual liaisons. He showed no signs of slowing down or settling down.

Warren Cowley, Viscount Huxley, was making a rare appearance, as he had been tucked away at the Bevan Sanitorium in Hertfordshire, receiving treatment for his sexual excesses. He was only in London this week to attend to business, and Asher had been shocked at the change in the man. More withdrawn than ever, he sat, nursing a scotch, barely speaking.

Next to Huxley was Damon Cranston, Marquess of Brookton and heir to The Duke of Chellenham. Damon would be taking over as the leader of their little clique. Damon was often referred to as "Dorian Gray" by society after the fictional Oscar Wilde character. Damon's scandalous reputation was the talk of London. But Asher had wondered, through the years, just how much of it was accurate?

Merritt Redfern, Viscount Tolwood and heir to the Earl of Shelton was not a full-blown member but part of their group as an apprentice—until he found a suitable bride.

By the end of the year, it could only be Asher, Gideon, and Damon left. Not that any of them were full-blown rakes at the moment, for Asher had the distinct impression most of the dalliances were all talk, complete fiction.

"I say, allowing your soon-to-be duchess to keep her investigative agency? Christian, you are progressive to the core," Merritt said, raising his glass. "I salute you."

Christian's fiancée owned and operated a successful investigative firm, The Galway Agency, with her sister and cousin.

"Thank you. As if I could dictate to Eleanora what to do, not that I would. The Galway Agency will go on. In fact, the business has been brisk. She may reduce her hours at some point, but that will be *her* decision." Christian reached for the decanter and freshened his drink. "Let's face facts, lads. A new century yawns before us. Do you think those of us with titles and societal standing will even factor into shaping the future? Our way of life is near its end."

"Bite your tongue," Damon scoffed. "There will always be a peerage."

"Perhaps, but the power our grandfathers and great-grandfathers wielded at the turn of this century? Gone forever. Good riddance, I say," Christian replied.

"How goes the bride search, Tolwood?" Gideon asked, his voice showing that he wasn't interested in knowing. He had changed the subject because the truth of their future wasn't something Gideon wished to discuss, let alone accept.

Asher understood completely.

Merritt sighed. "Still going. Finding someone to love and who will love you in return is blasted difficult. I may have to settle for an alliance."

"Why marry at all?" Brandon interjected. "We're supposed to be scandalous rakes."

Knight was a wealthy businessman of the gentry class. Gideon sponsored Knight, and they all accepted him into the club. Brandon Knight was the only non-peer in the current group.

It was true what Brandon said. They were *supposed* to be rakes. But, as Asher surmised before, he doubted many of them still embraced such an existence or even lived it to the full. That is, if they took a moment, to be honest with themselves.

They all had their various predilections when it came to carnal pleasures. Gideon? He frequented clubs that offered light birching. Damon? Orgies were his preference. Warren? Well, he had gone too far and sought treatment for his dissipation.

As for Asher? He found his pleasure in the East End: anonymous sex in the various back alleys. Oh, he was careful, as were all the rakes. He used protection. Why he sought out sex in such grubby circumstances, he could not say. Be damned if he would try and puzzle it out here.

"The way things are going," Gideon said, his deep voice rumbling. "We will have to recruit new members."

"Why even bother?" Christian stated. "Marriage may not be as horrible as you may think."

"Please spare us your cloying happiness," Damon replied in a dull voice. "Just because you found yourself caught in a marriage trap doesn't mean the rest of us wish it. Except for Merritt."

"And what of Althea?" Christian replied softly.

"What's this?" Asher exclaimed. Althea Galway was Eleanora's younger sister and partner in the investigative agency.

Damon's cheeks flushed. An actual reaction. Now, *this* was interesting.

"She means nothing to me. I wouldn't give a care if I ever saw her again." Damon threw back the rest of his drink and refilled his glass.

He was lying, of course, and all the men in the room knew it.

"Just as well," Christian replied. "She has said the same of you. Which proves that you both lie."

Damon flushed further, his jaw working furiously. Christian was correct. Could something develop there? Perhaps not, knowing Damon's stubborn and debauched nature.

"So, when are you leaving exactly, Knight?" Warren asked. It was the first time he had spoken in over an hour.

"December fifteenth," Brandon replied.

"Out for revenge regarding past hurts, correct?" Warren threw back his drink. "Take care, do not allow it to consume your life."

"Too late," Brandon replied, his voice firm.

Asher downed the rest of his scotch and stood. Enough of this conversation. "Shall we partake in a game of cards? There is a private room in the rear. There is also a small buffet set up."

"I say, I am famished," Merritt said.

"Christian? Stay and play. You're not under a self-imposed curfew, I trust?" Asher teased.

"Not at all. Cards it is. I hope roast beef is available," Christian replied, rubbing his hands together. "And duchess potatoes."

"I made certain to order it," Asher smiled. "I ensured all your favorites are on the menu, including Charlotte russe for dessert. And as an extra surprise, Eleanora sent along apple scones."

Christian laid his hand on Asher's shoulder and squeezed it affectionately. "You are a true friend."

Everyone stood and headed toward the back room.

Except for Warren.

Asher stayed behind. His friend was not well, physically or emotionally. The look of desolation on Warren's face concerned Asher. He had worried about his friend and thought of him often these past weeks he was away.

"What is it? What's going on?" Asher asked, his voice quiet.

"I am returning to the sanitorium. I have relapsed already. Speaking of consuming one's life, I'm a hopeless case and should be shut away permanently." Warren's voice was husky and anguished.

Asher shook his head. "I *am* sorry, my friend. Is there anything I can do?"

"There is one thing you can do for me. Leave this group, Ash. Stop seeking out thrills in the back alleys. Find someone to love, though I am aware that is not an easy task in this cold world. This existence is pathetic and soul-destroying. Be done with it before you become an empty, rotting husk like me. Or Gideon or Brandon. Damon is more than halfway there. Take my advice and save yourself."

Warren headed to the private room, leaving Asher shaken.

The stark warning had taken root.

www.ingramcontent.com/pod-product-compliance
Lightning Source LLC
Chambersburg PA
CBHW070102030726
47506CB00002B/570